THE BLOODY TOWER

As Daisy reached the top step, she saw a scarlet heap at the bottom. Puzzled, she started down. Then she realized the scarlet was a Yeoman Warder's cape.

And the yeoman was still inside it.

And sticking out of the middle of his back was a partizan.

Unbelieving, Daisy stared downward. The yeoman's head was turned at a strange angle, not only suggesting he was well and truly defunct, but also revealing the edge of a beard still rampant in death.

The Chief Warder! He might have stumbled or slipped on the steps in the fog last night, but the partizan was proof of dirty work. Even if Crabtree had been carrying it, he could hardly have stuck it in his own back. Who could have wanted to kill the kindly, boring old buffer?

Daisy Dalrymple Mysteries by Carola Dunn

Published by Kensington Publishing Corporation

THE BLOODY TOWER

A DAISY DALRYMPLE MYSTERY

CAROLA DUNN

KENSINGTON BOOKS
http://www.kensingtonbooks.com

The inhabitants of my Tower are fictional and bear no intentional resemblance to the actual residents of HM Tower of London in 1925, nor at any time before or since.

Map by Jonathan Bennett

KENSINGTON BOOKS are published by

Kensington Publishing Corp.
850 Third Avenue
New York, NY 10022

All Kensington titles, imprints, and distributed lines are available at special quantity discounts for bulk purchases for sales promotion, premiums, fund-raising, educational, or institutional use.

Special book excerpts or customized printings can also be created to fit specific needs. For details, write or phone the office of the Kensington Special Sales Manager: Attn. Special Sales Department. Kensington Publishing Corp., 850 Third Avenue, New York, NY 10022. Phone: 1-800-221-2647.

Kensington and the K logo Reg. U.S. Pat. & TM Off.

ISBN-13: 978-0-7582-2921-2
ISBN-10: 0-7582-2921-6

First St. Martin's Minotaur Hardcover Printing: September 2007
First Kensington Mass Market Paperback Printing: February 2009

10 9 8 7 6 5 4 3 2 1

Printed in the United States of America

Dedicated to all those who work to preserve Britain's and the world's history because, as Sir Walter Raleigh wrote while imprisoned in the Bloody Tower, "We may gather out of history a policy no less wise than eternal; by comparison and application of other men's forepassed miseries with our own like errors and ill deservings."

ACKNOWLEDGMENTS

I owe particular thanks to Bridget Clifford, Senior Curator of the Royal Armouries Library at HM Tower of London, who patiently answered my obscure questions and provided access to books and papers in the library collection. Thanks also to Natasha Woollard, PR Manager, HM Tower of London; Ken Wildwind, for sharing his extensive knowledge of the British Army between the Wars; Graham Howard, for going to the Tower especially to take photographs for me; and numerous Siblings in Crime and DLers, two groups whose collective expertise on everything under the sun never ceases to amaze, and whose willingness to help never fails to warm the cockles of my heart.

As always, any errors, omissions, substitutions, or alterations of fact for artistic purposes are entirely my responsibility.

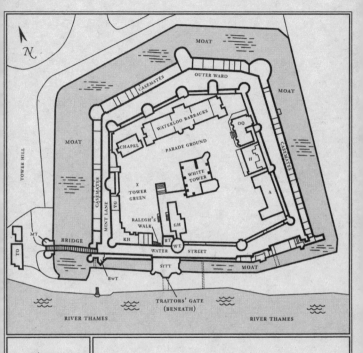

MOAT

OUTER WARD

CASEMATES

MOAT

MOAT

WATERLOO BARRACKS

OQ

CHAPEL

PARADE GROUND

H

CASEMATES

WHITE TOWER

TOWER HILL

X
TOWER GREEN

A

CASEMATES

MINT LANE

YG

RALEGH'S WALK

GH

KH

BT

WT

MT

BRIDGE

WATER

STREET

TO

StTT

MOAT

BwT

TRAITORS' GATE
(BENEATH)

RIVER THAMES

RIVER THAMES

Tower of London

1925

0 50 100 150
FEET

Legend

A	ARMOURY	MT	MIDDLE TOWER
BT	BLOODY TOWER	OQ	OFFICERS' QUARTERS
BwT	BYWARD TOWER	StTT	ST. THOMAS'S TOWER
GH	GUARD HOUSE	TO	TICKET OFFICE
H	HOSPITAL	WT	WAKEFIELD TOWER
KH	KING'S HOUSE	YG	YEOMAN GAOLER'S HOUSE
		X	SITE OF SCAFFOLD

—————— 1 ——————

"The Tower of London?" Alec, spreading marmalade on his toast, spoke with a sort of deliberate casualness. "That's rather a macabre subject to write about."

"One needn't go into the gruesome details," Daisy pointed out. "More coffee? The Americans will love it. Just think, 1078 A.D. to 1925, eight and a half centuries of history! They can't match that even if they go back to Christopher Columbus."

"True."

"Mr. Thorwald says he's willing to buy a series of three or four articles about the Tower for *Abroad* magazine."

"You've already written to him?"

"His answer just arrived." Daisy waved the telegram form from the top of the pile of letters by her plate. "See how keen he is? He telegraphed rather than waiting for a letter to reach me. I got the idea when we took Belinda to see *The Yeomen of the Guard* at Christmas."

After a moment's silence while he swallowed a bite, Alec voiced the question Daisy was expecting.

"What about the twins?"

She had her response ready. "I'll only be gone for a few hours at a time, as I shan't have to go out of town. That's why it's ideal. Honestly, darling, Nanny's perfectly competent. In fact, she's growing downright dictatorial. Since Mother went home to the Dower House—"

"And my mother retreated back to Bournemouth, thank heaven!"

"Exactly. Nanny no longer has their conflicting commands ringing in her ears. Isn't it odd how both of them insisted that no one on their side of the family ever had twins? As though there were something disgraceful about it," Daisy said indignantly.

"Yes, I never thought to hear Lady Dalrymple and my mother agree on anything except that we shouldn't have married each other. But don't try to change the subject, Daisy."

"Try! I thought I succeeded nicely."

"Only briefly. Quite apart from leaving the babies with Nanny—and I expect you're right about that—are you sure you're recovered enough from the birth to go exploring the Tower? As I recall, it's nothing but stairs, stairs, and more stairs, most of them steep and narrow."

"It's nearly the end of April already! They'll be two months old in a couple of days. I'm perfectly all right, just going quietly mad stuck here in the house with nothing to do but give Oliver or Miranda a bottle now and then, when Nanny deigns to permit. It was fun when Belinda was at home. She so enjoyed helping with them during the Easter hols. But now she's gone back to school . . ." Daisy sighed. "I'm glad she's enjoying boarding school, but I do miss her."

"So do I. Well, love, I'm not about to become the heavy-handed Victorian paterfamilias—"

"You'd better not try!"

Alec grinned. "No, that's exactly my feeling. But please don't traipse off if I have to go out of town, and make sure Nanny knows how to telephone me at the Yard."

"She can always ring up and ask for me at the Tower."

"I hardly think the Yeoman Warders will be willing to search that warren for—"

"Oh, but that's the best thing. That is, not the best but what, added to G & S, confirmed that I'm positively *meant* to write about the Tower. Mrs. Tebbit and her daughter are living there now, in the King's House, and they've invited me to lunch."

"Tebbit?"

"Your mother's friend. At least, one of your mother's fellow bridge players. The divinely outspoken old lady."

"With the rather limp daughter? Living in the Tower? Not, I take it, imprisoned for high treason?"

"Darling, as though your mother would be acquainted with anyone who might be suspected of high treason!" Daisy considered. "Mrs. Tebbit might commit lèse-majesté, perhaps, but one can't be arrested for that nowadays, can one? Anyway, it seems the Resident Governor, Major General Carradine, is some sort of cousin, and—"

"Tell me later, Daisy. I must be off." Alec gulped down the last drops of coffee, folded the *News Chronicle* and stuck it under his arm, and came around the table for a good-bye kiss. "Things are slow at present, so I'm hoping to clear up some arrears of paperwork before the Super has me arrested for dereliction of duty."

Daisy returned his kiss with verve before saying hopefully, "Does that mean you'll be home early enough to take me out for some driving practice? With what Mr. Thorwald is going to pay me, I'll be able to buy a secondhand car!"

Alec groaned. "I'll do my best. If you must have a car, it'll be just as well if you learn how to drive it without running over too many bobbies on point duty. We can't spare the men."

"Beast!" said Daisy, and pursed her lips for another kiss.

Daisy went up to the nursery. It had been Mrs. Fletcher's room while she lived with them, and Belinda had moved in when her grandmother moved to Bournemouth. Poor Bel had had to return to her tiny bedroom when the twins were born.

Not that the nursery was exactly large. In fact, it was definitely crowded with Nanny's bed and two cribs. A wardrobe, half occupied with shelves, stood against one wall. There was an armchair on one side of the fireplace and an elderly ottoman on the other, full of clean nappies. Its padded top was useful for changing wet and dirty ones. Later it could metamorphose into a toy chest. In the window was a small table with two rush-bottom chairs.

Remembering her own childhood, Daisy guessed that the rush seats wouldn't last long once the babies were up and about. Pulling bits out of them was irresistible.

Remembering her own childhood—The trouble was that she couldn't help comparing this nursery with the spacious day-nursery, night-nursery, and schoolroom at Fairacres.

She had chosen to marry a middle-class policeman, chosen a life in a semi-detached house in the suburbs. She was content with her choice, but she had to admit to herself that she had never for a moment considered how it would affect her children.

Knocking softly on the door—after all the nursery was also Nanny's bedroom—Daisy thought ruefully that she had made her bed and the twins were going to have to lie in it.

Ah well, they didn't know anything different.

Nanny Gilpin opened the door with a finger to her lips. Her face was pink beneath iron-grey hair sternly pulled back under a starched cap. Her plum-coloured dress, mid-calf in length, had a starched white collar and cuffs, and over it she wore a spotless starched white apron. In spite of all the starch, she was a kindly woman.

So, at least, said Daisy's friend Melanie Germond, who had recommended Mrs. Gilpin. Furthermore, her daughter, Bel's school-friend Lizzie, was still fond of her old nurse.

But Nanny Gilpin was undeniably old-fashioned. She expected absolute rule over the nursery, with parents admitted by appointment only. As she was, to all appearances, very good with the babies, Daisy was afraid of losing her and so catered to her whims, however, reluctantly.

She had told Nanny she was going out to lunch and wanted to see the twins before she left.

"You may come in, Mummy," Nanny whispered, "but I just put them down for a nap, so not a sound, if you please."

Daisy tiptoed over to Oliver's crib. He lay on his back, eyes closed, arms spread wide, hands relaxed. The soft down on his head had a distinct gingerish tone. He might end up a redhead, like his elder sister, but Nanny said it would probably change as he grew older.

He looked so tiny, so delicate. The doctor said twins were always smaller than the average baby, which made sense. Otherwise, how enormous she'd have been! They were both perfectly healthy though, thank heaven, and would catch up in height and weight in due course.

Oliver had kicked off his coverlet. Daisy leant forward to straighten it—then pulled back at a warning cough from Mrs. Gilpin.

"Now, Mummy, we don't want to wake him, do we?"

Daisy swallowed a sigh. Of course, Nanny knew best how to take care of babies, didn't she?

The baby's lips pursed in a sucking motion. One hand rose to insert a thumb in his mouth. It didn't mean he was hungry, she assured herself, as she had been assured.

Nanny moved forward in a purposeful way. Daisy hastily turned to Miranda's crib.

Miranda lay there quietly, good as gold, but her blue eyes were wide open. Catching sight of Daisy, she smiled. Daisy cast a quick glance behind her. Nanny was occupied with tucking in Oliver. Quick as a wink, Daisy scooped up her daughter in her arms for a quick kiss and cuddle before she was caught.

Miranda chuckled. Enchanted, Daisy kissed the top of her head, revelling in the softness of her dark fluff and sweet, milky smell.

"Now, Mummy—"

"She was awake, Nanny. I didn't wake her, truly."

"And how is she ever going to fall asleep if you pick her up?"

This was unanswerable. With an audible sigh, Daisy laid Miranda back in the crib, where she set up an earsplitting screech.

"You see?" asked Nanny accusingly.

Defeated, Daisy retreated.

Melanie Germond had also been invited to lunch with the Tebbits. She called for Daisy and they walked together through an April shower to the tube station.

"It's so brave of you to carry a red umbrella," said Melanie with a touch of envy.

"Brave?" Daisy queried, surprised. After her craven surrender to Mrs. Gilpin, she felt anything but brave.

"When practically everyone else's are black. People look at you."

"Why shouldn't they? Anyway, they're only looking at the umbrella, really, not at me."

"I suppose it's your upbringing." Melanie sighed. "We always had it drummed into us that one should never draw attention to oneself."

After living for a year and a half in St. John's Wood, Daisy was still discovering new facets of the difference between the middle classes and her own aristocratic background. She pondered. "I don't think we were ever taught anything so specific, certainly not that drawing attention to oneself is a virtue. I suppose it was sort of taken for granted that people would look at us, just because my father was Viscount Dalrymple. Unless we were among other people of the same sort, of course. Oh dear, that does make me sound stuck-up!"

"Daisy, that's not what I meant! No one could be less stuck-up than you."

"Well, I hope not. My brother had the umbrella made for me just before he went to France, to cheer me up. I think of it as a sort of outsize, year-round Armistice poppy."

"Oh, Daisy, I *am* sorry!" Mel said miserably. "I don't seem to be able to help putting my foot in it today."

"Bosh! I didn't have to tell you that." She grinned. "I could have just let you go on thinking me stuck-up."

"I don't. I never did. Do stop teasing, or I'll arrive with my face as red as your umbrella and everyone will stare at me."

Daisy gave her friend's face an envious glance. Mel had a perfect English rose complexion. Unlike Daisy, she had no need of powder to hide unwanted freckles. With just a touch of lip colour, and her unbobbed hair done up in a French pleat, she looked every inch the respectable bank manager's wife she was. Daisy was glad Alec had not followed his father into the banking profession. She could never have lived up to the requisite staidness. For one thing, a policeman's wife didn't have to entertain her husband's clients.

She suppressed a giggle. Alec's "clients" were crooks—but Mel wouldn't understand her amusement. "Not you, darling, you never blush, you lucky thing," she said, and folded her umbrella as they entered the shelter of the station.

"If you were stuck-up," said Mel, "you'd travel by taxi, not by the Underground."

"The tube is quicker than buses, and I'm a working woman, remember. In fact, this is a working occasion for me. I'm hoping to persuade the Resident Governor to give me special access for research. It would make for much more interesting articles than just parroting the guidebooks. Have you the right change for the ticket machine?"

At Baker Street, they switched to the Inner Circle line, and a few rattling, swaying minutes later, they emerged from the Mark Lane station at the top of Tower Hill.

The shower had passed over. The sun shone in a sky decorated with little puffs of white lamb's wool. Daisy and Melanie paused to look down towards the river, where the ancient palace-fortress spread up the hill towards them, a breeze gently waving the Union Jack atop the White Tower.

"It looks innocent as a picture postcard," Daisy remarked with a shudder.

"What do you mean?"

"Did you ever come here as a child? You're a Londoner; you must have."

"Yes, I suppose most London children come, but I don't remember much about it."

"We were brought once as a treat. Gervaise loved it, of course, all the arms and armour and bloodshed. You know what ghouls little boys are. Violet saw it as romantic, besides being fascinated by the Crown Jewels. But I had nightmares for weeks afterwards. All that chopping off of heads: I got it mixed up in my mind with *Alice in Wonderland*. In my dreams, I confused the Red Queen with Bloody Mary, and Alice with Lady Jane Grey."

"How horrible!"

"I even dreamt of ravens growing as tall as flamingos and turning into croquet hoops."

That made Mel laugh. "I do remember being afraid of the ravens," she acknowledged.

"I've been reading up on the history," said Daisy as they waited for the traffic policeman to let them cross to the gardens in the middle of Trinity Square. "Gower's *The Tower of London*, to prepare for the articles. I must admit I hoped it would dispel my early impressions of the place, but it simply put the endless executions in context."

"I don't know how Miss Tebbit can bear to live there."

"I doubt she has much imagination. And Mrs. Tebbit is capable of facing down any number of headless ghosts. Though I must say, it doesn't look at all sinister today."

Today, the picturesque scene ahead was more evocative of colourful processions of kings and queens on their way to Westminster Abbey to be crowned, escorted by throngs of nobles on brightly caparisoned horses. The blare of motor horns and glint of sunlight on polished brass headlamps conjured up trumpet fanfares and cheering crowds. Absorbed by the view, Daisy didn't notice the constable on point duty waving them across the street.

"Come on." Melanie tugged her arm. "Do you know him?" she asked as Daisy waved to the policeman.

"Who? Oh, the bobby? No, but learning to drive has given me a new appreciation for their intrepidity. Imagine standing there with all the taxis and 'buses and lorries and cars swirling about you, with nothing to protect you but long white gauntlets."

"Much worse than mere headless ghosts," Mel said with a smile.

They reached the gardens safely. The path led them to a reminder of the Tower's grim history, a fenced-off square commemorating the scaffold where public executions used to take place. Here, Daisy thought, the crowds would have jeered, not cheered, enjoying with equal glee a royal procession or a grisly death. Dutifully, she made a note of the inscription. Alec was right: The Tower was a morbid subject to write about. But it was too late now to change her mind.

They walked down Tower Hill, the pavement

separated from the dry, grassy moat by an iron railing and trees. Beyond the moat rose the outer walls. With their massive towers, arrow slits, and crenellations, they had a stern, forbidding look, but daffodils danced under the greening trees.

At the bottom, they stopped outside the ticket office and refreshment room, an inappropriate-looking wooden building.

"This was the site of the Lion Tower," said Daisy. "They kept the Royal Menagerie here for hundreds of years."

"Please, no history lessons," Melanie begged. "Do we need tickets?"

"Surely not. We're invited guests. No, look, the notice says you need them only for the White Tower, the Bloody Tower, and the Crown Jewels."

The walk swung left under a rounded Norman arch adorned with the royal lion and unicorn carved in stone, between two round towers. A stout Yeoman Warder stood there, a picturesque figure in his dark blue Tudor-style tunic and bonnet, lavishly adorned with red braid; on his chest was a crown, with G V R beneath. His eight-foot tasselled halberd was also Tudor and picturesque, though no doubt as lethal at close quarters as any modern automatic.

"Could you direct us to the King's House, please?"

A benevolent smile divided his short, neat grey beard from his moustache. "You'll be Mrs. Fletcher and Mrs. Germond? We was advised to look out for you." He turned to point the way. "You go across the bridge here, over the moat, then under the next archway. That's the Byward Tower. Keep straight ahead along Water Street, past the Bell Tower on your left. A bit farther on, you'll see the Traitors' Gate on your right. You turn left there, under the portcullis. There's a tunnel below the Bloody Tower to the Inner Ward. Just follow the signs to the Bloody Tower and the Crown Jewels. Can't miss it. You'll find another chap there who'll tell you the rest of the way."

They thanked him and continued over the bridge.

"His directions sounded like a history lesson," Melanie complained whimsically.

"Don't blame me. The White Tower is where they found the bones of the two little princes—"

"Daisy!"

"Sorry!"

"You won't start talking about murders and executions at lunch, will you?"

"Good heavens, no! That would be inexcusable in a duchess or a dustman."

"A duchess, perhaps," Mel retorted, "but my daily woman's husband is a dustman, and from what my housekeeper relays of her conversations, he regularly dispenses such tidbits from the evening paper over their supper."

"Really? Well, I assure you, no duchess of my acquaintance would dream of raising the subject before coffee."

Laughing, they passed under the Byward Tower arch, where a rigid sentry stood, clad in a red coat, white trousers, and red-cockaded white shako, and armed with a modern rifle.

"There's a military garrison here," said Daisy, "as well as the Beefeaters, who, I gather, regard that epithet as a mortal insult. Yeoman Warders, they are, so be careful what you say."

"I shall," Mel promised.

They watched as the soldier turned about, with much raising of knees and stamping of feet, marched a few paces, turned again, marched back, and re-sumed his position.

"I wonder how he knows when it's time to do that," Daisy said. "Did you hear a bugle or a whistle or anything?"

"No, nothing."

Daisy went up to the sentry. "I suppose you're not allowed to answer a question?" she asked.

His gaze never shifted from straight over her shoulder, but his lips twitched and he gave an in-finitesimal shake of the head.

"Ah well, never mind." She rejoined Melanie.

"Daisy, how could you?"

"Easily. How will I find out if I don't ask?"

They continued along Water Street.

Water Street was a cobbled street occupying the fortress's outer ward on the river side. High stone walls on either side were reminders of the Tower's historic function as a prison, but the inner wall's starkness was softened by a luxuriant creeper now putting forth bright green leaves. A few other people were wandering along, many studying booklets, which, judging by their overheard comments, pro-vided a brief history and description of the Tower. Ahead, a group stood by a railing on the right, being harangued by a Yeoman Warder. Several others turned left between a pair of sentries and dis-appeared under an arch.

"That must be the Bloody Tower," Daisy said.

As they turned in between the motionless sen-tries, she noticed behind each man a viciously spiked semicircle of iron protruding from the wall. She hadn't realized the torture had started before pris-oners even reached their cells. That was an aspect of the Tower she didn't intend to emphasize in her articles. She avoided drawing Melanie's attention to the fanged arcs, and also to the ironclad teeth of the portcullis suspended ominously overhead. Presumably it had good strong chains to support it?

A cloud passing across the sun made the tunnel suddenly dank and gloomy. They started up the slope, footsteps ringing on the cobbles.

Suddenly, a black apparition loomed ahead, silhouetted against the daylight. Daisy clutched Mel's arm. "What . . . ?"

"A Beefeater." Mel corrected herself: "A Yeoman Warder."

"Oh, of course." She felt an utter ass. The shape of the dark figure was peculiar, his long tunic suggesting a fashionably short skirt, his bonnet a truncated top hat. A bushy beard made his head look overlarge. But she wouldn't have jumped to the conclusion it was a ghost if she hadn't already managed to give herself the creeps. Not that she believed in ghosts.

He came down towards them, a tall, burly man, who seemed to Daisy to be eyeing them in a disagreeably appraising manner. The light was too dim to be sure. Besides, she was probably prejudiced by the unwarranted fright his sudden appearance had caused her. He was perfectly polite when they stopped him to ask for further directions.

In fact, he turned back to accompany them. Emerging from the tunnel, they continued up the cobbled slope. A crumbling section of ancient wall and a hideous modern guardhouse blocked the expected vista of the White Tower, the central keep of William the Conqueror's castle. Ahead, at the top of the slope, were two broad, shallow flights of steps. However, their guide ushered them through a gap in the wall on their left, up a couple of steps under a small arch. It was a murky spot, with high blank walls on two sides and a steep stone staircase on the third. Up this, the yeoman led them.

"So you're friends of Mrs. Tebbit, then, are you?" he said, his voice placing him as a Northcountryman, with the edges worn off by his sojourn in the army. "A very nice lady."

"Nice" was not how Daisy would describe Mrs. Tebbit. Amusing, interesting, thought-provoking, just plain provoking— In any case, it was not the yeoman's place to pronounce judgement, favourable or unfavourable, on members of the Resident Governor's household, even if he held some rank above the ordinary warder, as appeared by the White Tower insignia on his uniform. Nor did she like his tone, which seemed sly and insinuating, or the way he looked back at her and Melanie, apparently to judge their reactions.

Beside her, Mel pursed her lips in disapproval. They toiled upward in silence. In any case, they needed all their breath for the ascent. The warder waited at the top. Daisy thought she detected a touch of sardonic enjoyment as he watched their arduous ascent from the pit. Had he taken them that way just to amuse himself?

They came out level with the first floor of the Bloody Tower. Its entrance was just ahead, with a yeoman in a booth waiting to check tickets, his halberd leaning in the corner behind him. Another yeoman, unarmed, stood ready to escort visitors inside and tell them all about the murder of the young princes.

Their guide turned right towards a grassy slope with sycamores, just leafing out, surrounded by daffodils. Sparrows chirped noisily from the branches; a raven on the ground stared at them with bright, knowing eyes and greeted them: "Grawk!" The sun came out.

"Tower Green," said the yeoman. "The scaffold was just up there, where they used to cut off the heads of them as was favoured with a private execution. That black-and-white Tudor building there, built against the wall, that's the King's House. Just finished scraping off the old plaster coating, they have, that hid the timbers, and a sight better it looks."

It was indeed an attractive scene in the sunshine. Nothing could have looked less threatening. Daisy resolved to enjoy her lunch and try to ignore for the present the constant reminders of bloodshed.

2

A sentry stood at the door of the King's House. He remained immobile, expressionless, but his eyes slewed to watch them as Melanie rang the bell. They heard the bell ring inside, simultaneous with a bugle call from somewhere behind them.

A neat maid opened the door. She showed them up to the second floor—Daisy recalled Alec's warning about the Tower having an awful lot of steps—and into a spacious drawing room.

A high, wide, mullioned oriel window faced north onto Tower Green. Sunlight flooded in through a window in the opposite gable, overlooking Water Street, the outer wall, and the Thames. The ceiling was open to the slanting rafters, and dark beams chequered the white walls. This much, Daisy absorbed as a tall, painfully thin woman rose and hurried eagerly to greet them.

"I'm so glad you were able to come. Mother has been missing her friends in St. John's Wood." Miss Tebbit, in her mid-forties, wore her greying hair in a bun confined with a net, despite which wisps escaped in all directions. Her brown silk frock sagged at the hem. Admittedly, uneven hemlines were all the rage, but Miss Tebbit's just plain sagged.

A tart voice came from behind her. "There's no need to make me sound pathetic, Myrtle. Life is much more interesting here than in that fusty suburb. Just think, this very room is the Council Chamber where Guy Fawkes was questioned! But I'm delighted to see you, Mrs. Germond, Mrs. Fletcher. I hope you've come primed with all the latest scandal."

"Mother!"

Daisy was glad to see the move to the Tower had not banished the mischievous twinkle from Mrs. Tebbit's eyes. Ignoring, as usual, her daughter's feeble protest, the old lady introduced the Resident Governor. A slight, dapper gentleman with the erect bearing of a regular soldier, Major General Carradine had sprung to his feet when the visitors entered. He looked to be in his mid-fifties, his fair hair and moustache fading to salt-and-pepper, but still thick. He came forward to shake their hands with an affable smile.

"Welcome to my humble castle," he said. "May I offer you some sherry? Or a cocktail, perhaps?"

Melanie opted for sherry, while Daisy requested gin without the gin. "Spirits at midday make me sleepy," she explained.

Carradine laughed. "Vermouth coming up. Would you care for a dash of soda water in it?"

"That would be perfect. Yes, please."

He poured Cinzano and sprayed soda water, then handed her the drink. She took a sip. "Just right."

"I'll have the same," announced Mrs. Tebbit. "Never could abide sherry."

"But Mother, you've always—"

"And gin makes me bilious. Thank you, Arthur. Hmm, not bad."

He grinned at Daisy. In an undertone, he said, "I never expected inviting my cousins to live with me would provide such a source of amusement."

"She's splendid, isn't she? Your gain is our loss."

They chatted for a few minutes. Daisy liked him and thought he'd probably be amenable to giving her special access for her research. She was wondering whether to broach the subject at once or wait until lunch or after, when Mrs. Tebbit said commandingly, "Arthur!"

The general, looking a bit sheepish, excused himself to Daisy and went to join the old lady and Melanie. Miss Tebbit gravitated to Daisy's side, with her usual air of vague anxiety.

"Oh dear, Mrs. Fletcher," she said with a little gasp, "I do hope you won't think we've brought you here under false pretences."

"False pretences?" Daisy asked, astonished.

"The numbers!"

"Numbers? Are the general's daughters going to join us?"

"Oh yes, they promised."

"You and your mother moved here to chaperon them, didn't you?"

"Yes." Miss Tebbit wrung her hands. "But I'm very much afraid we shall be six ladies and only three gentlemen at table!"

Daisy laughed. "Well, I don't mind a bit, but isn't the Tower swarming with military men?"

"That's the trouble." She lowered her voice. "You see, Mrs. Carradine died when the girls were quite small, and her sister brought them up. Cousin Arthur was away a lot, of course, being in the army. Then after the War, he was offered this post, Resident Governor of the Tower, so they all came to live here. And his sister-in-law went and married the lieutenant colonel in charge of the Hotspur Guards battalion quartered here!"

"How very shocking of her."

"Oh no, I don't blame dear Christina in the least, even though Cousin Arthur says Colonel Duggan is not a pukka sahib. It's . . . it's not always very pleasant being an aging spinster, my dear."

"Not a pukka sahib?" Daisy asked, intrigued.

"He rose from the ranks, starting out as a common private. He got his commission and attained the rank of lieutenant colonel only because of the War, because so many officers were killed."

"He must be exceptionally competent, then."

"I wouldn't know about that, I'm afraid. In any case, when Christina married, Cousin Arthur sent the girls off to finishing school in Switzerland, so that was all right. But now they're seventeen and eighteen, such pretty girls, and they've come home, and as is only natural, they want to spend time with their aunt."

"Of course, since she brought them up."

"And, you see, the Hotspur Guards are presently our garrison again, and the colonel's quarters are positively haunted by young officers. The battalion will be quartered in the Tower for only a few months, I understand, or is it weeks? But in the meantime, Colonel Duggan just laughs, and Cousin Arthur has quarrelled with him, and, oh dear, it's very uncomfortable."

"And you can't invite any of the officers to lunch?"

"Exactly! So our numbers are all wrong. I know it's not what you're used to. . . ."

Daisy didn't like to reveal that these days she

usually ate lunch in the nursery with Nanny and the twins. "Who are the other two gentlemen?" she enquired.

"General Sir Patrick Heald," Miss Tebbit said impressively. "He's Keeper of the Regalia, which makes him a member of His Majesty's Household. And Cousin Arthur's assistant, Mr. Webster. He's a distant relative on the other side. He's sort of a secretary, really, but Cousin Arthur calls him his ADC, or sometimes his adjutant. Military terms, I believe."

"He's not a soldier, though?"

"No. And I must say," she added with a shadow of her mother's frankness, "it's very pleasant to have someone to talk to who is not obsessed with the army!"

"I can imagine it might be." Daisy looked round as the door burst open.

Two girls in tennis whites bounced in.

"Frightfully sorry we're late, everyone," the taller said breathlessly.

"But we won't be half a tick," vowed the other.

"We won't stop to bathe. . . ."

"Just a lick and a promise . . ."

"And a quick change . . ."

"And we'll be down for the soup."

They disappeared as abruptly as they had arrived, leaving Daisy with an impression of exuberant energy, pink faces, and blond bobs ruffled by exertion. Nothing could have been more at variance with the Tower's gloomy history.

"Allow me to introduce my daughters," said the general with pardonable sarcasm. "Those were Brenda and Fay. And allow me to apologize for their excruciating manners."

"Oh, I don't know," Mrs. Tebbit remarked. "They

did apologize on their own behalf. And tennis is healthy exercise these days, nothing like the genteel nonsense that was all girls were permitted in my young day. All we could manage, indeed, in our crinolines and corsets."

Carradine looked as if he was no longer so certain that Mrs. Tebbit's outspokenness was amusing. Perhaps he was also wondering whether Brenda and Fay had been playing singles or doubles. Daisy wanted to ask whether the amenities of the Tower included tennis courts, which would hint at doubles with military partners. However, she was afraid anything to do with tennis might prove inflammatory just now.

Before she could make up her mind, they were interrupted by the arrival of two men. The general introduced Sir Patrick Heald, Keeper of the Regalia, "A bit of a sinecure," he boomed in a voice unexpectedly deep for his short, tubby frame and round pink face. "I get free quarters in St. Thomas's Tower, a nice pied-à-terre in town, in exchange for minimal services to the Crown. Pun intended, ha ha!"

"You disappoint me, Sir Patrick," said Mrs. Tebbit. "I've been picturing you busily polishing the diamonds every day, or at least once a week."

"No, no!" He laughed jovially. "Leave that sort of thing to our good Curator under the stern eye of our friend here." He indicated the man who had come in with him.

General Carradine introduced him. "My adjutant, Jeremy Webster. Jeremy, Mrs. Fletcher and Mrs. Germond."

Webster bowed, his solemnity scarcely lightened by a perfunctory smile. A stocky man, he wore horn-rimmed glasses with lenses so thick, Daisy thought for a moment he must be blind. He had no white stick, however, and he had entered the room without hesitation. His mouth, wide and rather thin-lipped, in repose turned downward. This, with the spectacles, a sallow complexion, and a receding hairline, gave him a froglike appearance, but the effect was melancholy rather than disagreeable. He seemed about the same age as the general, perhaps a few years younger.

Jeremy Webster? Beatrix Potter's Jeremy Fisher inevitably sprang to mind. Daisy would have to take care not to address him as Mr. Fisher.

Her attempts at conversation elicited only monosyllabic responses until Miss Tebbit mentioned that he was also a writer.

"Also?" He turned his bottle-bottom lenses on Daisy with a perceptible brightening not unmixed with scepticism.

"I write articles for several magazines," she said defiantly. She had met such scepticism before. Either he didn't believe women were capable of doing, or ought to do a man's job, or he wrote something frightfully academic and considered that nothing else counted. "Both here and in America. What do you write?"

"I am preparing a treatise on the history of the Crown Jewels. Of interest only to scholars, I fear."

"Not at all. I'm interested. I'm writing about the Tower at present, and I'd be delighted to hear about your researches. I'd give you credit in the article, of course."

Webster gave her a suspicious glance, then reflected, frowning. "I might be able to give you one or two little-known facts," he said at last, grudgingly. "The Yeoman Warders merely repeat parrot-fashion what is already printed in the twopenny guidebooks, were visitors sufficiently enterprising to read them."

"That would be very kind of you."

"I'll have to think about it."

Daisy couldn't see what there was to think about, but the reappearance of Brenda and Fay distracted her. Their entrance was more sedate this time, as befitted their silk frocks and powdered noses. Their hemlines raised the latest knee-high fashion to the uppermost limit.

Close on their heels came a manservant, who announced that luncheon was served.

As they left the drawing room, Mrs. Tebbit nudged Daisy and pointed to a door. "That room is where Lord Nithsdale was imprisoned. He escaped disguised as his wife's maid." She chortled. "Quite a number of prisoners have escaped from this impregnable fortress, you know. It's to be hoped that Cousin Arthur doesn't mislay any."

"Mother, there have been no prisoners in the Tower since those German spies were shot in the War!"

Mrs. Tebbit sighed. "No, alas, but one can always hope. It would make living here still more amusing."

They all trooped down to the first-floor dining room.

Daisy and Melanie were seated on either side of General Carradine. Over the soup, he and Daisy came to an amicable arrangement about her research. He was pleased at the prospect of more American visitors, who invariably bought guidebooks and tickets to all the attractions, and took every available tour.

"Each of which costs them a gratuity," he said with satisfaction. "Or rather, a donation to our chapel, St. Peter ad Vincula. It'll keep my yeomen busy and happy. And best of all, the Guards won't

like it. The Hotspurs don't care to think of themselves as garrisoning a mere tourist attraction."

Miss Tebbit was right, Daisy realized: There was a
feud going on between the Resident Governor and
the garrison. Who'd have guessed that after eight
and a half centuries of grim history, the Tower still
seethed with malice and resentment?

Not that one could have guessed it from Sir
Patrick's chortles and Mrs. Tebbit's cackles at the
other end of the table. The unlikely pair were getting on like a house on fire.

As luncheon continued, Daisy felt Jeremy Webster's eyes—or rather, his spectacles—turned on
her. The glasses made it impossible to tell if he was
regarding her with earnest enquiry or stern disapproval, or some other, unguessable emotion. It
made her uneasy, but she tried not to glance his
way as she chatted with General Carradine and
with Brenda, seated on her right.

Brenda and her sister had recently "come from
a ladies' seminary," like the three "little girls" in
The Mikado. As with Yum-Yum, Pitti-Sing, and Peep-
Bo, no doubt the chief lesson learnt was how to
catch a husband. The War had prevented Daisy's
being "finished" on the Continent. She asked
Brenda how she had liked it.

"It was frightful. Too, too old-fashioned, really.
Would you believe, they taught us to waltz and polka,
but never a word about the fox-trot, let alone the
tango or shimmy."

"Shocking!"

Brenda grinned. "Then there was deportment,
and polite conversation. Mademoiselle D'Aubin was a
dragon and Frau Horst was worse, and I don't see why
we had to learn French and Italian, let alone German. But the tennis coach was a smasher. All the girls

were utterly potty about him. He was a pretty good teacher, too. Fay and I are quite keen on tennis."

"Can you play here at the Tower? There are courts?"

"Oh yes, a couple of grass courts, behind the Waterloo Barracks. I'll show you later, if you like, so that you can write about them. Do you play?"

"Only under threat of death. No, I'm not sporty, I'm afraid."

"A lot of the officers play, so we can always find partners. Some of them are pretty good. Lieutenant Jardyne has a smashing backhand, only he gets mad as fire if his partner botches a shot. You can practically see steam coming out of his ears, however much he tries to hide it. He's frightfully keen on Fay, you see, so he doesn't want her to see him fly off the handle."

Though Brenda claimed to have been taught the principles of polite conversation, she didn't seem to have absorbed the precepts. Daisy was accustomed to finding herself the involuntary recipient of confidences from the most unexpected people, but not generally in the middle of a luncheon party. What was more, she noticed that General Carradine's conversation with Melanie was faltering. From the corner of her eye, she glimpsed his set face. Time to change the subject.

She started to ask, "Did you ski in Switz—"

"Your father's quite right, my girl," Mrs. Tebbit interrupted. In spite of her loquacious neighbour, she, too, had overheard Brenda, and she had no inhibitions against sticking her oar in. "Right in this, at least," she added after a moment's consideration: "You're fools if you marry soldiers."

"I don't see why, Aunt Alice. Both you and our mother did."

"And look where it got us! Gilbert was sent out to Egypt and I was widowed at twenty-three. Your mother followed Arthur to India and died young of typhoid. Unless it was typhus—I never can recall the difference."

"Mother!"

"Quite right, Myrtle," said the old lady handsomely, "not a proper topic for the luncheon table. Or any other table. Nor is your love life, young ladies."

"I didn't—" protested Fay.

"Sorry, Aunt Alice!" Brenda said, without any visible sign of repentance.

Melanie, always rendered acutely uncomfortable by the possibility of strife, asked Fay whether they had visited other countries while on the Continent. The diversion worked. Both girls talked eagerly about the wonders of France and Italy; their father's face smoothed, and he joined Sir Patrick in recounting anecdotes about their respective travels with the army.

Melanie, some years older than Daisy, had been to the Continent before the War, but Daisy was the only person present who had crossed the Atlantic. Mel urged her to tell about flying across America. No one else had even been up in an aeroplane, so they were all enthralled.

It was the hitherto silent Webster who enquired as to why she had chosen to embark on such a perilous flight.

Daisy hunted for a way to answer without revealing Alec's profession. So many of even the most law-abiding people started looking at her askance when they found out she was a policeman's wife.

"My husband was a pilot in the War," she hedged, "and we happened to meet another English aviator. . . ."

"Mr. Fletcher is now a Scotland Yard detective," Mrs. Tebbit revealed with glee.

"Goll-ee!" breathed Fay, awed.

"He had no official standing in America, of course, but when we saw a crime committed, he had to give chase."

"And he let you fly with him?" Brenda asked, wide-eyed.

"I didn't exactly give him any choice in the matter."

General Carradine gave Daisy a reproachful glance.

Mrs. Tebbit promptly added more fuel to the flames. "Quite right, Mrs. Fletcher. Men always try to keep the best adventures to themselves. I only wish I'd insisted on going to Egypt with Gilbert. At least I would have seen the pyramids and the sphinx for myself."

"Oh, Mother, but you might have been killed, too, and then where would I have been?"

The old lady gave her daughter a critical look. "Who knows, perhaps you might have blossomed without me to hold your leading strings."

Myrtle Tebbit seemed alarmingly likely to burst into tears. Melanie opened her mouth, no doubt with some anodyne remark prepared, but Jeremy Fisher sprang to the rescue.

"Miss Tebbit is all that is ladylike," he announced. Though he was refuting Mrs. Tebbit's comment, his inscrutable stare was turned on Daisy.

She had a vague impression that he had been watching her with particular intentness since she had revealed Alec's profession. Was he involved in some sort of fishy business? Could his treatise on the Crown Jewels possibly be cover for preparing a plan to steal them?

No, she was letting her imagination run away with her. Seeing crime everywhere was another hazard of being a police officer's wife.

Melanie, in desperation, had started to talk about the seasonable weather. Mrs. Tebbit, perhaps remorseful about her mockery of her daughter, responded by quoting " 'Oh, to be in England, now that April's there.' "

" 'When all at once I saw a crowd / A host, of golden daffodils,' " put in Fay.

" 'Spring, the sweet Spring, is the year's pleasant king.' " That was Daisy's contribution.

" 'The year's at the Spring, / And day's at the morn,' " said Sir Patrick. General Carradine stared at him in astonishment.

" 'Whan that Aprille with his shoures sote . . .' " Brenda began.

"Show-off," said Fay.

"The Prologue to the *Canterbury Tales*," said Miss Tebbit. "Do you know it all by heart?"

"Just the first line," Brenda admitted.

"I used to be able to recite the first eighteen lines, though I doubt if I ever pronounced it right."

"Won't you give it to us?" begged Fay.

"Oh, I couldn't possibly!" Miss Tebbit faltered, in a panic. "Not in company."

"I should like to hear it," said Webster solemnly.

Miss Tebbit shot an agonized glance at her mother.

"It's up to you, Myrtle," said that lady. "If you think you can remember it, I'm sure we should all be pleased to hear it. As I recall, the first bit is quite pretty. But don't go any further. Some of the rest is decidedly racy."

This brought a blush to her daughter's cheeks.

"Do go ahead, Miss Tebbit," Daisy encouraged

her. "I couldn't possibly quote it all by heart, let alone spell it, but I may be able to prompt if you get stuck."

Setting down her spoon and fork—they had moved on to apple tart and custard by this time—Miss Tebbit stood up. Hands clasped before her like a little girl repeating her lesson, she proceeded to regale them with Chaucer's paeon to spring.

Brenda started the applause, and Fay joined in with enthusiasm. "Spiffing, Aunt Myrtle," she said.

They were nice girls, Daisy decided, though their manners left something to be desired. While Mrs. Tebbit was not likely to set a good example, she wouldn't hesitate to correct them. The rough edges would smooth away with practice, if their social horizons were widened beyond the ranks of the garrison's officers.

The general had sat through the recitation with a blank face. "Do you mean to tell me that's written in English?" he asked.

"Old English, Daddy. Even older than Shakespeare. Didn't you read it at school?"

"No, we were too busy cramming Latin and Greek, I suppose."

"A fine thing it is when a man knows more of the language of Rome and Athens than his own!" scoffed Mrs. Tebbit.

General Carradine sighed. " 'I am the very model of a modern major-general,' " he quoted wryly.

Another reminder of G & S. Daisy countered with "The flowers that bloom in the Spring, tra-la," and the conversation returned to April and the weather.

But what slipped into Daisy's mind now was an uncharacteristically gruesome verse from *The Yeomen of the Guard:*

The screw may twist and the rack may turn,
And men may bleed and men may burn,
O'er London town and its golden hoard
I keep my silent watch and ward!

Oh well, she thought, *it's far too late now to change my mind.* She was committed to writing about the Tower, gory history and all.

3

Mrs. Tebbit led the ladies out of the dining room, leaving the gentlemen to smoke and discuss Tower business.

At the bottom of the stairs up to the Council Chamber, Fay said, "Mrs. Fletcher, do let me show you Ralegh's Walk, where he used to take the air when he was a prisoner in the Bloody Tower. There used to be a door through from upstairs, before the Victorians built those hideous houses on the Governor's garden."

Daisy was sure to see Ralegh's Walk on her tour, so why on earth did Fay want to show her now? She was sufficiently curious to agree. "Thank you, I'd like to see it, if you don't mind us disappearing for a few minutes, Mrs. Tebbit."

"Sorry, Aunt Alice. We'll be back by the time Daddy comes for his coffee, promise." Down in the hall, she took a jacket from the coat tree. "Better grab your coat, Mrs. Fletcher. It's always windy up there."

As Daisy followed her out past the sentry, Fay

went on: "I expect I should have asked Aunt Alice before I invited you, but all that's frightfully *vieux jeu*, isn't it?"

"Is it? I'd have called it common courtesy. But perhaps I'm old-fashioned."

"Oh no! You being a writer and marrying a policeman—wasn't your father a lord?—not that that makes any difference these days, of course. But still, Brenda and I think you're frightfully up-to-date. As a matter of fact, we're having a bit of a time of it, trying to work things out. You see, so much of what they taught us in Switzerland was utterly pre-War, we're never quite sure. . . ."

"Your aunt . . . ?"

"Aunt Christina taught us proper manners before she married the colonel, but we were younger then and things are a bit different when you're grown-up, aren't they? And now there are always officers in their quarters and everything is rather free and easy, if you know what I mean. Not a bit formal. I don't suppose you'd give us a few hints, would you? As you're going to be around here for a while?"

"I'm perfectly willing, but I don't know that I'm the best person to ask. You and your sister may think I'm 'up-to-date,' but lots of people would call me unconventional."

"That's all right. We don't want to be rude, but we don't want to be conventional, either."

"Then, if I may be so blunt, don't go running after officers."

"There's nothing else to do here. And they're so adorable in their fancy uniforms."

"If you've read your Jane Austen," Daisy said tartly, "you know that's as old-fashioned as the hills."

"Jane Austen? I've heard of her, I think, but we

didn't read anything by her at school. It was mostly poetry, hence our facility at producing quotations. Novels were rather frowned on."

"Since, I assume, you have no need to earn your living as I did, you might try expending some of your time and energy in filling the holes in your education. No modern young woman should be content with an inferior education. Oh dear, I do sound pi!"

"Only slightly," Fay said with a giggle. "But we honestly do admire you, so . . ." She waved to the yeoman on guard at the Bloody Tower entrance and he saluted her with a grin. Popularity with the Hotspur officers apparently didn't preclude popularity with the warders. "Here, it's up these steps."

More steps. They climbed up onto the wall of the inner bailey. The top was wide enough for two people to walk abreast, with the upper door to the Bloody Tower at one end. The other end was closed off by a gate marked PRIVATE. Beyond this, potted plants created a pleasant, if small, balcony area, with windows and a door opening onto it from the dwellings built for the warders by the despised Victorians. The shoulder-high parapet provided some protection from the wind.

"All right," said Daisy, "what's this all about?"

Fay looked guilty. "I'm dying for a gasper." She took a silver cigarette case from the pocket of her jacket and offered it to Daisy.

"No thanks, I don't."

"You see, Aunt Alice is a game old bird, but she won't stand for me smoking, and nor will Daddy. They'd notice the smell indoors, in spite of those foul cigars he smokes. It's no good just stepping out of the front door, because they might see me through the window, and there's no back door to the King's House because of it being built against the wall." She lit a cigarette and leaned against the parapet, smoking.

"So that's why you were so keen to bring me up here."

"I suppose that's not very couth, either, come to think of it. Sorry. But I did think, too, that you'd like to see Ralegh's Walk."

"Certainly. I hope you're going to explain it to me."

Fay pointed to the building at the far end of the section of wall. "That's the Bloody Tower, where he was imprisoned. Sir Walter Ralegh, I mean. They let him come out through that door there to take the air on the wall, and he'd walk along to call on the Governor at the other end. There are flats for warders in this house here that's in the way now, and I don't suppose Sir Walter would care to visit them. That's really all I know about Ralegh, except that he dropped his cloak in a puddle so that the Queen wouldn't get her feet muddy—frightfully romantic!"

"And he was the one who introduced tobacco from the Americas," Daisy told her dryly.

"No, was he? Jolly good for him! This is really the best place for a smoke. One doesn't want to huddle in a hidden corner—too uncouth! Here one can always pretend to admire the view."

"Tell me about it."

Fay peered over the parapet. "There's St. Thomas's Tower, where that frightful Sir Patrick lives, when he's around. It's built over Traitors' Gate. And that monstrosity is Tower Bridge, of course." She waved her cigarette at the scene, then took another puff. "Oh blast! That awful, slimy man is watching."

With one hand, she stubbed out the cigarette be-

hind her back, while with the other she waved to a
man in the Yeoman Warders' blue and red who was
standing on top of the nearby Wakefield Tower.
Daisy recognised the bushy beard of the man who
had showed her and Melanie the way to the King's
House.

He sketched a salute and turned away.

"From that distance," said Daisy, "I doubt if he
could tell you were smoking, even if it was any of
his business."

"I swear he can see through walls," said Fay gloomily, "and you never know, he just might happen to
mention it to Daddy."

"Who is he?"

"The Yeoman Gaoler. Sergeant Major Rumford.
They're all sergeant majors, come to that, but he's
second in charge after the Chief Warder. Oh, blast
that bugle," she said as a call rang out. "It always re-
minds me of the Rupert Brooke poem."

" 'Bugles calling for them from sad shires'? Wil-
frid Owen."

"That's the one. I don't think I really want to
marry a soldier." Fay shivered. "It's cold. Let's go
down."

When Daisy and Fay reached the Council Chamber, Sir Patrick, the general, and his ADC had just
arrived. They drew back to let the ladies pass, then
followed them in.

Brenda jumped up. "Fay, Mrs. Germond has invited us to a tennis party! Isn't it kind of her? Aunt
Alice says we may go. Daddy, you should be thrilled
to death. We'll actually meet some young men who
aren't soldiers."

"That is indeed very kind of you, Mrs. Germond."

"Spiffing!" Fay exclaimed. "We'd love to come."

"It depends on the weather," Melanie warned.

She looked a trifle harassed. Daisy wondered whether Mrs. Tebbit had somehow managed to make it impossible for her not to issue the invitation.

"The sun is shining madly," said Fay with conviction. "Not a cloud in the sky. It's going to be fine for days."

The maid brought in coffee. General Carradine, having brought Daisy her cup and sat down beside her with his own, said, "I've been thinking about who's best to show you around the place. I believe Rumford's the man, my Yeoman Gaoler, second in command of the warders. He knows everything there is to know."

Daisy gave a murmur of appreciation, managing not to say she'd been told Rumford could see through walls. Fay caught her eye and pulled a face, Webster looked even more melancholy than usual, and Sir Patrick pulled a comic face expressive of distaste.

"I'm afraid he'll expect a gratuity," the general warned Daisy.

"Oh yes, for the chapel."

"I wonder," Brenda mused, "how much of Sergeant Rumford's gratuities actually reach the chapel."

"You mustn't say such things," her father snapped, "even in jest. It's a serious matter. Pocketing tips can get a man dismissed."

"Sorry! I didn't mean anything by it."

"Anyway, that's all right," Daisy put in hastily. "My American editor is pretty generous about expenses."

"Good, good." Carradine rubbed his hands together. "I'll have a word with Rumford this afternoon. Would tomorrow suit you? We'll hope the weather holds."

"Arthur," said Mrs. Tebbit commandingly, "I trust

you mean to invite Mrs. Fletcher to watch the Ceremony of the Keys. You'd have to stay the night here afterwards, my dear, as it takes place at ten o'clock and all the gates are locked."

"I'll have to consult Alec about that."

"Anytime. Just let us know. We'll be here."

"Thanks. I expect I'll be popping in and out for at least a week to make sure I've got it all right."

Then Melanie started making time-to-leave noises. General Carradine offered to send the ladies home in his car and sent his batman to fetch it.

Fay and Brenda escorted Daisy and Melanie back to the exit under the Bloody Tower.

"Mrs. Fletcher," said Brenda, "we'd like to introduce you to our aunt. Will you come and have lunch or tea or dinner or something one day when you're here?"

"If she invites me, I'd be happy to."

"And you, of course, Mrs. Germond," Fay put in quickly. "You could come specially. I know Aunt Christina will want to meet both of you."

As they passed under the portcullis and emerged from the tunnel, three officers came towards them. They all wore khaki uniform. Catching sight of the Carradine girls, the youngest cried out, "Well met!" Then, seeing the others with them, the three men stood aside to let them pass.

"Mrs. Fletcher," said Fay urgently, "these are particular friends of ours. May we introduce them?"

"Would you mind awfully, Mrs. Germond?" asked Brenda.

Daisy and Mel nodded and smiled.

Brenda first introduced Captain Macleod, a doctor in the Army Medical Corps and in charge of the Tower's hospital. In his mid-thirties, he was dark-haired, pale, too thin for his height, with a somewhat saturnine expression even when he smiled. The white line of a scar on his cheek did nothing to mar his good looks. Indeed, Daisy thought it might add a dangerous attraction in a young girl's eyes.

In fact, Fay seemed to have difficulty tearing her gaze from the doctor to introduce Captain Devereux.

The captain was a few years younger than Macleod, but old enough to have fought in the War. He had a devil-may-care air Daisy had seen before in soldiers who had gone through hell in the trenches, the reverse of shell shock but, in its way, equally abnormal. Such men often found it difficult to take anything seriously. Life and death had lost their importance.

With a grin, he presented the third officer to the ladies. "This stripling is Jardyne, a mere lieutenant, as you can see. Macleod and I are doing our best to whip him into shape."

Jardyne, fair, tall, and robust, smiled as he said, "How do you do?" but Daisy noticed a flash of anger in his eyes. She recalled that Brenda had said he was keen on Fay and did his best to hide his temper from her. He had cause enough for annoyance at present, what with his beloved making sheep's eyes at the doctor and Devereux making fun of his juniority.

Was there such a word? If not, there ought to be, Daisy decided.

"I say, Miss Fay," he said, "we were walking on the wharf and Dev has had a dashed good notion. How about you and Miss Carradine taking a boat trip on the river with us this afternoon? It's such a beautiful day." He hesitated. "Mrs. Fletcher and Mrs. Germond are welcome to come, too, of course."

"Kind of you," said Melanie, frowning slightly, "but we're just leaving."

"Yes," Daisy corroborated, "but why don't you invite Miss Tebbit? I bet she hasn't had such a treat in years, if ever."

"Aunt Myrtle?" Fay blurted out. The girls, the lieutenant, and the captain stared at Daisy in shock.

Dr. Macleod's smile became more saturnine than ever. "Yes, why don't you?" he drawled. "Sick call will sound in a couple of minutes, so I can't go along to play gooseberry. In fact, I should invite Mrs. Tebbit, too, if I were you."

"The old lady?" Lieutenant Jardyne was aghast.

Brenda pulled herself together. "Yes, why don't we?" she said brightly. "Thank you for the suggestion, Mrs. Fletcher."

At that point, the Bentley arrived from the far end of Water Street, driven by the manservant dressed in a chauffeur's peaked cap and motoring coat. The doctor and Captain Devereux handed Daisy and Melanie in and the car set off at a stately pace towards the Byward Tower. Daisy glanced back and saw the girls and the officers disappear under the Bloody Tower. They crossed paths with Sir Patrick. His face set in a frown, quite unlike his joviality in the King's House, he crossed the lane and unlocked a door in the wall on the other side.

Daisy's thoughts flitted involuntarily to Jeremy Webster, and the possibility that he had designs on the Crown Jewels. Was it possible the Keeper of the Jewel House suspected him?

"Who on earth am I going to invite to play tennis with Fay and Brenda?" Melanie demanded.

"You'll dig up someone. Did Mrs. Tebbit force you to invite them?"

"Shhh!" She made a slight gesture towards the chauffeur.

"Oh, for heaven's sake. Did she?"

"Not as blatantly as you forced those young men to invite the Tebbits. But you were quite right, of course. Most unsuitable for the girls to go off alone with the officers."

"You'll be doing a good deed inviting them to meet other people. That struck me as an explosive situation back there."

"Oh Daisy, you do have a tendency to dramatize!"

"Well, maybe. Perhaps it's just that I find the Tower rather sinister. I dare say it's only the influence of those childhood nightmares, but I almost wish I'd never thought of writing about it. And all those steps!"

The early-morning post brought an invitation from Mrs. Duggan to lunch in the colonel's quarters that very day. Daisy rang up Melanie. She had also been invited but had a prior engagement.

Daisy decided to accept anyway. Curiosity having overcome distaste, she wanted to observe the feud from the other side of the fence.

Approaching the Middle Tower at ten o'clock, when the Tower opened to the public, Daisy saw a tall, burly warder with a bushy beard chatting to the yeoman on guard. Her heart sank. She had hoped she was mistaken, that the Yeoman Gaoler, whom Carradine had chosen for her guide, the Sergeant Major Rumford whom Fay accused of spying on her, was not the man she had taken an instant dislike to.

Not that I have any real cause for mistrust, she scolded herself. The unfortunate manner that had put her off could well be responsible for Fay's accusations also. She must try to be fair.

As she drew closer, the bearded warder glanced round towards her, and she wondered if he was, in fact, the same man. She didn't remember so much grey in the lush beard. The eyes she recalled as sharp, even hard, now crinkled at the corners when he smiled at her. His nose was different, too, she thought. It was difficult to be sure; one tended to observe the costume, not the man. She noted his insignia—crossed keys on three chevrons, rather than the White Tower.

"Mrs. Fletcher?" His voice confirmed that he was not the warder she had expected. This was a native of London, not a Cockney, but perhaps from the Borough, south of the river. "I'm Crabtree, Chief Yeoman Warder. Mr. Rumford had to take care of some unexpected business, so I hope you won't mind starting your tour with me."

"I shall be delighted," said Daisy, with somewhat more emphasis than she had intended.

Mr. Crabtree, for all his friendliness, was a very tedious companion, alas. In his flat voice, he recited the history by rote, and told Daisy nothing that she hadn't already read. When they went through the arch under the Byward Tower, he pointed out the postern door leading to the Queen's Stair, the only entrance to the Tower after the gates were locked at night, for the sole use of the monarch. But he couldn't tell when or why it was last used, or even which queen it was named after.

He even made the sinister Traitors' Gate sound dull. As he talked, Daisy lent half an ear to another warder who was giving the same talk, word for word, to a small group of visitors. The tourists asked a few questions, then moved off along the lane just as Crabtree finished his lecture.

The other came over. "Message for you, Mr. Crabtree," he said.

"What's up, Mr. Pierce?"

"General Heald wants to show Mrs. Fletcher his gewgaws hisself." Pierce touched his hat to Daisy as he uttered her name. "I'll go tell him you're heading that way, and he'll meet you in the Wakefield Tower in ten minutes."

Crabtree pulled out his watch. "Right you are. He'll use his private entrance, I expect."

They grinned at each other, sharing indulgence for the foibles of the brass-hats. Daisy had noticed that the Chief Warder was on excellent terms with all the Yeoman Warders they had come across.

Pierce went off towards St. Thomas's Tower.

"No good waiting for the general here, ma'am," said Crabtree. "He'll go over by the bridge from his quarters. The Yeoman Gaoler's going to come and find us in the Wakefield Tower soon as he can get away."

They crossed the lane towards the Bloody Tower. Prompted by the sight of the motionless sentries on either side of the gate, Daisy asked, "You were a soldier, weren't you, Mr. Crabtree. Tell me how the sentries know when it's time to do their little march up and down."

Crabtree laughed. "It's up to them, madam. It's blinking hard work standing absolutely still, you wouldn't believe, even two hours on, two hours off. So when you feel a twitch coming on, or a cramp, or your legs going numb, you're allowed to do a little stamping about in a regulation manner. We don't want 'em dropping like flies."

"How sensible."

"Of course, in daylight, with people about, they're always being watched. But at night—well, you see those rings of spikes sticking out from the walls just behind those chaps? Horrible things! Those were put there by the Iron Duke when he was Constable of the Tower. 'Wellington's Armchairs,' they're known as, or 'Lazy Soldiers.' "

Delighted, Daisy scribbled in her notebook. That was the first morsel of interesting, unusual, and therefore useful information she'd received today.

4

*T*he entrance to the Wakefield Tower was guarded by both a Yeoman Warder and a Hotspur sentry. Because of the sentry's requisite impassivity, Daisy couldn't tell whether they were at daggers drawn. For all she knew, the feud between the two factions might have been grossly exaggerated.

The Chief Warder greeted the yeoman, "Anyone up there now, Mr. Biggle?"

"Just a couple with small kiddies, went up a few minutes ago. Don't s'pose they'll be long. Waste of a shilling, if you ask me, taking the little ones up."

"Right you are. Mrs. Fletcher here's a friend of the Governor, don't need a ticket. A journalist she is, too. Member of the press."

Mr. Biggle saluted, looking properly impressed. Pleased by Crabtree's recognition of her professional credentials, Daisy warmed further towards him. He couldn't help being boring.

"I won't take up any more of your time, Mr. Crabtree," she said. Mentally crossing her fingers behind her back, she thanked him for getting her tour off to a good start. Wondering whether she ought to tip him, she decided his rank was too exalted, even in the interests of Saint Peter ad Vincula.

Ad Vincula? What was a *vincula*? Her school had considered Latin too exacting for female brains. Perhaps Sir Patrick would know.

She went into the tower. Another two warders were posted in the ground-floor guardroom, their halberds—no, they were called partizans, Crabtree had told her—leaning against the wall, close at hand. Daisy nodded to them and started for the steps, only to meet Sir Patrick bustling down.

He was closely followed by a small boy at a gallop, who, in turn, was followed by a plaintive female voice. "Not so fast, Johnnie! You'll take a tumble for sure!"

Daisy and Sir Patrick stepped aside to let the anxious mother collar her son.

The Keeper of the Regalia shook Daisy's hand with enthusiasm. "Delighted, dear lady, delighted. It's not often I get a chance to show off my little baubles. The yeomen handle tourists, and very nicely, too, and I leave my curator to cope with the general run of journalists, don't you know. Excellent fellow, very hard worker. I gave him a few days off while I'm in town. Told him I'd take care of you."

Daisy wasn't sure whether she was above the general run because her husband was a Scotland Yard detective or because her father had been a viscount. Nor was she sure that Sir Patrick would prove the best person to tell her about the Crown Jewels. But she expressed her appreciation, and, as a man's shoes and trousers appeared descending the stairs, she asked, "I've been wondering, what does *vincula* mean, as in 'Saint Peter ad'? Do you happen to know?"

"*Vincula?*" Sir Patrick looked blank. "Good heavens, that's quite a poser. Something to do with flowers, isn't it? Periwinkle, that's it, the Latin name for periwinkle. I dabble a bit in gardening down at my country place."

Daisy's botanical Latin was as sparse as her classical or church Latin, but what Saint Peter had to do with periwinkles was unclear to her. A second opinion was called for, she felt.

Amid objurgations from the anxious young woman—"Stop wriggling, Maryanne, or you'll make your dad trip!"—the father reached the bottom, a girl child on his shoulders. The family departed.

Daisy preceded Sir Patrick up the winding stair. She came out into a spacious, high-ceilinged octagonal room. In the centre was a plate-glass enclosure, reinforced by steel bars, behind which lurked a fabulous treasure of gems. On each side of the room stood yet another armed Yeoman Warder.

"Plenty of guards," Daisy observed with a smile.

"Good heavens, yes. Can't be too careful. Wouldn't want any funny business on my watch." The Keeper scowled suspiciously at the man who came around the display at that moment. "Look at him, for instance. No part of his duties!"

Peering through bottle-bottom glasses at a sheaf of papers in his hand, the Resident Governor's ADC was oblivious of Sir Patrick's inimical stare.

"Good morning, Mr. F—Webster," said Daisy.

Webster looked up. "Uh . . ."

"Mrs. Fletcher," Sir Patrick reminded him testily. "You made the lady's acquaintance yesterday."

"Oh, ah, good morning, Mrs. Fletcher."

"You must be working on your dissertation on the Crown Jewels," Daisy suggested, wanting to deflect Sir Patrick's suspicion, the more so since she had had the same unworthy thought.

"I am. I have here notes of ancient descriptions of the royal regalia, and some sketches made by an artist of original paintings of kings and queens. I intend to prove that the ruby now set in the King's State Crown cannot possibly be that given to the Black Prince by Pedro the Cruel and worn by Henry the Fifth at Agincourt."

"Balderdash!" Sir Patrick was furious. "Of course it is the same stone."

Leaving them to their argument, Daisy wandered over to a sort of large alcove in one wall. One of the yeomen followed her.

"Henry the Sixth's oratory, madam, where he was murdered at his prayers. Stabbed, he was. They send flowers on the anniversary every year still, Eton and King's, Cambridge, the colleges he founded. White lilies and white roses. And his ghost walks—"

Sir Patrick overheard. "Balderdash!" he cried again.

"Stuff and nonsense!" muttered Webster. "Ghosts indeed!"

The Keeper glanced at him with a more kindly eye, then turned his disapproving gaze on Daisy. Busy scribbling down this useful tidbit in her own personal version of Pitman's shorthand, she announced, "Readers love ghosts."

The yeoman winked at her.

"Mrs. Fletcher," said Sir Patrick severely, "allow me to point out the various items of the Regalia and tell you something of their history. Unhappily, as Mr. Webster has pointed out, they are not the original crowns worn by the kings and queens of England before the Commonwealth. Those were destroyed or sold by Cromwell. These are, however, set with the same stones, as well as the Koh-i-Nor and the Stars of Africa cut from the Cullinan diamond."

Daisy dutifully admired the orb and sceptre and a multiplicity of crowns. The first two were constants, but no monarch, apparently, was content to be crowned with his predecessor's headgear. It reminded Daisy of ladies who wouldn't be seen dead at Ascot in last year's hat. She didn't voice the thought. Sir Patrick might consider it lèse-majesté and have her clapped up in one of the convenient dungeons.

Light reflecting off the polished glass made it difficult to appreciate the splendours of the collection. Daisy concentrated on noting down the few snippets of information she hadn't already gleaned from her history book. The Keeper was more conversant with the Regalia than she had expected, since he had described his position as a "sinecure." He told the stories well, too, making a fine dramatic tale of Captain Blood's failed attempt to steal the Crown Jewels.

But she couldn't help noticing that he kept a watchful eye on Jeremy Webster as he told it.

Webster was oblivious of the scrutiny. He went on poring over his notes and sketches and peering into the glass case, until a sudden *ping* startled him. He delved into an inner pocket, in the process scattering papers on the floor. While one of the yeomen picked them up for him, he brought out a repeater watch, opened and consulted it, and moaned, "Oh dear, I shall be late."

Oh, my ears and whiskers! thought Daisy as Jeremy Fisher, now playing the part of the White Rabbit, grabbed his papers and dashed for the stairs.

Then he stopped abruptly and took a step backwards, looking appalled.

Sir Patrick gasped.

From the stairwell a huge curved axe-head rose up, on the end of a pole. After it came a blue Tudor bonnet, beneath which was a face Daisy recognized, much of it concealed by a huge bushy beard. The Yeoman Gaoler stepped into the room. With a bland glance at Webster, who scuttled past him and disappeared, he said, "I thought Mrs. Fletcher might like to see my ceremonial axe."

The Keeper gave him a dirty look. "Mrs. Fletcher, this is Mr. Rumford, whom General Carradine has picked to give you a tour of the Tower. I'll say goodbye for now, but I hope to see you again while you're working here."

With a slight bow, he shook her hand, then abandoned her. Taking from his pocket a large iron key, he unlocked a door across from the stairs; he disappeared through it, and locked it behind him with a click audible through the thick oak. Meanwhile, the yeoman at the oratory had sneaked round behind Rumford's back and vanished downward after Webster. The remaining yeoman stood stiffly against the wall, holding his partizan with the butt resting on the floor.

No one wanted to be in the same room as Rumford and his axe.

He couldn't be physically dangerous, Daisy told herself a trifle nervously. He wasn't going to attack with that horrible instrument of death, or he wouldn't be allowed to walk around carrying it, wouldn't hold the position of Yeoman Gaoler. No, Fay claimed he had a nasty habit of being able to "see through walls." That was an unendearing trait,

enough to make people avoid him, especially anyone with a guilty conscience.

Did Webster really have designs upon the Crown
Jewels? What about Sir Patrick? As Keeper, he had
far greater opportunities to abstract the odd diamond.

Stuff and nonsense! She was letting her imagination run away with her, all too easy in the melo-
dramatic atmosphere of the Tower. Besides,
Rumford's inquisitorial scrutiny was enough to make
anyone feel guilty.

"Good morning," she said. "I'm looking forward to seeing everything."

The Yeoman Gaoler turned out to be a good
guide, if not exactly likeable. He considered most
of those who had ever been shut up in the Tower to
be rogues or fools, or both, and his opinion of the
monarchs and judges who had imprisoned them
was not much higher. Daisy found his cynical atti-
tude a refreshing contrast to the usual maudlin
melodrama.

However, he extended his scorn to the present
residents. Not that he gossiped either about them,
or to them when their paths crossed while he showed
Daisy around, but anything he did say had a dero-
gatory twist to it. He had a low opinion of his fellow men.

His fellow men returned the favour, judging by
the way every yeoman not pinned to his post did
his best to be elsewhere when Rumford approached.
Even the officers Daisy had met yesterday altered
their course to avoid him.

Daisy hoped they were not avoiding *her.* She had
rather forced them to invite the Tebbits on their
river excursion.

In any case, the result was quite satisfactory, as she was able to concentrate on her work without distraction. The Yeoman Gaoler did indeed know all the interesting stories, even the ghost stories, though he assured her he didn't believe in ghosts.

"There's them that won't go into the Salt Tower after dark," he said derisively. "One of the warders swears he was nearly throttled by invisible hands. It's true dogs won't go near the place, but if you ask me, those invisible hands came out of a bottle."

"Like the djinn," said Daisy.

"Like gin, could be. Like one kind of spirits or another, and not the ghostly kind."

By lunchtime, Daisy had had quite enough of ghosts, prisoners, escapes, executions, steps, and Rumford. Slipping a couple of half-crowns for Saint Peter into his ready palm, she asked for directions to Lieutenant Colonel Duggan's quarters.

The Officers' Quarters building faced the parade ground, next to the Waterloo Barracks, behind the White Tower. A mere eighty years old, the garrison's two grandiose buildings weren't part of the historic tour. Daisy was halfway across the parade ground, enjoying the almost summery warmth of the sun in a cloudless sky, when Fay and Brenda caught up with her.

"Mrs. Fletcher, we're glad you could come."

"Aunt Christina is so much looking forward to meeting you."

"Have you had a frightful morning?"

"With Rumford?"

"On the contrary, he was most helpful and obliging. As your father said, he knows everything."

"Oh yes." Brenda shuddered. "Always poking and prying."

"And *watching*!"

"Daddy can't stand him, really."

"Nor can Uncle Sidney."

"It's about the only thing they agree on."

"Here we are."

"This way."

"You'll like Aunt Christina."

"She's a dear."

Daisy was bustled into a cramped sitting room, its plain furnishings a reminder that Duggan was not a gentleman of private means. The austerity was relieved by a vase of narcissi, flower paintings on the walls, a number of family photographs in silver frames, and several well-filled bookcases. Two men in uniform rose as they entered. Another pair were standing by a tray of drinks. Fay and Brenda escorted Daisy across the room and presented her to their aunt rather as if they were retrievers bringing home a particularly fine pheasant.

Mrs. Duggan was a small, plump woman with a shy smile. "I'm so happy you were able to come at such short notice," she said in a soft voice. "The girls insisted that after three hours of history, you would be sorely in need of sustenance."

She introduced her husband, a stalwart figure of about fifty with very upright military bearing and old-fashioned mutton-chop whiskers. While Colonel Duggan poured Daisy a drink, Brenda said, "You met the others yesterday, Mrs. Fletcher— Dr. Macleod, Captain Devereux, and Lieutenant Jardyne."

"We thought you'd prefer it if we invited officers you'd already met," said Fay.

"Besides," said the captain, a glint of mockery in his eyes, "Jardyne and I wanted to see you again to thank you for suggesting that we include Mrs. and Miss Tebbit in our river cruise."

"I'm afraid it was very interfering of me, none of my business."

"No, no, I mean it. The old lady and I got on like a house on fire. I believe I've found my soul mate."

"Dev hardly spoke to the rest of us," Brenda confirmed with a slight pout.

"But I did round up a couple more chaps to keep you entertained," Devereux reminded her.

"We didn't need those two idiots," Jardyne protested.

"Oh, but it was fun," said Fay, who had no doubt kept all three young men dancing attendance while her sister languished after the captain and Miss Tebbit languished alone. "We must do it again sometime when you can come, Dr. Mac."

"Not really my kind of thing, Miss Fay." Today the doctor seemed to be on edge, nervy. Several times he almost took a gunmetal cigarette case from his pocket, then dropped it back.

"You'll have better luck if you ask him to take you to the races," said Jardyne, not quite openly jeering.

Macleod flushed darkly. Fay was obviously on the point of following the young lieutenant's advice when, to Mrs. Duggan's obvious relief, luncheon was announced.

The dining room furnishings were as Spartan as the sitting room, but Daisy was more interested in the food, which was excellent. She sat next to Colonel Duggan. He was an inarticulate man, but having asked her about her writing, he listened with apparent interest. He ate a hearty meal, and was pleased when Daisy did likewise, pressing her to take another slice of this or spoonful of that.

"I like to see good vittles appreciated," he said

gruffly. "A soldier on campaign goes without often as not. I can't abide waste."

So Daisy took another potato and some more parsley sauce. She *had* been walking up and down stairs all morning.

At the other end of the table, Mrs. Duggan was finding it hard going with the doctor, whose nerviness led him to taciturnity rather than garrulity. In between, though, Fay and Brenda flirted merrily with Captain Devereux and Lieutenant Jardyne. Daisy noticed that Fay couldn't resist an occasional glance at Macleod to see if he was reacting. He wasn't.

When the ladies retired, the two younger men showed signs of wanting to accompany them. Colonel Duggan called them to order.

In the passage—it could hardly be dignified with the word *hall*—Mrs. Duggan said to the girls, "Off you go and powder your noses. I want a word with Mrs. Fletcher in peace."

"Oh, Aunt Chris, don't tell her anything too dreadful about us!"

"As though I should do such a thing, Fay." Mrs. Duggan's tone spoke of her affection for her nieces. "Run along now. Just give us ten minutes without your chatter."

"Chatter! We were going to practise polite conversation." Brenda's mock-indignant protest was voiced over her shoulder as they obeyed.

As soon as Daisy and Mrs. Duggan were settled with coffee in the sitting room, the latter said anxiously, "I do hope you won't mind if I ask your advice. I need the opinion of someone who can see the girls objectively. I . . . I feel I'm in an odd position, having acted as their mother for several years but not *being* their mother, and no longer being re-

sponsible for them. I can't quite offer uncondi-
tional mother love, but neither can I view them as
an unconcerned outsider. Do you see what I mean?"

"Yes," said Daisy, "absolutely. I'm in sort of the
same position as regards my stepdaughter—but she's
such a good little girl. . . ."

"You wouldn't say Fay and Brenda are good?"

"Oh yes, from what I've seen, they're charming
and good-hearted and . . . well, as silly as girls that
age usually are. I dare say Belinda will be just the
same at seventeen."

Mrs. Duggan sighed. "I still *feel* responsible. Especially as it's in my home they're meeting young
men their father disapproves of."

"Is there any particular reason for disapproval?"
Daisy asked cautiously. She tried hard to repress
her curiosity, but she couldn't resist another question: "That is, any particular young man . . . ?"

After a moment's hesitation, her hostess said,
"To be frank, the three you have met are my greatest worry. Most of Sidney's young officers are perfectly acceptable. Not that there's anything wrong
with Lieutenant Jardyne, if only he didn't fancy
himself madly in love with Fay."

"He has a jealous temper, I suspect."

"You've observed it, too? Oh dear! It's a pity she
isn't fond of him, so that he'd have no cause for
jealousy."

"I don't think it works that way. He'd find some
reason, if that's the way he's inclined. I'd be glad
she doesn't care for him."

"Really?" Mrs. Duggan brightened, then drooped
again. "I expect you're right, but I *cannot* believe it's
preferable that she should pine for Dr. Macleod.
He's an excellent physician, no doubt, but there's
something about him. . . ."

"No need to worry. I've seen no sign that he has the slightest interest in her. I'd be more concerned about Brenda and Captain Devereux."

"Captain Devereux has several medals for bravery in the War."

"I'd be surprised if he hadn't. He's a perfect Byronic hero, and I bet Fay and Brenda read Byron at that finishing school of theirs. But I rather doubt Byronic heroes make good husbands. Byron himself certainly didn't."

"N-no," said Mrs. Duggan uncertainly.

"I've advised Fay to read Jane Austen. I can't really justify interfering any further."

"Do you think I ought to talk to Miss Tebbit about them?"

Daisy bit her lip to suppress a snort of laughter. The only thing less useful than talking to Miss Tebbit would be talking to Mrs. Tebbit, who would doubtless treat the whole business as a great joke. "Have you met the Tebbits?" she asked.

"Briefly. I called, of course, when they first came here. But it's so difficult, Arthur having taken against me for marrying Sidney. We can't exchange more than the most formal visits."

"I can tell you this much. Miss Tebbit sincerely sympathizes with you. However, I shouldn't count on much assistance with the girls from that quarter."

Brenda and Fay came in then, along with the men. Daisy stayed a little longer, chatting and observing, but she was anxious to get back to her babies. Tomorrow, unless Alec was sent off to some out-of-the-way corner of the provinces, she was to witness the Ceremony of the Keys and stay the night at the King's House. The Carradine girls were just going to have to take care of themselves.

5

*D*aisy shivered as she walked down Tower Hill in the dusk. It was chilly, but her shivers had more to do with the veils of mist rising from the river, swathing the Tower in mystery, so that its menacing bulk loomed larger than ever. Hoots and whistles from shipping on the Thames added to the eerie atmosphere.

Public visiting hours were over, the ticket office and refreshment room closed. The gates onto the wharf would be locked, by now. The world outside had changed, but the Tower was still a mediæval town, huddled behind walls to keep out unwelcome travellers.

One of the pair of sentries at the Middle Tower challenged Daisy. She was glad to see the unmistakable silhouette of a Yeoman Warder approaching in the hazy gaslight under the arch.

"Mrs. Fletcher? The Governor sent me to meet you." He spoke to the sentry, who lowered his rifle to the ground.

"Thanks," said Daisy. "For a moment, I was afraid I was supposed to know a secret password."

"No fear, madam. Wouldn't be secret then, would it? 'Sides, you wouldn't want to walk alone around here on a nasty night like this. Lovely weather for ghosts, it is."

"Yes, isn't it?"

They went through the arch and across the bridge. Fog flowed along the moat channel as if the Thames were returning to refill it. Tendrils twisted up to twine about the gas lamp in the middle of the bridge.

"Getting thicker. We'll have a pea-souper by morning, I shouldn't wonder."

Daisy was dismayed. She didn't want to have to choose tomorrow between being stuck in the Tower and trying to find her way home through one of London's infamous yellow fogs. The mixture of smoke from countless coal fires and the river's natural exudations could become almost as impenetrable as it was unbreathable.

Under the Byward Tower arch, a yeoman was on guard. From the right came the sound of jollity. Seeing Daisy glance that way, her yeoman said, "The Warders' Hall, madam." He turned to the door on the left. "I'll just pop in here and tell Mr. Crabtree you've arrived, if you don't mind waiting a half a tick."

"Please give Mr. Crabtree my regards." Daisy hoped he meant "half a tick." If he was gone any longer, she'd seek refuge among the merry warders in their hall.

But he returned very quickly, conveyed the Chief Warder's respects, and accompanied her along Water Street, under the Bloody Tower, and round to the King's House.

To Daisy's surprise, Colonel and Mrs. Duggan were dining with the Resident Governor.

"I don't believe in family feuds," Mrs. Tebbit told her loudly. "Such a lot of childish fuss and bother over nothing! Besides which, I'm far too old to rein in those resty fillies, and Myrtle's quite incapable of managing them on her own."

"Oh, Mother!" Miss Tebbit succumbed to a fit of coughing.

General Carradine turned purple. The Duggans looked uncomfortable. Jeremy Webster remained as impenetrable as a pea-souper. Fay and Brenda grinned.

Mrs. Tebbit winked at them. "If Mrs. Duggan is willing to lend a hand, let her, say I."

While Carradine fussed over drinks, the back of his neck gradually returning to its normal colour, Fay and Brenda converged on Daisy.

"Isn't she marvellous?"

"We simply adore her."

Though the girls were oblivious of constraint, the others struggled to make polite conversation. Mrs. Duggan made a brave attempt to chat with Miss Tebbit, who coughed periodically and dabbed at her eyes, apologizing and saying she hoped she was not coming down with something. Mr. Webster and Colonel Duggan remained speechless, the latter harrumphing now and then, which gave a curious effect of ventriloquism, as if the croaks of the fictional Jeremy Fisher were issuing from Duggan's mouth. Fortunately, dinner was soon announced.

On the way downstairs, Daisy recalled Mrs. Tebbit's mention of Lord Nithsdale's escape from the room at the head of the stairs. Once seated, she asked General Carradine if he could tell her the details. The story turned out to be a favourite of his.

Everyone listened to the tale of how Lady Nithsdale, hearing her husband had been arrested for his part in the Jacobite rebellion of 1715, rode from the North through icy winter weather to plead for his life. Failing to move George I, she had persuaded the Governor of the Tower to let her visit the prisoner.

"The evening before the execution," Carradine related, "she brought several women friends with her to the Tower, and women's clothes hidden under her cloak. It's said the earl wasn't happy about dressing as a woman, but his wife convinced him of the necessity. She used rouge to redden his eyes, as if he'd been weeping, and with a shawl over his head and the others around him bemoaning Nithsdale's fate, they all trooped down the stairs and away. He escaped the country dressed as a servant to the Venetian ambassador."

"A good story," said Colonel Duggan. He laughed. "That must have taken the Governor and the warders down a peg, letting him run off like that."

The general glared at him. If looks could kill, the colonel's dinner would have gone to waste.

Mrs. Tebbit flung fuel on the flames. "It sounds to me as if someone must have been bribed. Not the Governor, I dare say," she added with a vestige of discretion, as her cousin appeared about to burst a blood vessel. "A Yeoman Warder or two."

"The very first prisoner at the Tower escaped," said Webster, his enigmatic glasses making it impossible to gauge his intent, pacific or inflammatory. "He was a churchman, Ranulf Flambard, Bishop of Durham. He had a rope smuggled to him in a cask of wine, made his guards drunk, and climbed down from the White Tower."

"Oh, yes," Daisy put in, "the rope was too short, wasn't it? He fell but then picked himself up and scurried away. But that was when the Tower was still a royal palace—that is, when the royal family still lived here—centuries before the Yeoman Warders existed. Mr. Rumford, the Yeoman Gaoler, told me about it. You said he knows everything, general, and there wasn't a single question I asked that he didn't have the answer to. You couldn't have chosen a more helpful guide."

She succeeded in turning his attention from escaping prisoners. At least he ceased to look apoplectic, though his expression could hardly have been described as cheerful. "Glad the fellow made himself useful," he muttered, and sank into a depressed silence.

Mrs. Tebbit glanced around the table. "What a lot of long faces," she declared. "You all dislike him? What's wrong with the man?"

"I've only spoken to Mr. Rumford once, briefly," said Mrs. Duggan. "I can't claim to know him."

"He really was very knowledgeable and amusing," Daisy reaffirmed. "But I must admit I found the Chief Warder more likable. Mr. Crabtree's information was less useful for my purposes, but he was very pleasant and friendly. I gather he plays a major part in the ceremony tonight, general?"

At last she'd hit on a topic that offended no one. Both garrison and Yeoman Warders, as well as the Resident Governor himself, had their parts to play in the seven-hundred-year-old ritual. Everyone at the table had something to say, though all agreed one had to watch it to appreciate it. Even when Mrs. Tebbit pointed out that on such a foggy night the solemnities would no doubt be interrupted by a good deal of coughing, Carradine kept his good humour—through gritted teeth at times, Daisy suspected.

Having been invited for dinner and the night because of the ceremony, Daisy had expected company when she went out to view it. However, the night was much too unpleasant to expect an old lady to venture forth, and Mrs. Tebbit ordered her daughter to take her cough to bed. The Resident Governor's part in the proceedings demanded that he stay at home to receive the King's Keys from the Chief Warder. Daisy hadn't much faith in either Brenda or Fay abandoning the comfort of the Council Chamber for the cold, clammy fog for the sake of mere manners, though Fay might for a cigarette. Jeremy Webster had some papers to be dealt with before morning; Colonel Duggan had military duties awaiting his return.

"You go along, Sidney," Mrs. Duggan proposed, "and I'll watch the goings-on with Mrs. Fletcher."

"I'd love to have your company," Daisy said gratefully. "I expect I'd get lost out there alone in the dark and the fog."

Fay and Brenda exchanged a shamefaced glance.

"We hadn't thought . . ."

"Of course we'll come with you, too."

"It's going to be beastly outside."

"Would you like to borrow a woolly hat?"

"And a muffler?"

They rushed off and returned with a selection of warm gloves, scarves, and hats.

"Come on, let's go."

"They start at seven minutes to ten."

"On the dot."

"The gates are locked at ten."

"After which no one can enter or leave the Tower."

"Absolutely no one."

"Not even Daddy."

"Except the King."

"They're like a music-hall act, aren't they?" said their aunt fondly.

Well wrapped, the ladies set out. The fog had thickened, but it still smelt of river muck, not yet of coal smoke and petrol fumes. Only the nearest of the gas lamps scattered about the Inner Ward were visible, haloed beacons that cast little light.

"I don't fancy going down the shortcut in this," said Brenda, shivering.

"We'd probably break our necks on those steep steps," Fay seconded her.

"They'll be invisible."

"And slippery."

"We'll go round," Mrs. Duggan agreed.

"Oh yes, let's." Daisy remembered the sinister impression of those walled-in steps in broad daylight.

They walked along the wall and round the end, then down the two wide, shallow flights of steps, Fay and Brenda hanging on to each other and giggling. The steps were indeed slippery, as was the cobbled slope leading down to the Bloody Tower archway. Lamps at either end of the tunnel only rendered the darkness underneath more complete. Daisy, gloved hands deep in her pockets, felt Mrs. Duggan's hand slip through her arm.

"I hate this place," the colonel's wife whispered, "even in the daytime. I can't help thinking about the little princes murdered just over our heads."

"Almost four and a half centuries ago," said Daisy comfortingly, wishing she hadn't been reminded.

As they passed under the portcullis, invisible above, they heard fog-muffled marching footsteps coming after them. Daisy glanced back and, by the light at the far end, caught a fleeting glimpse of shakoed silhouettes before they disappeared into the darkness.

"The escort," Brenda explained.

"The sergeant of the watch," Fay elucidated.

"And three privates."

"One's a drummer."

"That's his official title."

"But he plays the bugle."

They both laughed, their youthful insouciance driving away any lingering ghosts.

The marching footsteps stopped under the Bloody Tower. The four ladies continued, turning right along Water Street, walking close to the wall, towards the Byward Tower. For all they could see of it, the tower might as well not have existed.

Its lamp came into view, and at the same time two yeomen materialized, coming towards them. Except for the Tudor bonnets, their uniforms were hidden by scarlet capes. They walked with solemn tread, on official business now. As they came closer, Daisy recognised the Chief Warder's beard. His companion carried a lantern, its candle doing absolutely nothing to illuminate the scene.

She and her companions turned to trail the yeomen. At the Bloody Tower, they halted, and Crabtree's voice rang out, "Escort for the Keys!"

Followed by the five Hotspur Guards, they marched back along Water Street, under the Byward Tower and across the moat to the Middle Tower. As they reached it, a large motor-car nosed through the arch, its acetylene lamps creating two glowing spheres of fog. Their dazzle hid the driver, but Daisy recognized Sir Patrick's voice: "Just in time, eh, Crabtree? The damn fog suddenly thickened at the top of the hill."

The silver Hotchkiss crept past.

The second yeoman helped the Chief Warder close the great gates. Crabtree locked them with a huge key from his huge bunch of keys as the sentries and escort presented arms. With Daisy and her friends doing their best to keep out of the way but in sight, Yeoman Warders and Hotspur Guards returned to the Byward Tower.

"Quick," Fay urged, "we don't want to be locked out on the bridge overnight!"

She and Brenda skipped through; Mrs. Duggan and Daisy slipped through after them. The closing and locking were repeated. Here the second yeoman was left on guard. Crabtree and his escort and their four shadows returned to the Bloody Tower.

From under the arch a challenge rang out: "Halt! Who comes there?"

"The Keys," Crabtree responded.

"Whose keys?"

"King George's Keys."

"Pass, King George's Keys. All's well."

Back through the tunnel they went, less eerie now with the tramp of marching boots ahead. At the top of the slope, a ghostly platoon awaited them, arrayed on the steps with the Officer of the Guard in front, his sword drawn.

"Guard and escort, present arms," he commanded.

"That's Billy Playdell," Brenda whispered in Daisy's ear. "He's our croquet champion."

Crabtree took two steps forward, raised his bonnet, and called out, "God preserve King George!"

"Amen!" bellowed the Guardsmen.

Through the fog came the fog-deadened sound of a clock striking ten. The drummer raised his bugle to his lips and played the "Last Post." Always a melancholy sound, in this setting it was positively ghostly.

"That's the end," said Fay. "Mr. Crabtree takes the keys to Daddy now. Why don't you go with him, Mrs. Fletcher, and we'll see Aunt Christina home."

"Good idea," her sister agreed. "Mr. Crabtree!"

The Chief Warder came to meet them. "Now, Miss Brenda, you know I'm not supposed to do nothing this minute but deliver the King's Keys to the Governor."

"Oh but, it's such a foul night, we can't let Mrs. Duggan try to find her way home alone, can we?" Brenda coaxed.

"My sister and I will go with her, Mr. Crabtree—"

"But you wouldn't want Mrs. Fletcher to have to traipse all that way with us, would you?"

"Or to go to the King's House by herself in this fog?"

"When you're going straight there."

Crabtree shook his head, but he said, "No indeed. I'll be honoured to escort Mrs. Fletcher."

Daisy shook Mrs. Duggan's hand and promised to meet again soon. Aunt and nieces disappeared up the steps into the fog.

"We'll take the shortcut, madam, if that's all right with you."

"Yes, it shouldn't be too bad going up, though we funked it coming down."

"Very wise, madam. A nasty night it is for sure, but I've got my lantern to show us the way."

"It's a very fine lantern," said Daisy, with a dubious glance at the remaining stub of candle and its wavering flame.

"Presented by the Artillery Company in '19, when they were garrisoned here. They gave us a nice inkstand for the Warders' Hall, too. Good chaps, that lot."

In contrast to the present garrison? Daisy wondered. With luck, Mrs. Tebbit's caustic comments on the futility of family feuds might alleviate the discord between Yeoman Warders and Hotspur Guards for the rest of the battalion's residence here.

"You'll see better if I go first, madam, so the light hits the steps ahead of you."

Daisy followed him up. The candle end did help a little, but she couldn't see a thing beyond its light. She heard someone, though, someone with a bad cough standing at the top of the steps—there hadn't been much coughing during the ceremony, perhaps because coal smoke hadn't yet suffused the fog. As they neared the top, the fuzzy globe of a gas lamp dimly illuminated a Tudor bonnet and a red cape like the Chief Warder's.

A hoarse whisper: "Evening, madam." *Cough, cough.* "Evening, Mr. Crabtree. Can I 'ave a word wi' you?"

"Not just now, Mr. Rumford. I have the Keys, and this lady . . ."

"That's all right," said Daisy. She could just make out the lamp on the corner house, the one that now blocked Ralegh's Walk. "I can find my way now." She almost offered to take the King's Keys to the general, but decided that would be a breach of etiquette.

"Only take 'alf a mo." Rumford started coughing again.

"All right, then, if you don't mind waiting, Mrs. Fletcher. I promised the young ladies to see you home."

The Yeoman Gaoler pulled Crabtree a couple of paces aside. Daisy couldn't hear what he said, but the Chief Warder replied, "Right you are. You sound bloody 'orrible all right."

Rumford went off, his cough still echoing back after he'd vanished.

"Gassed," said Crabtree briefly, rejoining Daisy. "He's mostly right enough, but the fog brings it on."

Daisy made sympathetic noises, wondering why he sounded disgruntled. Perhaps Rumford used his damaged lungs to pass off some of his duties on his superior, but the cough had sounded bad enough to be a reason, not an excuse.

The King's House was easy enough to find now. Crabtree knocked on the door. General Carradine's batman opened it and there was a moment's confusion while the general stepped forward to receive the keys while the Chief Warder stepped back to usher Daisy inside. They sorted themselves out, the keys were handed over in due form, and Daisy thanked Crabtree.

As the batman closed the door, Carradine demanded, "Where are my girls, Mrs. Fletcher?"

Daisy explained, adding, "It was very thoughtful of them, wasn't it?"

"As long as they don't hang about with the officers when they get there."

"I'm sure they intend to come straight home, as straight as is possible in the fog." She hid a smile as she envisioned an officer or two offering to escort the young ladies home and, in turn, having to find their own way back to their quarters.

They went upstairs, where Mrs. Tebbit immediately echoed her cousin: "Where are the girls, Mrs. Fletcher?"

Again, Daisy explained.

"Hm, very proper. I suppose you gave them the hint."

"Not at all. It was their own notion."

"Well, I ascribe it to your influence anyway. They seem to consider you a model to be emulated. There is something to be said for an aristocratic young lady who is also a modern working woman."

"Oh, Mother!"

Half an hour later, Fay and Brenda turned up, damp and chilled and calling for cocoa.

When the household retired to bed, Daisy found herself wakeful. While the details of the ceremony itself had not particularly inspired her, the idea that it had taken place in more or less the same form for seven hundred years was impressive. The ancient setting and the atmosphere of mystery lent by the fog made it unforgettable.

Yet when at last she slept, her dreams were haunted not by huge bunches of giant keys but by visions of the little princes murdered in the Bloody Tower. As with Alice and Anne Boleyn, Queen Mary and the Red Queen, the princes became confused with her own twins.

When she awoke next morning, she was desperate to see her babies. Not that she believed dreams foretold the future; she just wanted to see them.

Though it was still very early, she thought the posterns at least might be unlocked by now. She got up and dressed. To sneak out would be very bad form, but she couldn't help herself. She tore a page out of her notebook and wrote a grovelling apology to Mrs. Tebbit, whose maternal feelings were probably not strong enough to help her understand. With any luck, she might be amused.

Slipping down the stairs, Daisy left the note on the hall table, unbolted the door, and stepped out.

A brisk, blustery breeze had driven off the fog, thank heaven. Passing the sentry posted near the Resident Governor's front door, she thought he gave her as much of a strange look as was consonant with his duty. Ignoring him, she made for the shortcut stair.

As she reached the top step, she saw a scarlet heap at the bottom. Puzzled, she started down. Then she realized the scarlet was a Yeoman Warder's cape.

And the yeoman was still inside it.

And sticking out of the middle of his back was a partizan.

6

*U*nbelieving, Daisy stared downward. The yeoman's head was turned at a strange angle, not only suggesting he was well and truly defunct but also revealing the edge of a beard still rampant in death.

The Chief Warder! He might have stumbled or slipped on the steps in the fog last night, but the partizan was proof of dirty work. Even if Crabtree had been carrying it, he could hardly have stuck it in his own back. Who could have wanted to kill the kindly, boring old buffer?

Ought she to go down and see if he needed help? No, her first-aid skills were minimal, and she was practically sure it was too late. Besides, she didn't want to see.

Shock struck. Daisy nearly sank down on the nearest step, but she had to go for help before the Tower community awoke and started its daily routine. She forced her leaden legs to carry her up the few steps she had descended.

She couldn't get back into the King's House without rousing the household. The modern lock on the front door had clicked shut automatically behind her. The sentry on guard beside that door was the only person in sight. His job was to stand as still and silent as a lead soldier, responding to no overtures from the wandering public, until he was relieved. What would he do when faced with a hysterical woman reporting a murder?

Daisy was going to find out. She had no choice.

Alec gazed down at his son in his arms. Busy sucking on his bottle, Oliver gazed back, his wide eyes just the same shade of blue as Daisy's. He snuffled like a little pink pig with a squashed nose. His chin was practically nonexistent and his scalp showed through the fine down on his head. Were all babies so unattractive? Belinda, for instance: Alec couldn't remember his beloved daughter—elder daughter—ever looking so . . . so unfinished.

He glanced over at Miranda, snuffling at her own bottle on Nanny's arm. She stopped suckling for a moment and blew a bubble. He hoped that when they were a little older he'd be able to tell which was the boy and which the girl without asking.

The cook-housekeeper peeked around the door, then came in, breathing heavily after climbing to the second floor. "Telephone, sir. It's the Yard," she said importantly, but in a hushed voice so as not to startle the babies. "That Mr. Crane."

Alec groaned. "Thank you, Mrs. Dobson." He detached the bottle from Oliver's mouth and laid him carefully in his cradle, where he promptly set up a banshee howl.

"Poor lamb!" Nanny's severity was aimed at Alec, not the howler. "They don't like interruptions.

That's why we don't care for daddies in the nursery."

"Sorry." Alec fled. He'd rather deal with his superintendent, happy or unhappy, than with an unhappy baby.

As he crossed the landing, he heard Mrs. Dobson beg in a tentative voice, "Couldn't I finish off giving him his bottle, Nanny?"

Down in the hall, Alec picked up the telephone. "Hello, Fletcher here."

"This is Crane. We have a situation, a deuced awkward situation."

"Sir?"

"Murder at the Tower."

Alec's heart plunged into his slippers, then bounced back a little. "The Tower of London? Surely that's the City force's territory, sir."

"Alas, no. It's still a royal palace. You're a historian, aren't you? You know how much trouble the monarchy had with the City of London through the ages. They've never let the City police near the place. But all the Yeoman Warders are sworn Special Constables of the Met, three dozen of them or so, and their top chap seems to have been bumped off."

"The Resident Governor? Great Scott!"

"No, no, the Chief Warder. That's bad enough, isn't it? He was a Special, too."

Bad enough indeed, but not Daisy's host, thank heaven. Still, Daisy had spent the night at the Tower. Superintendent Crane must be ignorant of that fact, or he would surely have mentioned it—not to say raved about it. However, he was bound to find out. Alec decided the information had better come from him, and sooner rather than later.

"I see, sir. I . . . I'm afraid Daisy stayed at the King's House last night. The Resident Governor's residence."

There was a long silence at the other end of the wire. Then Crane's voice arrived with a note of cautious hope: "I must have misunderstood you, Fletcher. Tell me you didn't say Mrs. Fletcher stayed at the Tower last night."

"I'm sorry, sir. I did. She did." Part of Alec wanted to rush to Daisy's side, to comfort and protect; another part wanted nothing whatsoever to do with any murder case she'd managed to get herself mixed up in; and there was a bit left over that wanted to wring her neck. "In the circumstances, I expect you'll prefer someone else handling the investigation, sir."

"Not on your life!" Superintendent Crane exploded. "If *you* can't control your own wife, who the devil else do you suppose has the slightest chance? Get over there immediately."

"Yes, sir."

"You'll have a battalion of Hotspur Guards to contend with, too, and their lieutenant colonel. You can guess how those chaps'll feel about civilian interference. I'll send your sergeant—Tring, isn't it? And I suppose you'll need a DC or two. The place may be swarming with Specials," he added dryly, "but I imagine they'll all be suspects."

Alec breathed a silent groan. "DC Piper, please, sir." It wouldn't hurt to have a detective constable who thought Daisy was the cat's pyjamas, just in case any of the Yeoman Warders considered *her* a suspect. "And Ross, if he's available."

"All right, you shall have them. A police surgeon is on his way. Now get on with it. And Fletcher, for pity's sake, don't upset General Carradine. Just remember, he's not only a general; as Resident Governor, he represents the Crown."

Crane rang off. Alec dashed back upstairs to finish dressing. He put on his Royal Flying Corps tie, hoping it might smooth his way with the military. After a quick word with Mrs. Dobson in the hall, he was opening the front door when the telephone bell sounded again.

"I'm glad I've caught you, Fletcher. I've just reported to the AC, and he tells me there's another general at the Tower."

This time, Alec let his groan be heard. "Who's that, sir?"

"Sir Patrick Heald, Keeper of the Regalia. Bad luck that he's in residence at present, as he lives mostly at his country house. Officially, he's a member of His Majesty's Household. And he's a friend of the Assistant Commissioner."

Alec took the tube to Mark Lane. At this hour, the trains were crowded, but probably quicker than driving. As he made his way up from the depths, a breathless voice behind him called, "Chief!"

He was pleased to see Ernie Piper. The young DC's phenomenal memory for detail would help him keep straight the names of the dozens of Yeomen Warders they were going to have to interview. With him was DC Ross, whose much longer stride accounted for Piper's puffing and panting.

"We been chasing you up I dunno how many steps, Chief."

"Good practice. According to my memory and my wife, the Tower of London consists mostly of steps. Morning, Ross."

"Good morning, sir." Ross hadn't worked with Alec often enough to address him as Chief. "Mrs. Fletcher's involved in the case?"

"Peripherally, I trust. She was staying with the Resident Governor last night. I doubt she had anything to do with the victim—the Chief Warder, I gather."

"I wouldn't give you odds on that, Chief! Mrs. Fletcher's bound to know exactly what's going on," said Piper.

"We'll see."

Hadn't Daisy said something about the Chief Warder, when she was telling him about her tour of the Tower? He couldn't for the life of him remember what. Not for the first time, he wished he'd listened to her more closely.

They walked down the hill under spitting rain and a sky that threatened worse to come. A gusty wind blew scraps of paper about their feet. Alec passed on what little information he had from Superintendent Crane, mostly concerned with not offending the eminent gentlemen involved.

"I should warn you also," he added, "that many, if not most, of our suspects are likely to come from the ranks of colleagues of ours."

"Colleagues, sir?" Ross exclaimed.

"All Yeoman Warders are Special Constables of the Metropolitan Police. By the way, don't for pity's sake call them Beefeaters, unless you want more murder done. My wife says they regard the term as an insult."

"They must get insulted a lot, then," observed Piper. "Most people don't know any better."

"I didn't," Ross admitted.

"Well, you do now. You two are going to have to handle initial interviews with them, and I don't want any missteps. Besides, every single one is a sergeant major, so they outrank you. Think you can cope?"

"If you can cope with a couple of generals, Chief, and one of them a Sir into the bargain, me and Ross'll manage a few dozen sergeant majors, never fear."

"All right. To start with, we want some idea of the character of the victim—at least, how the others regarded him—and as many alibis as possible for the time of death, to weed them out a bit."

"Do we have a time of death, sir?"

"Not yet. With luck, the doctor will get there before us. If not, we'll surely be able to narrow it down. Actually, for all I know, he was in bed and his wife hit him with a frying pan."

"Shouldn't think so, Chief. If it looked like being that simple, they'd've told the Super so and he wouldn't have sent you, even with Mrs. Fletcher being there."

"He didn't know she's there." Alec saw Piper and Ross exchange a glance, and realized he sounded irritable. They were not to blame for Daisy's association with yet another murder case. "No, you're right, Ernie. It must be more complicated than that."

They reached the bottom of the hill. At the ticket office, a grim-faced Yeoman Warder in blue was posting a notice informing the public that the Tower was closed today to anyone not on official business.

Alec accosted him. "We're on official business. Police. I'm Detective Chief Inspector Fletcher."

The man came to attention and gave a crisp army salute, an odd effect combined with his fancy dress. "Sergeant Major Liston, sir. Glad to see you, and I hope you catch the sodding bastard what did it! General Carradine is expecting you, if you'll just come with me, gentlemen. Oh, half a tick. I better give you some of our visitors' guidebooks. They have a plan of the Tower, so's you can find your way about."

He popped into the ticket office and brought them three green brochures. Among the advertisements for Sapon soap, Beefeater gin, Mazawattee tea ("It's British-grown!"), and Thos. Cook & Son was a plan of the Tower.

"We won't make you pay your tuppence for the guidebook, sir." Liston led them onward.

Beneath the royal arms carved in stone, two sentries of the Hotspurs guarded the first archway—the Middle Tower, according to the brochure. They didn't challenge Liston and his companions. No doubt they had seen the yeoman go out with his notice, but Alec wondered whether anyone who managed to filch or copy a suit of the picturesque Tudor uniform would be able to march in without question. Or out, for that matter.

As they walked across the moat bridge, he said, "Tell me about the Chief Yeoman Warder. I don't even know his name."

"Crabtree, sir. He was regular army, sir, like the rest of us, done our twenty years afore we get a billet here. Crabtree was Regimental Sergeant Major, so it weren't no surprise when he got picked for Chief Warder, nor there weren't no grumbling, neither, for a nicer bloke you never met. It fair flummoxes me who'd want to do him in."

"Married?"

"A widower, sir, no children. His better half died in the 'flu."

Alec, who had lost his first wife in '18, in the influenza pandemic, felt an instant kinship with the victim. Yet he had a feeling that what Daisy had said of him was uncomplimentary. Was Liston's encomium a case of *nil nisi bonum?* Alec hoped so, because if it were true, if Crabtree really had no obvious enemies, he had no starting point for the investigation.

"Can you show me on this plan where the body was found?" he asked.

The yeoman pointed. "Hereabouts. It's just a staircase, so it's not shown, not properly."

"What exactly happened?"

"I didn't see, there being a ruddy horde of Hotspurs posted all around by the time I got there, but what I heard was, he was found at the bottom of the steps with a partizan stuck through him."

"A partizan?"

"One of them halberds—pikes—we carry when we're on guard duty or on parade."

"I don't suppose you know whether it was his own."

"Couldn't've been. His is a mace with a model of the White Tower on top, wouldn't stick into nobody. Not likely he have anyone else's with him, neither, but s'posing he did, he'd have a ruddy hard job stabbing hisself in the back!"

"His back, was it?"

"That's what I heard, sir."

Alec tried to imagine a man holding a pike missing his footing on steps, perhaps tripping over the pike, and somehow falling in such a way that the pike followed him down and impaled him. He didn't see how it could happen. He dismissed the speculation, for the present. Very likely the medical evidence would rule it out anyway.

He noted that Piper, while keeping up with their brisk pace over the bridge, had his notebook out and, with typical thoroughness, was writing down everything Liston said.

They came to the Byward Tower. Again, a pair of Hotspur Guards stood sentry outside the massive gate, closed except for a postern door. Alec and his men followed their guide through and found themselves in the gloom under the arch. A yeoman was on guard within, his partizan in his hand.

"The 'tecs from the Yard, Mr. Fairway," said Liston.

Fairway sketched a salute. "And a good thing, too. The general's in the Warders' Room, sir," he told Alec, pointing to a door on the left.

Liston knocked on the door, then opened it. "It's the police, sir."

The circular room, its ceiling vaulted, had narrow cross-slit windows high in the walls. It was well lit by a gasolier and warmed by a coal fire. As Liston ushered in the detectives, three men stood up.

Alec recognized one immediately from Daisy's description. He couldn't remember his name, though, only that she had called him "Jeremy Fisher," after Beatrix Potter's frog. The one who had been sitting on the corner of the big desk, swinging his foot and resting one hand on a black bag, wore the uniform of a major in the Medical Corps. He was the only one Alec was really interested in talking to at present, but the man behind the desk was not to be brushed off. Obviously in command, he came round and shook hands, saying, "I'm General Carradine. Dr. Macleod and my assistant, Webster. We're very glad to have you."

"DCI Fletcher, sir." Alec had met a good many generals in his time. To his relief, Carradine was not the red-faced, blustering sort. In fact, he had a shrewd look in his eye, which could make him easy to work with—or hard to trap. With any luck, he'd have an unshakable alibi. "I've brought these two detective constables with me, and my sergeant, Tring, should be arriving any moment, as well as a police surgeon."

"Liston, you'd better get back to the Middle Tower and make sure they have no trouble getting in." He raised his eyebrows at Alec. "Fletcher, eh?"

"My wife has been a guest of yours, sir. I did suggest to my superintendent that he should send someone else, but he insisted."

"I'm sure he sent the best man for the job. Mrs. Fletcher is being well cared for, I assure you. You never saw such a flock of women hovering with tea and hot-water bottles."

"Why? What's wrong with her?"

"She did find the body, my dear fellow," said the general reproachfully.

"Great Scott!"

"A bit of a shock for a gently bred lady, naturally, though she refused to see Macleod. Oh, but of course, you didn't know. She asked me not to mention her presence when I rang up the Yard."

Alec decided it was best, for the present at least, not to enquire into what the devil Daisy had been doing wandering about the Tower before anyone else was up and about. "I see," he said, not seeing at all.

"You'll want to see her, of course."

"Of course, sir, but first I must talk to Dr. Macleod. Doctor, I take it you've examined the body?"

Macleod grimaced. "Not pleasant, but I dealt with a great deal worse in France."

"No doubt. When you've told me your conclusions, I must see it for myself." He turned back to the Resident Governor. "I gather the scene is under guard, sir?"

"I had Colonel Duggan post some of his men to

keep people away. The Tower is ultimately under my authority. And all that goes on here is ultimately my responsibility as well, which is why I would like to be present while you talk to the doctor. However, it's for you to decide."

"You're welcome to stay. I'm afraid I'll have one or two questions for you after I've heard from Dr. Macleod."

"Naturally, I'll do anything I can to assist you. This is a terrible business. Poor Crabtree, of all people!"

"Let's get on with it, then," said Macleod impatiently. "I have sick people waiting for me." He didn't look very well himself, tired and jumpy. Perhaps he'd been up half the night with his patients.

"By all means," said Alec. "Do sit down, Doctor. I take it this is a suitable place for me to use, general, at least for the present?"

"Yes, yes, do make use of the desk. This room is the Chief Warder's lair. You'll see his Wait Book there by the inkstand. Poor Crabtree!"

Alec went to sit behind the desk, while Carradine, the doctor, and Webster took three of the leather-seated chairs. Piper and Ross had moved to one side, standing against the wall, Piper ready with notebook and one of his supply of well-sharpened pencils.

"First of all, Doctor, can you give me some idea of the time of death?"

"I'm no expert. He'd been dead for several hours. Somewhere between ten and two, I'd say. The former is not a medical estimate. I'm assuming he turned up on time with the King's Keys."

"Yes indeed," Carradine confirmed. "But why—"

"We'll get to that later, if you don't mind, sir. Two A.M., Doctor?"

"That's the latest possible, in my opinion. No doubt the police surgeon will narrow it down for you."

"Possibly." In Alec's experience, police surgeons came in two varieties: those who were as vague as Macleod, or vaguer, and those who gave a precise time within a quarter hour, without any possible justification by the evidence. "Any chance that he didn't die instantly?"

"None. He broke his neck. The partizan was a gratuitous extra, but if he was not dead already, that wound would have caused fatal bleeding."

"Did both occur at the same time, roughly?"

"With a number of Special Constables about, I was not permitted to move the body, scarcely to touch it. It was cold, but rigor was scarcely beginning to set in, possibly due to the chilling effect of lying on cold stone. And that's all I can tell you."

"Very helpful. The police surgeon should be able to give us an answer, or the pathologist. We may have one or two more questions for you later, Doctor, but this gives us somewhere to start. Thank you for your time."

With an abrupt nod, Macleod stalked out.

"Damn rude," the general muttered. "What Fay sees in the blighter, I cannot understand. But there, I'm only her father."

Alec tactfully ignored this aside, which didn't seem to have anything to do with the case. "Now that we have some idea of the time," he said, "I'd like my men to interview all the Yeoman Warders, with a view to eliminating as many as possible as soon as possible. Where would you suggest as a suitable place?"

"They'd better go across the way to the Warders' Hall. They'll find a list of yeomen pinned up in there. Many of them will be there already, and they have my permission to send for the rest as needed. Fairway's on duty out there. He'll direct you." He nodded towards Piper and Ross, then turned to his aide. "That had better go in the Daily Orders, Webster."

Webster made a note as the detective constables departed.

"You say Crabtree was on time with 'the King's Keys.' What exactly does that mean?"

"Mrs. Fletcher didn't tell you about the ceremony she came to see last night?" Carradine asked dryly.

"She mentioned it, of course." Alec grinned. "Either she didn't go into detail or I didn't listen as closely as I should have."

"Doubtless," Webster put in unexpectedly, "Mrs. Fletcher reserved a full description until she had witnessed the event."

"She knows I prefer an eyewitness report to hearsay. I take it, general, you witnessed Crabtree doing something with these keys at ten o'clock last night?"

"He handed them over to me, at the door to the King's House, after locking the gates. It's the end of the ceremony. What I can't make out is why he then went off down those steps. He'd finished his duties for the day."

"He didn't need to come back here to his office?"

"No," said Webster, "and his quarters are in the opposite direction, next to the Yeoman Gaoler's House. It wasn't a pleasant night for a stroll."

"Perhaps he was going to the Warders' Hall," Alec suggested.

"The men do gather there in the evenings for a

pint or two," Carradine conceded, "but Crabtree didn't drink. He told me, when I was considering him for the position of Chief Yeoman Warder, that he's—that he was a teetotaller and usually spent his evenings reading the Bible. I couldn't make him Chapel Clerk because he was a nonconformist, but he was willing to turn out for church parades."

"Mightn't his religious propensities have offended his fellow yeomen?" Alec asked.

"Oh no. He was a student, not a teacher, he assured me, and he considered every man must find his own route to salvation. I'd have heard complaints if he'd tried preaching, I assure you. The men wouldn't have stood for it. No, a quiet man, he was, but very well respected."

A most unlikely victim of murder, Alec thought. Digging out a motive was going to be difficult, unless Piper and Ross came up with a completely different picture of the man.

1

"No, thank you," said Daisy, regarding with dismay yet another cup of hot, sweet tea. Besides disliking sugar in her tea, she was about to drown in the stuff. She swung her legs off the sofa. "Truly, I'm completely recovered."

"Your colour is much improved," observed Mrs. Tebbit, "though I do think the glass of brandy would have effected a quicker recovery."

"The brandy didn't go to waste, Aunt Alice."

"Daddy swallowed it with one gulp."

"What a shocking thing to happen," twittered Miss Tebbit for the hundredth time, "and when you were our guest, too."

"Poor Mr. Crabtree!"

"If only it had been that horrid Rumford instead."

"What a very unchristian thing to say, Brenda," Miss Tebbit said reprovingly, then spoilt the effect by adding, "At least, I think it must be, mustn't it?"

"Not really, Aunt Myrtle."

"Because we're wishing even harder that it *wasn't*

Mr. Crabtree than we're wishing it *was* Mr. Rumford who was murdered."

"I wish you wouldn't use that horrid word, Fay."

"But it was murder, Myrtle. No good closing our eyes to the facts," said Mrs. Tebbit.

"It looked to me like murder," Daisy cautioned, "but I could be mistaken. The police may decide otherwise. The general did say he wouldn't tell the Yard I'm here, didn't he?"

"He promised."

"Daddy always keeps his promises."

"But I don't see why you didn't want your husband to come."

"We're desperately keen to meet him."

"He must be frightfully dashing. . . ."

". . . To catch a viscount's daughter."

"Now that," said Mrs. Tebbit roundly, "is an appallingly vulgar remark!"

Fay and Brenda glanced at each other, then looked in appeal at Daisy, who nodded. They were profuse in their apologies.

"You see, we have met two or three lords' daughters before . . ."

"Though none of them was half as nice as you, Mrs. Fletcher."

". . . But never a policeman."

"I believe that is about to change," announced Mrs. Tebbit, who was seated by the window of the small downstairs sitting room, watching comings and goings on Tower Green in a way she would surely have condemned in the girls. "Here comes Mr. Fletcher."

"Oh blast!" said Daisy.

They heard the doorbell ring, the maid's footsteps in the hall, the click of the front door's latch, the murmur of voices. The girls sat up straighter, their gazes fixed on the sitting room door.

It opened and the maid announced, "Detective Chief Inspector Fletcher, ma'am."

Alec looked very tall and stern standing on the threshold, but Daisy hoped the glance he flashed her held as much concern as exasperation. He ought to know by now that it wasn't her fault if she had a tendency to stumble across bodies. It was Fate, that's what it was, and she didn't like it any better than he did.

He advanced into the room. "Good morning, Mrs. Tebbit. Good morning, ladies."

"You are already acquainted with my daughter, Mr. Fletcher. These are my young cousins, Fay and Brenda Carradine."

"Gosh, are you going to question us, Mr. Fletcher?"

"Too thrilling!"

"We do hope so."

"Not that we know anything."

"But we'll do anything we can to help."

Alec's lips twitched. "I expect I'll want to talk to you all. However, since my wife was first on the scene—weren't you, Daisy?—I must have a word with her first. In private," he added as Fay and Brenda folded their hands in their laps and settled back with the obvious intention of catching every word.

"We'll go up to my room," Daisy proposed.

"Oh no," Miss Tebbit exclaimed, jumping up, "dear Mrs. Fletcher, you mustn't move after such a dreadful shock. We'll go upstairs."

"And what about your poor old mother's aged legs, Myrtle?"

"If you *must* mention them, Mother, there's nothing wrong with them whatsoever. Come along, girls."

"So old-fashioned," sighed Mrs Tebbit, following the others. "But perhaps she's developing a trace of a spine at long last."

Alec saw her out and closed the door firmly behind her before coming to join Daisy on the sofa. He took her in his arms and gave her a comforting and altogether most satisfactory kiss.

When it came to an end, she asked hopefully, "Do I look pale and interesting, darling?"

"Not at all. You're your usual robust self, and I'd like to know why, when you're obviously in the thick of things, you left it to *me* to break it to the Super that you're here."

"I hoped if the general didn't mention me, Mr. Crane might send someone else and need never know I found the body. Is he very upset?"

"More resigned, I think, love, though he put up a bit of a show. All right, let's start at the beginning and get your part over with. First, why on earth were you wandering about Tower Green at that time in the morning?"

"I woke up early and suddenly wanted more than anything else in the world to see the twins. So I wrote a note of explanation to Mrs. Tebbit and sneaked out. A disgraceful breach of etiquette, but I didn't think she'd really be offended. She's marvellous."

"She's quite a character. Mother always disapproved of her, although she played bridge with her. Go on."

"You've seen the steps, haven't you? They're the shortest way out, from here. We didn't use them going down last night because of the fog. Was it foggy at home? I suppose it was just near the river, but you could barely see your hand in front of your face, so we decided the steps were too steep and dark and slippery to be safe. This morning it was sunny. From the top I saw a red bundle. I thought one of the yeomen had dropped his cape. I'd gone down a couple of steps before I realized . . ."

"That he was still wearing it."

"Yes. I saw the hat—they call it 'a bonnet'—and his beard, and then the partizan. I don't know why I noticed that last."

"I expect you didn't want to see it, which is perfectly understandable. Did you go on down? Did you touch anything?"

"I know better than that, darling!" Daisy said tartly. "I guessed he was dead, from the angle of his head. If not, I wouldn't have known what to do to help him, anyway, so it seemed best to go for help. Poor old Crabtree! He was a bore, but a nice old bore."

"Ah, that was it. I was sure you'd told me something about him. You knew right away who it was?"

"I could see his beard. It's rather conspicuous. Rumford, the Yeoman Gaoler, has a similar growth, but nowhere near as grey. Besides, I'd seen Crabtree in his red cape just the night before, doing his bit at the Ceremony. He kindly walked me back to the house."

"Which way?"

"Up those steps. He had a lantern of sorts. All you could see of the gas lamps was a fuzzy ball of light that didn't illuminate anything. It was frightfully eerie, particularly with Rumford waiting in the murk at the top, coughing like a foghorn."

Alec frowned. "This Rumford character keeps popping up. What did he want?"

"I don't know. He and Crabtree stepped aside to exchange a word or two, so I didn't hear what they said. Crabtree seemed a bit irritated, but not at all alarmed. He came back to me, Rumford went off coughing, and—"

"Which way did Rumford go?"

Daisy thought. "I couldn't swear to it, but I think along the wall. Not down the steps; certainly not the way we went, which would be the quickest way to his house, and much the easiest in the fog."

"How do you know where he lives?"

"He's the Yeoman Gaoler, darling, so he lives in the Yeoman Gaoler's House. It's right next door to the King's House, on the west side of Tower Green, opposite those beastly steps. Come to the window and I'll show you." She pointed out Rumford's front door. "As his title implies, his predecessors kept prisoners in the house, but then, there don't seem to be many spots at the Tower that didn't house prisoners at some time or other. Even this house."

"Is this relevant, Daisy?"

"Sort of. After all, he's second in command of the Yeoman Warders, so I presume he's next in line for the Chief Warder's job. And he was wandering around in the fog last night, perhaps luring poor Crabtree to his doom. And he's not a very nice man."

Alec grinned. "I can't arrest him for murder just because you don't like him."

"The thing is, no one seems to like him, which suggests he has some serious character flaw, doesn't it?"

"Or an unfortunate manner. Don't worry, Piper and Ross are interviewing the Yeoman Warders now. We'll find out where your sinister Mr. Rumford was at the time the deed was done."

"What time was that?"

"Daisy, you know I can't tell you—"

"Oh, come on, darling, I promise I shan't go around asking people what they were doing between the hours of ten and whatever."

"No." Alec sighed. "Your ways of ferreting out information are rather more subtle—and don't interpret that as permission to meddle! The police surgeon examined the body just before I came here. He puts it somewhere between eleven and three. Not before eleven, certainly, and probably later. That fits pretty much with the opinion of Dr. Macleod, who examined the body earlier but in less detail, besides being no expert. The autopsy should be more precise, with luck, especially if we can find out when Crabtree last ate." He paused as a maid brought in a tray with tea and biscuits.

"Miss Tebbit thought the gentleman'd like tea, madam."

Daisy thanked her. She set the tray on a table and went out.

"*Miss* Tebbit, not Mrs. Perhaps she is beginning to think for herself. Perhaps the Tower inspires her. Pour your own, will you, darling?"

Alec filled two cups and handed one to Daisy.

"No, thanks! I must have drunk about a gallon already. I'll take a biscuit, though. I'm ravenous. I haven't had breakfast. Please make a note of the time, in case I'm murdered." She shuddered. "Sorry! The Tower is so full of horror stories, I must be getting a bit blasé."

"My fault." Alec gave her a one-armed hug, to the imminent danger of the cup of tea in his other hand. "I shouldn't have mentioned that particular aspect of the investigation. I don't suppose you noticed which direction Crabtree went after handing over the keys?"

"No. General Carradine was asking me where Fay and Brenda had got to. They went with me to watch the ceremony, you see, and their aunt, too—"

"Their aunt?"

"Mrs. Duggan, the one who brought them up and then married an officer, the man who happens to be in charge of the garrison at present. The girls decided to escort her home because of the fog. The Officers' Quarters are on the far side of the White Tower."

"So the Carradine girls were also wandering about the place in the night."

"You can't suspect them, darling. They're just a pair of rather silly, though quite nice, girls. Besides, they weren't gone more than half an hour. A couple of young officers escorted them home. I didn't see them, and the girls didn't mention their names."

"So now we have two unknown officers wandering about the place in the night!"

"There are soldiers about all the time. They change the guard at regular intervals, though they're marched from place to place by the sergeant of the watch, not wandering freely. But it doesn't seem likely to me that the feud has anything to do with the murder."

"Great Scott, what next? What feud?"

Daisy explained about the ill feeling between the general and the colonel who had stolen his sister-in-law, and how it had spilled over into relations between garrison and warders. "I don't think it was ever very serious, though. In any case, Mrs. Tebbit sabotaged it by inviting the Duggans to dinner last night. That's why Mrs. Duggan was with us at the ceremony."

"Damn the ceremony! Carradine says the keys

were put into his hands at ten o'clock. Does that agree with your recollection?"

"It always happens at ten. Duke of Wellington's orders. It will still happen at ten in a hundred years, or a thousand, for all I know. Tradition is sacrosanct."

"We have to find out what Crabtree was doing between ten and eleven, or later."

"Fay and Brenda might have seen him."

"Yes, I'd better talk to them now, while I'm here." He finished the last of his tea and got up to ring the bell.

"You will see Mrs. Tebbit, won't you, darling? She'll be so disappointed if you don't."

"My job does not include giving old ladies a thrill! But yes, I'll have to ask her a few questions at some point. No hurry. I just hope she doesn't insist on chaperoning the girls."

"Gosh, no," Daisy agreed with a giggle, "I can't imagine trying to interview them with her sitting in—and butting in." She gave him her guileless look, the one that so often encouraged people to tell her their inmost secrets. "I'm sure she'd be satisfied if I stayed with them."

"Unfortunately," Alec said, grimacing, "you're probably right."

"I won't say a word, and I'll take notes for you."

When the maid arrived, he told her to ask the young ladies to join Mrs. Fletcher and himself. Fay and Brenda bounced in a few minutes later.

They sat down and regarded Alec with eager expectation.

"Can we really help, Mr. Fletcher?"

"What do you want to know?"

"I gather you two young ladies were out and about after the Ceremony of the Keys?"

"Yes, we took Aunt Christina home."

"But we didn't push Mr. Crabtree down the stairs."

"We liked him."

"He was a nice old buffer."

"Not like—"

Alec broke into the double act. "But did you see him?"

"Not after he went off with Mrs. Fletcher."

"To take the keys to Daddy."

"Did you see anyone else out and about?"

"We couldn't see much at all."

"Visibility was extremely limited," said Brenda grandly.

"One could have got lost crossing the parade ground."

"So we went round the side."

"Keeping close to the wall of the White Tower."

Alec consulted his map.

"And we heard footsteps behind us."

"So we hurried up."

" 'Like one, that on a lonesome road—' "

" 'Doth walk in fear and dread—' "

" 'Because he knows, a frightful fiend—' "

" 'Doth close behind him tread.' "

"Fay looked back."

"And it was only one of the warders."

"All she could see was his silhouette against the last lamp."

"But I could tell, because he was wearing their fancy dress."

They glanced at each other.

"Which was odd, come to think of it."

"They usually change into mufti as soon as the public leaves."

"At five o'clock."

"Except the Chief Warder, because of the Keys."

"He has to stay dressed up for that."

"And the Byward Tower guard does, too, come to think of it."

"You and your aunt went straight from the ceremony to her residence? No stopping on the way?"

"There isn't anywhere to stop," said Fay.

"We walked pretty briskly because of the cold."

"Even before the frightful fiend."

The yeoman they saw couldn't have been Crabtree, Daisy thought. The old man couldn't have caught up with them after going with her to the King's House.

Alec's frown suggested he had come to the same conclusion. "You didn't notice where your frightful fiend went?"

"No, we lost him after the White Tower."

"We could hardly see the lamp on the Officers' Quarters building."

"Where Aunt Christina and Uncle Sidney live."

"Uncle Sidney sent a couple of officers to escort us home."

"Or rather, they volunteered."

"Do you know their names?"

Fay and Brenda exchanged an amused look.

"Oh yes, Mr. Fletcher, we know all the officers."

"They were Lieutenant Jardyne and Captain Devereux."

"Thank you."

"Do you think they might have seen the murderer?" asked Brenda, wide-eyed.

"On their way back?"

"After they left us here?"

"It's always possible. I take it you didn't see anyone as you walked back from your aunt's?"

"Not a soul."

"The fog was thicker than ever."

"Thank you," Alec said again. "That's all for now. I may have more questions for you later."

"Anytime!"

The girls departed, but the door had not quite closed behind them when Fay turned to ask, "Mr. Fletcher, are you going to interrogate Aunt Alice—Mrs. Tebbit?"

Brenda's face appeared over her sister's shoulder. "Because she's simply dying to be interrogated."

"Does she have something specific to tell me?"

Fay glanced back at Brenda, who said, "I don't think so."

"But you never know."

"Aunt Alice is a dark horse."

"It's no use trying to guess what she might have to say."

Alec looked at Daisy, who shrugged and gave a slight shake of her head. It seemed to her unlikely that the old lady, a recent arrival at the Tower, could know anything useful.

"Please tell Mrs. Tebbit," he said, "that I may need to speak to her later. If she has specific, relevant information to offer, a message to the Warders' Room in the Byward Tower will reach me."

"Right-oh." They disappeared.

Alec asked apprehensively, "Is that what the twins are going to be like when they're older? Reading each other's minds and finishing each other's sentences?"

"I've heard that some twins develop their own private language. But perhaps that's only identical twins."

"Let's hope!" He stood up. "Next stop the Duggans, I think. He's a colonel?"

"Lieutenant colonel. Risen from the ranks, I gather."

"In a Guards regiment? I'd have said it was impossible! Surely unprecedented. 'The Gentlemen's Sons,' they call themselves, or used to. Before Waterloo, the other regiments called them 'Hyde Park Soldiers,' but they gave a good account of themselves there." Alec had a degree in history, specializing in the Georgians. "And in our latest little shindig, too."

"He must have done something truly spectacular, not merely competent."

"It would have been a field commission, probably a lot of officers killed in his unit. I'd have thought they would have made him transfer to a different regiment, though. And then to keep promoting him, even if he never makes it to full colonel! Hmm, this could make him easier to deal with, or harder."

"I wouldn't have said he's the sort to stand on his dignity. I see you have on your RFC tie."

"Every little bit helps. I'm off. You're free to go home to Oliver and Miranda, love. If you think of anything else you need to tell me, it can wait until I get home this evening."

"Right-oh," said Daisy. "I'll pop up and say goodbye to the Tebbits. Only think, if I'd waited until a decent hour this morning to do just that, someone else would have found poor Crabtree."

Mrs. Tebbit brushed aside Daisy's apologies for her unceremonious early departure. "Young women are excessively maternal these days," she said. "In my young day, one left babies strictly to the nurse. Oh, don't look at me like a dying cow, Myrtle. I don't suppose it would make a ha'p'orth of difference to you if I had turned myself into a milch cow for your benefit."

"Mother, how can you!"

"With the greatest of ease. Has your husband left the house already, Mrs. Fletcher?"

"Yes, I'm afraid so. The girls mentioned that you wanted to speak to him, but he has to deal with the basic stuff first. He'll come and see you later. Was there some specific information you wanted to give him? Because I could probably pass it on."

"No," said Mrs. Tebbit regretfully. "I did think . . . But after all, it wasn't Crabtree who was making a nuisance of himself; it was the other fellow, the one who looks just like him."

"Rumford?"

"That's the one. A nasty piece of work if ever I saw one."

"Making a nuisance of himself to you, Mrs. Tebbit?"

"Certainly not. To Arthur. However, since Rumford has not been murdered, it's of no significance."

Miss Tebbit was shocked—again. "Mother, surely you wouldn't have told the police about Cousin Arthur and that horrible man!"

"I was of two minds about it," Mrs. Tebbit conceded. "It would have been a great bore to have to move back to St. John's Wood so soon if Arthur had been arrested. I'm happy not to be faced with that choice. Well, Daisy, you have presented your apologies very prettily, and by now you must be more anxious than ever to dandle your infants. Off you go."

On her way downstairs, Daisy tried to decide whether Mrs. Tebbit had been speaking merely for effect, as she was wont to do. In any case, her information seemed irrelevant as well as unreliable, and not worth relaying to Alec.

8

Alec stepped out of the front door of the King's House and paused to look around. To his right, just beyond the window of the room he had left a moment earlier, stood a sentry. The window was closed because of the drizzle, now falling in a determined way, but had it been open, he could scarcely have failed to hear every word spoken within.

Glancing up, Alec saw a gas lamp above the front door. However dark the night or thick the fog, a sentry posted there would surely have noticed anyone leaving or entering the house that way.

There was no back door, since the house was built directly against the wall surrounding the inner bailey—the Inner Ward, as they called it. The door farther along, under the balcony terrace, was probably the servants' entrance. It, too, was lit by a lamp and at present within full sight of the sentry. But on a foggy night?

His gaze turned on the Guardsman, Alec contemplated the stiff figure. Staring straight ahead in the prescribed fashion, was he conscious of anything but boredom? Under Alec's scrutiny, whether

aware of it or not, he shifted his weight uneasily
from foot to foot. Suddenly, without warning, he
performed a precise turn, marched several paces
away from Alec, turned again with knees raised high
and a great deal of stamping, and returned to his
post. Before he turned again to face forward, his
eyes met Alec's.

All Alec saw there was curiosity. Had the man
taken his little walk just so as to examine the ob-
server?

Checking his wristwatch, Alec saw that it was not
the hour, nor the half hour, nor even the quarter.
The Royal Flying Corps had not gone in for much
fancy marching, having more important matters
on their minds, so he didn't know if the gyrations
took place at regular, prescribed intervals. If not,
anyone sneaking out of or into the King's House
would have risked coming face-to-face with a Hotspur Guard.

He considered asking the sentry. The man was
once again rigid, his gaze fixed on the middle distance directly ahead of him. Better not to present
him with the dilemma—To speak or not to speak—
when Colonel Duggan could supply the answer.

There were sentries all over the place, including
at the top of the fatal stair. That was presumably not
a regular post, or the murder could not have taken
place. But the Tower was not only a tourist attraction; it was still a military fortress and a prison—
Daisy had said German spies were kept here, and
shot here, during the War—and the repository of
a vast fortune in jewels. It was well guarded.

Therefore, the fog had played an important rôle
in this murder.

Alec walked past the sentry and along the row of
attached houses facing Tower Green. The one next

door was very narrow and lower than its neighbours on either side, as if squeezed in between. Then came three more, Victorian brick, without half the charm of the King's House's Tudor half-timbering. They were yeomen's residences, he had been told. Halfway between the end of the row and the front door of the King's House, a lamppost stood on the other side of the paved way, on the edge of the lawn. Another lamp was attached to the corner of the end house.

Daisy and the Carradine girls had both mentioned being barely able to see one lamp from the next last night.

Alec stopped at the corner and turned to look back diagonally across Tower Green. On the west side beyond the King's House were more yeomen's houses. If he remembered correctly, the second was the home of the Chief Warder, the victim.

From his front door, Crabtree had had a choice of routes to the spot where he was found. He could have gone round the top of the Green, past the site of the scaffold, and down the broad steps towards the Bloody Tower. But then, why turn aside to the shortcut? In any case, on a dark, foggy night, the alternative would have been much more attractive, round the lower edge of the Green with houses on his right all the way, then down the shortcut steps. That was obviously the way he had chosen, assuming he had come from his house.

His duties of the day finished, why would he have left its shelter on such a foul night? "Who knew he was going to be out and about?" Alec said aloud.

"That's the big question, Chief?" DS Tring, with the soft tread peculiar to men whose bulkiness is largely muscle, had come up beside him unnoticed, the rumble of his deep voice the first sign of his arrival. "He didn't have to make a final round before turning in?"

"I understand he finished his duties at ten, and that it was his custom to go home and read the Good Book, rather than carousing with his mates in the Warders' Hall. He was a widower, no children."

"Ah." Tom Tring ruminated. "You don't reckon someone just happened to spot him and seized the occasion to give him a shove?"

"No."

"No, it don't smell that way to me. For one thing, there's that bloody great pike—beg pardon, partizan—sticking out of his back."

"Not to mention the fog."

"Malice aforethought."

"Who knew he was going to be out and about?" Alec repeated. "Who wanted to get rid of a man who was, by all accounts, inoffensive and well respected?"

"The man who expected to step into his shoes? But it's not that important a position, is it? It's not like he has the key to the Crown Jewels?"

"Not to my knowledge, but my knowledge is not yet very extensive. It's something we'll have to check. I believe the choice of Chief Warder is up to the Resident Governor, though, and he might have any number of reasons for passing over the second in command. I doubt anyone could count on inheriting the post."

"Unless he has some sort of hold over the Governor."

"Blackmail? We can't count it out. So far, there doesn't seem to be anything we can count out. The first thing I'd like to do is count out the residents of the King's House."

"That'd be the Governor's place, where

Mrs. Fletcher was staying?" Tom's eyes twinkled. "I can see it'd make life easier if they were eliminated."

"*You* know Daisy didn't do it," Alec said ruefully.

"*I* know Daisy didn't do it. But that's just why we have to prove it. In our present state of ignorance, she has as much motive and opportunity as anyone else."

"But not means, Chief. Where'd she have got hold of a partizan?"

"Difficult, but not impossible, alas. Each yeoman is supposed to keep his at home when not in use. Apart from ceremonial parades, they're used only in certain duty posts—at the main gates, for instance, and the Wakefield Tower, where the jewels are kept. As each man is at a given post for a week, he often leaves his weapon there, rather than lug it back and forth. There are usually a few standing about at the entrance to the Warders' Hall. A partizan isn't something a visitor can casually walk off with unnoticed, so they don't take any particular care."

"More's the pity," said Tom mournfully. "Would have been nice if we could limit our suspects to the yeomen."

"No such luck. But there is one oddity: The Carradine girls report a yeoman, or someone in yeoman's dress, following them around the back of the White Tower yesterday evening."

"No idea who?"

"Too foggy. Look here. . . ." Alec pointed out the sentry, the doors to the King's House and the late Chief Warder's house, explaining his observations and deductions.

"So you want me to have a word with the servants at the King's House?" Tom proposed. "Good job, too. I could do with a cuppa."

"You've finished on the steps, I take it."

"Everything fingerprinted and photographed and gone off to the Yard for developing. Body on its way to the pathologist. The officer of the watch kindly let me leave sentries posted top and bottom until you're done with the scene. Incidentally, he mentioned that the guards on duty don't use these steps, being they're too steep and narrow to march properly. From the Guard House, they go round by the others, which is why no one found him before Mrs. Fletcher. Here she comes now."

Daisy came out of the King's House, raising her red umbrella. In the moments before she noticed Alec and Tom, Alec saw her assessing gaze move from point to point that he himself had noted and had just described to Tom. Inevitably, now that the shock had subsided, her curiosity was aroused. Thank heaven she was eager to get home to the twins.

She saw them and came towards them. "Hello, Tom."

He tipped his hat. "Morning, Mrs. Fletcher. Stirred up another hornets' nest, haven't you?"

She smiled at him, having long ago learnt that the twitch of his moustache hid a teasing grin. "So much for early to bed and early to rise. Alec, I've been thinking."

"You surprise me."

"Don't be beastly, darling. The thing is, it wasn't the sort of night for hanging about on the off chance of a certain person turning up. Someone must have known Crabtree would be there at that time."

"We did get that far ourselves."

"Congratulations! I suppose you also worked out that the obvious person is Rumford, the Yeoman Gaoler? The one who spoke to Crabtree earlier, when he was taking the keys to General Carradine? He could have been making an appointment."

"And can you explain why he should want to meet on the steps in the small hours of a foggy night when their houses are next door to each other?"

"Oh!" Daisy was crestfallen. "I didn't know Crabtree was Rumford's next-door neighbour. Some of the yeomen's houses are in the casemates, actually inside the outer walls. But the view is the inner wall across a narrow lane. I suppose it's logical that their chief should have a nice view of the Green."

"I don't know that logic has much to do with the traditions of the Yeoman Warders. There's no reason you should guess, but that's how it was."

"Pity. I'd still like to know what he said and where he went afterwards."

"We'll ask him," said Alec, "but I can't promise to tell you."

Daisy sighed, then turned a considering look on the house beside which they stood, and its attached neighbours. "Someone might have watched out for him from one of these windows. Suppose he went home after dropping off the keys, and came out again later—"

"Daisy, I thought you were in a hurry to get home to the babies."

"I am, I am."

"And you're feeling all right?"

"Yes." She looked very well, but the red umbrella cast a deceptively healthy pink glow on her face. "The girls—Fay and Brenda—offered to go with me to the tube, but I'm perfectly all right."

"You'd better take a taxi, all the same." Alec felt in his pocket for change.

"I have enough cash, thanks, darling." She looked as if she were going to kiss him. Tom's presence wouldn't have stopped her, but either the complication of her dripping umbrella and his dripping hat or the blank stare of the nearby windows dissuaded her.

"Go carefully, Mrs. Fletcher," Tom admonished her. "These cobbles get slippery."

As she departed, she said over her shoulder, "Oh, by the way, it may not mean anything, but this house has two back doors."

"Back doors?" said Tom blankly to Alec, watching Daisy hurry past the fatal stairs.

"I would guess she was suggesting that had someone kept a lookout for Crabtree from this house, he could then have sneaked out through a back door, reducing the chance of being seen by the sentry."

"Ah. Might as well take a dekko while we're on the spot."

They turned around the side of the house. At the back, against the inner bailey wall, a staircase went down to a tiny area and a door that must lead into a windowless cellar.

"One," said Tom. "Where's the second?"

"It must open onto the wall up there. I'll go and see, but you'd better get on with the King's House staff." He knew that, far from ruffling feathers, Tom would soon have them all eating out of his hand, especially the women. "Then go over to the Waterloo Barracks. I hope by then to have arranged for you to talk to last night's sentries."

"All of 'em, Chief?"

"Those who were on duty at the King's House at least. Ernie and Ross can handle the rest when they're done with the yeomen."

Consulting his map, Alec climbed the steps to

the top of the wall. This was Ralegh's Walk, apparently. Before the construction of the Victorian residences, the prisoner had been able to stroll along the wall from the door of the Bloody Tower at one end to the King's House at the other. Now a wrought-iron gate marked PRIVATE gave access to a few yards of wall top apparently used as a balcony, blocked at the other end by a two-story house wall with a door in it.

Conceivable, he thought, but unlikely that the murderer had come out that way to follow his victim. At the other end, the Bloody Tower had no window in the upper floor on this side, though the floor below had two, as well as the main entrance, where a sign read TICKET HOLDERS ONLY. Was it locked at night? It would make a good place to lurk unseen, for someone with a luminous watch who knew roughly when to expect Crabtree.

He looked over the rampart, towards the river. Tower Bridge loomed large to his left. From inside the Tower one didn't notice it, but in height the bridge dwarfed even the White Tower, the mercantile structure eclipsing the royal fortress's ancient preeminence. Closer, just across Water Street, was the wide, flattened archway of Traitors' Gate. On either side of the gate stood a stone tower, outposts of St. Thomas's Tower, connected by a brick and timber building constructed over the arch. On the near side, adjoining the Bloody Tower and blocking the view along Water Street, was the bulge of the Wakefield Tower, home of the Crown Jewels.

Had the Chief Warder possessed a key to the Wakefield Tower? Surely General Carradine would have mentioned it, would have been distraught about the possibility of its having been stolen, even in the midst of shock at the murder. Shock had odd effects on men's minds, though. Something else to be checked.

As if summoned by his thoughts, the Resident Governor appeared as Alec descended the stair. In broad daylight, even with the drizzle turning to rain, and even with his hat pulled low, he was recognizable by the time he came level with the sentry at the top of the shortcut steps. So was his faithful shadow, the frog-faced Jeremy Webster.

They both looked up at Alec's hail.

"Fletcher! Dare I hope?"

"Sorry, sir, it's a bit early for results. In fact, I'm just beginning to realize how ignorant I am about the Tower and how it's run, all the stuff they don't put in this otherwise admirable brochure of yours. I don't suppose you could spare Mr. Webster to go about with me, just for a while, to act as a sort of walking guidebook. If you would be so kind, Mr. Webster?"

His glasses spotted with raindrops in the shadow beneath his hat, Webster looked more enigmatic than ever, and a trifle supercilious. He did not speak, neither consenting nor demurring when the general agreed to lend his services. Alec understood why Daisy found him a trifle unnerving.

He decided it would be tactful to warn Carradine about Tom's presence in his house. "By the way, sir, my sergeant, DS Tring, is talking to your servants," he said.

Carradine looked taken aback, but after a moment he said quite mildly, "I suppose you are bound to suspect everyone."

"Not so much suspect as need to rule out."

"Even your wife?"

"Even my wife. To be honest, Daisy's the main

reason we're starting with the King's House and hoping to eliminate everyone residing there. If we can't, I may have to hand over the reins to someone else."

"I trust not," the general said dryly. "Better the devil we know, if you'll excuse the phrase, not to mention that clearing Mrs. Fletcher will also clear myself, along with my household."

"And that," Alec admitted with a wry smile, "is the other reason we're starting there. Without the cooperation of the Resident Governor, the investigation would be ten times more difficult."

"Believe me, I'll cooperate." With grim jocularity, he added, "I don't know if you realize it, but if I have to keep the place closed to the public for more than a couple of days, there will be the sort of ructions that will inevitably lead to questions in the House."

In fact, any case where the CID of the Metropolitan Police was called in had the potential to lead to questions in Parliament. This one, however, involved a royal palace, an ancient monument of national importance, and the murder of one of those picturesque, romantic beings the public called Beefeaters. Talk about fodder for the press!

"We always work as fast as possible, sir," Alec assured the unhappy Resident Governor. "Trails grow cold. Unfortunately, there's never enough manpower available. I was hoping to use some of your Special Constables, once we've sorted out their alibis, but perhaps I'd better ask Superintendent Crane to spare me a few more men."

"No, no, I have every faith in your efficiency, my dear chap. Let's at least wait until we see how it looks by the time you knock off this evening."

He went off, leaving Alec with Webster.

"First question: Is the Bloody Tower locked at night?"

"No. It holds nothing of great value."

"I assume the Wakefield Tower is locked. Did the Chief Warder have a key?"

"Certainly not."

"Who does?"

"The Keeper of the Regalia has one, of course. That's General Sir Patrick Heald. The Resident Governor is responsible for the other. Except when there's work to be done inside, cleaning and so on, I lock the door as soon as the Wakefield Tower closes to the public, take the key to the King's House, and lock it in the safe."

"So, in essence, you control the second key."

"Yes," said Webster frostily. "However, I cannot see that this fact has any bearing whatsoever on the murder of Crabtree."

"Nor can I," Alec agreed. Nonetheless, it was interesting, if only because the man was so defensive about it.

9

*A*lec gave the fatal stairs a cursory examination. Though he learnt nothing new, he wanted to look again after seeing Tom's photographs, so he left the sentries on guard.

He learnt much more as he walked with Webster to the Officers' Quarters building. The Resident Governor's adjutant was able to answer every query unless it pertained solely to the garrison. After a few minutes, he warmed up enough to actually volunteer information instead of having it prised from him by a direct question.

"The soldiers are ultimately under General Carradine's command," he explained, "but he doesn't interfere in the day-to-day running of the garrison. The lieutenant colonel in charge of whichever battalion of whichever Guards regiment is currently posted here requests the governor's permission for any unusual activity."

"The battalions come and go? So the soldiers haven't time to develop an intimate acquaintance with the Yeoman Warders."

"On the whole, no. They don't mix much. How-

ever, our warders served in many different regiments and may have known members of the garrison before they left the regular army."

"I assume you have records of where each warder
came from."

"Certainly. Their last postings at least. I believe
there was considerable reassignment during the
late War."

Which meant that though, en masse, the Hotspur Guards and the Yeoman Warders were not on
familiar terms, any particular one might have known
any other for many years. Unless an obvious suspect turned up soon, the victim's service history
would have to be delved into. Contemplating the
possible network of connections leading from it,
Alec blenched.

By this time, he and Webster were crossing the
Parade Ground. On their left stretched the vast
Waterloo Barracks, a curious hybrid typical of Vic-
torian architecture, classically symmetrical but sport-
ing Gothic towers and battlements and oriel windows.
On their right loomed the massive Norman White
Tower.

"What business would a yeoman have going this
way at ten o'clock at night?" Alec asked.

Webster frowned. "None. Someone was seen here
last night? In costume, presumably, or he'd not likely
be recognized. Very odd. They all change out of it
as soon as possible when they get off duty."

"You'd expect the Chief Warder to change as
soon as he'd handed over the keys?"

"Definitely."

Crabtree's behaviour was not the least puzzling
aspect of this case. Supposing he had gone out to
meet someone by appointment, why had he not
changed into civvies first?

They reached the Officers' Quarters, a smaller version of the barracks.

"Police," said Alec to the sentry, and started up the steps.

Webster hung back. "You won't want me in there with you," he said gruffly. "If you need me again, I'll be at the King's House." He turned and stumped off before Alec could thank him.

"Froggy hopped it in a hurry," observed a grinning Hotspur officer, a captain in khakis, who was leaning against the doorpost, cigarette in hand. Alec's face must have showed his distaste for the jibe, for the captain added, though with only the slightest diminution of the grin, "Sorry! Friend of yours, is he? He can't help his face, I suppose."

Recognizing Eton and Sandhurst in his voice, Alec wondered about the relationship between this mocking scion of the upper classes and his risen-from-the-ranks colonel. Himself at a disadvantage halfway down the steps, Alec continued upward as he announced himself. "Detective Chief Inspector Fletcher, Scotland Yard."

"Oho, police!" The captain's grin vanished and he straightened. "The Beefeater's unexpected demise, I presume. Joking aside, what a rotten business! The poor old fellow had earned a bit of peace and quiet. I'm Devereux. What can I do for you, Chief Inspector?"

"I'm looking for Colonel Duggan."

"He's at the barracks. I'll show you the way."

"Thanks. But I might as well speak to Mrs. Duggan while I'm here. Do you know if she's in?"

"I believe so. Word is that you chaps have stopped up all the rat holes and confined us to the Tower," Devereux drawled. He eyed Alec's RFC tie but didn't comment. "In the absence of the lady's husband

and my commanding officer, ought I to insist on being present to protect her from police misconduct?"

Ignoring the persiflage, Alec responded with professional blandness, "If Mrs. Duggan desires a witness, I shall wait until the colonel is available. However, given her acquaintance with my wife, I doubt—"

"Don't tell me you're the other half of the formidable Mrs. Fletcher!" The captain laughed. "What a team you must make. Right-oh, I'll hang about till you're done with the colonel's lady and then provide a military escort to the barracks." He pointed out the way to the Duggans' rooms.

Daisy formidable? Alec wondered what on earth she had said to the brash Guardsman. And was mockery his normal manner, or was it a shield to hide his thoughts? Yet what possible quarrel could Captain Devereux of the Hotspur Guards have had with the unfortunate Chief Warder, by all accounts a kindly and mild-mannered man?

Crabtree had been Regimental Sergeant Major, though. No man rose to that position without being as tough as the Iron Duke himself.

Alec knocked on the door.

A slightly nervous female voice enquired, "Who is it?"

Identifying himself, he heard bolts being drawn back as he continued speaking. "Mrs. Duggan? I'd like to ask you a couple of questions."

"Do come in, Mr. Fletcher." She twiddled a bolt, as if uncertain whether to shoot it closed again. "Sorry about all this. I'm not usually nervy, but Sidney—my husband—told me to lock the door when he left, and I started thinking. . . . You see, no one could have had any reason to kill poor

Crabtree, which means someone did it without reason. And since he killed Crabtree, he might go after anyone at all. Do sit down."

They sat, she with her hands clasped tight in her lap.

"You were acquainted with Crabtree?"

"He came to the Tower about the same time we did."

"When was that?"

"When my brother-in-law Arthur came home from Mesopotamia—he served there during the War—and was appointed Resident Governor. You see, my younger sister and Crabtree's wife both died in the influenza epidemic, such a horrible time, just when the War was finished at last and we thought all the dying was over. He and I used to talk sometimes. He became a bit obsessed with trying to work out why God had sent such a . . . a *scourge*—that was the word he used—upon the world after the horrors of the War, and whether it was a punishment for the War. As if the War wasn't punishment enough in itself!"

" 'Obsessed'?" Alec queried with interest. Obsession was a not uncommon factor in murder, in either killer or victim.

"Not in a mad sort of way," Mrs. Duggan hurried to assure him. "He didn't go around preaching fire and brimstone, or even talk about it to anyone but me, I think."

"Do you know what church he belonged to?"

"None, not then. He called himself a 'Seeker,' and he went to Quaker meetings sometimes, because, he said, they understood about 'seeking.' But he went to the Tower Chapel, St. Peter ad Vincula, without any qualms when his duty required it."

Not the picture of a religious fanatic, so probably unconnected with his death. "Did he join some group later?"

"I don't know." She blushed. "I'm afraid we didn't really chat anymore after Sidney's battalion was sent here and I got to know him. Then we were married, and the battalion moved to other duties. Since we came back, I haven't done more than pass the time of day with poor Crabtree."

"You have greatly illuminated his character for me. Now I'd like to get to specifics. Last night, you attended the Ceremony of the Keys with my wife and your nieces?"

"Yes. It was such a nasty night, I thought Mrs. Fletcher would like some company."

"Kind of you. I don't need a description of the ceremony, but if you could tell me what happened after you parted from Daisy?"

"All right. I thought I wouldn't go as far as the King's House, and I was perfectly happy to walk home alone, in spite of the fog." Mrs. Duggan shuddered. "I wouldn't do it now, not for anything. In any case, the dear girls insisted on coming with me, as Crabtree had to go to the King's House with the keys and was happy to accompany Mrs. Fletcher. It wasn't then that he was attacked, though, was it?" she faltered.

"No, no, thank heaven! It was later. You and the girls—sorry, that's a very informal way of referring to your nieces, but I've picked it up from Daisy."

"Oh, please, it doesn't matter in the least. We couldn't see even as far as the barracks, just across the Parade Ground, so we stayed close to the White Tower."

Alec was fairly sure the girls hadn't invented the "frightful fiend," but he had to avoid suggesting his existence to Mrs. Duggan. "Did anything happen on the way?" he asked.

"Happen? Not to say *happen*."

Eyebrows raised, Alec gave her a look of enquiry.

"It wasn't anything really. On a less eerie night, we wouldn't even have noticed. We heard footsteps behind us and Fay—or was it Brenda?—one of them looked back. Fay, it was. She said one of the yeomen was coming along our way. So, you see, it was nothing."

"Did you notice where he went?"

"I didn't see him at all. I didn't look round. And what with the girls' chatter, and once we passed the White Tower we could hear the river shipping whistling and hooting, if he made any sound, I didn't hear it. I'm sorry I can't be more helpful."

"Have you any idea where he might have been heading for?"

"No." She gave a helpless shrug. "Certainly not here. The Hotspurs and the Yeoman Warders don't mix much, and there wasn't any reason for Arthur to send Sidney a message. Oh, but. . . . No."

"Oh but what?" Alec said encouragingly.

"It may have been my imagination. I did wonder if I heard a cough, before I heard the footsteps."

"Is that significant?"

"Probably not. Only, the next building is the Tower's hospital, so he might have been going to ask for cough mixture."

Daisy had said something about a cough. The yeoman waiting at the top of the fatal stair for a word with the victim had been coughing, and he, too, had been wearing his costume at an unlikely hour. The hospital was not labelled on the brochure's plan, Alec saw, doubtless because it was of no interest to tourists. It would have to be looked into.

"That seems very likely," he said. "Did you notice the time when you reached home?"

"No," she said, absurdly guilty, as though she should have guessed she was going to be interrogated on that point. "I didn't look at the clock. Sidney might have noticed. It must have been shortly after ten, because the ceremony is always exactly on time. For fear of disturbing Wellington's ghost," she added with an unexpected touch of whimsy.

Alec smiled. "The Iron Duke was quite a martinet, they say, but I should have thought you had plenty of other ghosts here."

"We do," she retorted, "if you believe everything the yeomen tell visitors. And another was added to their number today, I'm afraid. Mr. Fletcher, you will catch the murderer, won't you?"

"I expect so. We usually do, and in a closed community such as this, it's largely a matter of sifting information. So the more information we have, whether it seems relevant or not, from as many people as possible, the sooner we'll get there. You're being extremely helpful."

"I'm happy to help. I like your wife so much. Such a comforting person."

As a reason for assisting the police with their enquiries, it was not what Alec would have chosen. He reminded himself with relief that Daisy was safely on her way home to the twins and unable to meddle further.

"Tell me what happened next, after you got back here. Ten o'clock on a foggy night and your nieces were on the wrong side of the Inner Ward."

"Sidney was in—a commanding officer has most

irregular hours!—and he said at once that he'd walk the girls back. But some of the boys, the younger officers, were here for cocoa, and—"

"For cocoa?" Astonishment diverted Alec from his purpose.

"Some of them really are boys, you know. And there's such a temptation in the evenings, when they're off duty, to drink too much alcohol in the mess. So I always have cocoa and biscuits available for any who want it. I think of their mothers."

"Admirable!"

"Well, Sidney jokes about it, but it can't hurt, can it?"

"On the contrary." Alec, who already liked Mrs. Duggan, in spite of his duty to be objective, warmed still further to the little lady. He hoped he was not going to have to arrest anyone near and dear to her. "A thermos bottle of cocoa kept me going through many a cold flight. But to get back to last night . . ."

"Naturally, all the boys at once volunteered to escort Fay and Brenda. Sidney said two were sufficient, and he sent Captain Devereux and Lieutenant Jardyne. I said to him later that it would have been better not to pick Lieutenant Jardyne, because he is quite dotty about Fay and apt to make a bit of a nuisance of himself, but Sidney said, and of course he was quite right, that Captain Devereux would keep him in order. Captain Devereux sometimes *seems* a little thoughtless, but he's really very reliable."

"Both officers returned for their cocoa?"

"As a matter of fact, Lieutenant Jardyne didn't. I heard Captain Devereux tell one of the others he'd gone off in a sulk."

Another loose end wandering about in the fog!

With any luck, Jardyne had gone back to the mess and got drunk in company. Suppose he hadn't, though. Suppose he had met Crabtree and quarrelled with him. . . . It was difficult to imagine what a youthful officer and a mature Yeoman Warder might find to quarrel about. He'd worry about that later, if necessary. More to the point was that he'd have had somehow to provide himself with a partizan. Malice aforethought, Alec and Tom had concluded.

He asked Mrs. Duggan, "Do you happen to know which regiment Crabtree served in?"

"Yes indeed, because it was the Hotspurs."

Aha, the plot thickens! Alec thought. "Did your husband go out again?" he asked.

"Not last night. Sometimes on a fine evening, we take a stroll along the walls, but yesterday was a night for sitting by the fire. He had no duties to call him out. Sidney is most conscientious about performing all his duties to the letter, and beyond. You see—I expect someone has told you—he started out as a common soldier and was commissioned in France."

"So I've heard. How did that come about?"

"Well, he was already a warrant officer before the War. He earned the Military Cross. I think it was in '15. Then he saved an officer's life at risk of his own. He won't tell me about it—he says it would give me nightmares, but he got the DCM for it, so he must have been very brave, mustn't he?" She giggled, suddenly looking remarkably girlish. "But the significant part is that the man he saved was the son of a field marshal, who was terribly grateful."

"I see."

"And so many officers were killed over there, or

put permanently out of action, that Sidney was given a temporary commission. The field marshal made his commission permanent and has helped him rise through the ranks, though in a different Guards regiment. He'll never be a full colonel, not in the Guards, he says, but that's all right. He's going to retire soon anyway, so even this horrible murder can't harm him. Besides, it's not as if he's in charge of the Tower. That's Arthur's pigeon."

"Very true," said Alec. He took his leave and went in search of the lieutenant colonel.

He found Captain Devereux waiting for him, still lounging against the doorpost, smoking. The rain was falling more gently now. A break in the clouds had produced a magnificent rainbow over the Royal Chapel of St. Peter ad Vincula and the site of the scaffold.

"We are told a rainbow is a symbol of a covenant," Devereux murmured. "One wonders just what is being promised us." Even as he spoke, the bright arc faded.

Alec was reminded of Crabtree's search for a meaning for Plague following on the heels of War. He doubted the captain would turn to Bible study for an answer.

"Did you know Crabtree before he became a Yeoman Warder?" he asked.

"Good Lord, yes! He was my drill sergeant major when I was a wet-behind-the-ears sublieutenant. But I assure you I didn't hold it against him for a decade and then push him down the stairs. In fact, I wouldn't be alive today but for one or two tricks he taught us." His momentary earnestness carried conviction. "If there's anything I can do to help you catch the bastard who killed him, Chief Inspector, I'm your man." The habitual mockery returned: "I can at least be your Virgil. Let me show you the way to Colonel Duggan's office."

"I'm no Dante," said Alec, accompanying him down the steps. He couldn't claim to have read the *Inferno* or whatever it was—and he wondered whether Devereux actually had—but at swapping vague references, he could hold his own. "Reports in verse are frowned upon at the Yard."

Devereux laughed. "An educated copper with a sense of humour," he marvelled. "What is the world coming to?"

"No doubt we shall find out in due course. Would you mind telling me how you spent yesterday evening?"

"As you will no doubt find out, Chief Inspector, if you haven't already, I was watch officer. That means I slept fully dressed on a damn uncomfortable cot in the Guard House, with men tramping in and out past my door at all hours, just in case the sergeant of the guard came across something he couldn't cope with. A most unlikely contingency, and one that did not occur last night, leading me to the conclusion that no one noticed the Chief Warder's body."

"A reasonable conclusion. So you were safely tucked away in the Guard House all night, with numerous witnesses."

"Oh, no, I'm afraid not," said Devereux sardonically. "The watch officer's room has its own door to the outside. One is expected to sortie at some point during the small hours to make an unannounced inspection."

"Which you did?"

"Which I did."

10

Daisy, having seen with her own eyes that Miranda and Oliver were safe and sound, woke them by kissing them, to Nanny's displeasure. However, she was permitted to give each a bottle. Feeding them made her realize she was ravenous. Somehow, between one thing and another, she had had no breakfast, though she was wallowing in tea.

She went down to the kitchen. Mrs. Dobson was pinning on her second-best hat, to go to the shops, while giving the daily help instructions for what was to be accomplished during her absence. They both looked round and said, "Good morning, madam."

"Good morning, ladies. Mrs. Dobson, I missed breakfast. I'll just get myself some bread and butter and marmalade."

"That you won't, madam!" The hat came off with a swish. "Sit yourself down right there and I'll have eggs and bacon for you in a trice. Well, what are you waiting for?" she said severely to Mrs. Twickle. "You can get on with the bathroom while I'm busy in here."

Cowed, the charwoman went off with her pail and mop and scrubbing brush.

Daisy also did as she was bade. She had no qualms about eating in the kitchen. As children at Fairacres, her family home, she and Violet and Gervaise had popped into the labyrinthine kitchens for a picnic or a snack whenever they escaped their nursemaids, governesses, and tutors.

Melanie Germond would have been shocked. It was one of the odd differences between the customs of the aristocracy and the professional middle classes that Daisy felt she had at last more or less mastered.

At first, when Daisy married and came to live in St. John's Wood, Alec's mother had been a complicating factor. The elder Mrs. Fletcher held so stringently to the most restrictive rules of Victorian propriety that Daisy found it difficult to distinguish between her quirks and the somewhat more relaxed etiquette of modern middle-class life. A year ago, Mrs. Fletcher had moved to Bournemouth. Daisy felt she now grasped which commandments were carved in stone and which she could safely ignore, at least as long as she didn't draw her lapses to anyone's attention.

Her struggle made her sympathize with Fay's and Brenda's confusion over appropriate manners. They had been very sweet earlier when she returned to the King's House in a state of shock. She was sorry she had abandoned them. Perhaps she should go back—but Alec would be furious if she reappeared in the middle of his investigation.

Mrs. Dobson emerged from the larder and set about preparing breakfast. "Weren't it a general you was going to stay with, Mrs. Fletcher?" she observed. "You'd think a general's household could spare a body a bite of breakfast before you left."

"It wasn't their fault. There was . . ." Daisy hesitated. She really didn't care to discuss the murder with the housekeeper, though Mrs. Dobson was used to the subject, given the master's profession, and would read about it in tomorrow's newspaper. "They had some trouble at the Tower," she said vaguely. "Mmm, the bacon smells heavenly, much better than when one actually eats it."

"It's the best back bacon," said Mrs. Dobson, bridling, then conceding the point. "But it's like coffee and frying onions—the taste's always a bit of a letdown after the smell."

Having served Daisy, she put her hat back on, adjured Daisy to leave the washing up for Mrs. Twickle, and set off to do the shopping. Daisy enjoyed the bacon; it tasted better in the kitchen, where the smell lingered, than in the dining room, she decided.

With a slightly guilty feeling for disobeying Mrs. Dobson's orders, she put her eggy plate into the sink and ran water onto it. In the days between the War and marriage, when she had shared a bijou residence in Chelsea with her friend Lucy, she had scrubbed many a plate on which egg yolk had congealed. It didn't seem fair to leave such a mess for poor bullied Mrs. Twickle.

She went to the office she shared with Alec now that the house was full of babies. Her article was nearly finished, but she had to add a bit about the Ceremony of the Keys, now that she had seen it. Americans seemed to believe London was always smothered in fog, so her description should please them. People always liked to have prejudices confirmed.

Writing about the ceremony inevitably brought vividly to mind its chief figure. She couldn't concentrate on the proud yeoman bearing his part in the ancient tradition. All she could see was the man she had found crumpled at the foot of the steps.

She did, after all, need to talk to someone about it, though not Mrs. Dobson.

Melanie would be ideal. She knew some of the people involved. But Mel would be shocked to the core that Daisy was mixed up in another murder. Sakari, on the other hand, would be interested and sympathetic, and would be a calming influence on Mel.

Daisy abandoned her typewriter and went out to the hall to telephone her friends. Mel was free and delighted to come over for morning coffee, as she wanted to discuss the forthcoming tennis party for the Carradine girls. She wouldn't want to talk about tennis when she heard the news, but Daisy cravenly didn't warn her.

Sakari knew at once from Daisy's voice that something was wrong. "What is up, Daisy? Is it Belinda?" Sakari's daughter, Deva, was one of Bel's best friends, along with Melanie's daughter, and the three were at the same boarding school.

"No, Bel's quite all right."

"That is fortunate. I was about to offer to lend you the car and chauffeur to go to her, and my lord and master claims to have some pressing need for them later today." Mr. Prasad was something important at the India Office. "But you are troubled. I will come at once, of course. Shall I pick up Melanie on the way?"

"Yes, please, Sakari. Bless you."

Daisy went to put on the percolator. Looking in the biscuit tin, she found only crumbs. She hoped Mrs. Dobson would be back before the others arrived. One couldn't invite one's friends to have their shoulders cried on and not offer biscuits to go with their coffee.

Not that she meant to cry on anyone's shoulder, but she just couldn't get the picture of Crabtree's body out of her mind. With any luck, talking about it would help. Thinking back over the various cases she'd stumbled into, she couldn't remember ever having felt so isolated.

The feeling ended the moment Sakari walked through the door and enfolded her in an exotic-scented rose-and-gold embrace. "Dear Daisy, we have decided that you must have discovered another body."

"Sakari has decided." Mel kissed Daisy's cheek. "I can't believe it."

"I'm awfully afraid it's true. Come and sit down, and I'll tell you about it. If you don't mind."

Mel couldn't suppress a quiet sigh.

"She cannot help it, Melanie," Sakari said as they followed Daisy into the sitting room.

"I know. It's just that . . . these things never happen to other people."

"I'd much rather they didn't happen to me, I assure you. I won't talk about it if you'd rather not, Mel, but you've been to the Tower and met some of the people, so I thought perhaps you could help me get things straight in my mind."

"Oho, you are sleuthing, Daisy!" Sakari made herself comfortable on the sofa, a plump bird of paradise in her colourful sari, and accepted a cup of coffee. No Mrs. Dobson; no biscuits.

"Not really sleuthing. I've finished my work there, so I have no excuse to go back. Let's talk about something else. Your tennis party, Mel."

"Daisy, I'm sorry. I can see you're upset and you need to talk about the . . . the murder. I'm sure

otherwise you'll develop inhibitions, or something."
Mel smiled at Sakari. The Indian woman was a devotee of lectures on all subjects under the sun and still occasionally brought forth words of wisdom from a talk on psychology she had attended eighteen months ago. "It happened at the Tower?"

"Who was killed?" Sakari asked.

"The Chief Yeoman Warder." Daisy told them about the ceremony and how Fay and Brenda had coaxed Crabtree into escorting her through the fog to the King's House.

"Not the one who showed us the way!" Mel exclaimed. "The one whose manner we didn't care for? I remember he had some special insignia on his costume."

"The oily one? No, he's Yeoman Gaoler. He's second in charge, but he doesn't play any rôle in the ceremony."

"My dear Daisy," said Sakari, "I see no difficulty. Clearly, the murderer is this oily man, of whom even Melanie speaks ill. He wishes to be Chief."

"Well . . ." Daisy hesitated. "He *was* out and about, in spite of the frightful fog. But if he was planning murder, surely he'd have kept out of sight."

"Ah, I see what it is." Sakari laughed. "This obvious solution is too simple. You want a mystery!"

"Of course not! I just don't think he's stupid."

Melanie hastily intervened to keep the peace. "How did you come to be mixed up in the affair, Daisy?"

"I found him." She explained about getting up early because of her urgent need to see the twins. As mothers, they quite understood, though Melanie was rather shocked that she had departed without taking leave of her hosts.

"I know, it was disgraceful of me. I found the

Tower disturbing from the first, I must admit, so perhaps spending the night there was just too much for my poor nerves."

"Nonsense," said Sakari briskly. "You do not suffer from nerves, nor from an excess of inhibitions!"

"I did leave a note," Daisy pleaded in exculpation, "and I apologized profusely when I returned, once I'd recovered a bit from the shock. They almost drowned me in tea. Another cup of coffee?"

As she poured, Melanie asked, "You don't think Miss Carradine and Miss Fay are suspected, do you? I should hate to be responsible for introducing someone suspected of murder to my friends, especially the young people at the tennis club."

"Alec has to start by suspecting everyone. Even me, so perhaps you ought not—"

"Daisy, you must not tease Melanie. Her concern is natural. Whatever Alec may say for form's sake, he cannot really suspect you, but this does not hold true for the young ladies."

"No, but can you honestly imagine, Mel, either Fay or Brenda, or even the two together, creeping out of the house in the middle of the night to stab a man with a halberd and push him down a flight of steps?"

Mel gasped. "No! Is that what happened?"

More worldly, or more cynical, Sakari said, "To meet a young man, perhaps, with whom she did not wish to be seen."

Daisy shook her head. "On a fine night, yes, but last night down by the river we had a foul, clammy fog. Not at all inviting for lovers."

"Who else is available to be suspected? The general, of course, and the Tebbits."

"The Tebbits! Oh, surely not!"

"Now who's teasing?" Daisy reproved Sakari. "Mel,

darling, you're an angel to put up with us. But I don't suspect the Tebbits, though they'll be on Alec's list, along with everyone else at the Tower. Several hundred people. No one outside could get in after ten o'clock, though come to think of it, someone could have come in earlier and hidden."

"My dear Daisy, this is altogether too many. We shall not consider any possible outsiders."

"We can eliminate those in the Outer Ward, too, which is where most of the Yeoman Warders live. There are only three ways through the inner wall, and all have sentries posted who would take note of anyone going through."

"Excellent."

"But there are still several hundred."

Sakari groaned. "I give up. We shall have to leave the investigation to Alec and his excellent men."

"I'm sure we should," Melanie said hopefully.

Daisy was still pondering the question. "It seems to me unlikely that the murderer should be one of the garrison. The Hotspur Guards, that is. They don't on the whole have much to do with the yeomen."

"And the yeomen, you say, live outside the wall," said Sakari triumphantly, "so we are left with the inhabitants of the King's House. And since we have eliminated the Tebbits and the young ladies, we are left with the general. That was easy."

"No, no, I said *most* of the yeomen live between the outer and inner walls, not all of them. Besides, there's Mr. Webster, General Carradine's secretary, in the King's House, too. He's quite peculiar. I don't think I'm letting his appearance influence me, am I, Mel?"

"Not entirely. He is a bit odd."

"And he's obsessed with the Crown Jewels. Suppose Crabtree came across evidence that he was plotting to steal them." Daisy reflected on the extensive display of gold and precious gems. "Well, some of them."

"Surely not," Mel protested. "They must be well guarded."

"Yes, but presumably they were thought to be well secured when Colonel Blood tried to run off with them. He was only stopped by a lucky chance."

"Colonel Blood!" Sakari was all agog. "You are inventing this, Daisy! Or your guide was having you on." Occasionally, Sakari's precise speech blossomed into unexpected idiom.

"No, I've read about it, too."

"Tell us."

"It was soon after the Restoration, after they'd remade all the crowns Cromwell sold or destroyed—"

"Not a history lesson!" Mel moaned.

"But yes, a history lesson," said Sakari. "How else am I to understand? Don't look so dismayed, Melanie. It is all right. I have learnt about your Commonwealth and cutting off the head of Charles the First, although I was not aware of the Lord Protector's destruction or sale of the Regalia. You may continue without the history lesson, Daisy."

Daisy laughed. "It doesn't really matter when it happened, I suppose. Colonel Blood dressed up as a parson and brought his supposed wife to see the crown. The Keeper showed it to her, and she pretended to faint. Being a kindly man, the Keeper let them into his private quarters. That led to a developing acquaintance with the Keeper's family, and eventually to Colonel Blood offering to marry his nephew, a young man of means—or so he claimed—to the Keeper's daughter. Naturally, the Keeper and his wife were delighted."

"Some things never change," Sakari observed.

"The wedding day arrived. In those days, people didn't get married in church, so Colonel Blood brought his nephew and friends to the Tower. His wife, he said, had been delayed but would join them shortly. While they waited for her, he suggested, they might pass the time looking at the jewels. So the Keeper unlocked the room and took them in. As soon as he closed the door, they hit him on the head with a mallet and gagged him. They started breaking up the treasures and stuffing them into pockets and down their breeches."

Sakari chuckled. "This scheme could not have been attempted in the time of the doublet and hose, nor that of skintight pantaloons."

"No, they needed baggy breeches and cloaks to carry it off. But as it happened, the Keeper's son came looking for his father. Seeing him unconscious on the floor, he raised a cry of 'Treason! The crown is stolen!' The ruffians made a break for it, but they were all captured."

"And had their heads chopped off?"

"No, that's the oddest thing. Colonel Blood's sheer cheek amused Charles the Second, and he became a favourite at court."

"How extraordinary," said Melanie. "But Daisy, I simply can't imagine Mr. Webster doing anything so outrageous."

"Nor can I. If he's plotting, his plot will be much more subtle. Anyway, the jewels are kept in a sort of cage now, with guards all over the place, not just one man. In fact, I don't think the present Keeper has much to do with them, at least on a daily basis. It's more of a ceremonial post. I did wonder . . ." Daisy hesitated. "Sir Patrick—that's General Sir Patrick Heald, the Keeper of the Regalia—did appear to regard Webster with suspicion."

"There you are, then." Sakari was delighted. "The sinister Webster is the murderer."

"I can't see how Crabtree could have found him out, though, and if he did, I'd expect him to have taken the information straight to General Carradine, not to tackle Webster himself. There are the servants living in the King's House to be considered, too. I don't know anything about them. And it *could* be one of the Guards, however unlikely."

"What about the Yeoman Gaoler?" Melanie asked. "Where does he live?"

"In the Inner Ward, next door to the King's House. It all keeps coming back to him, doesn't it? Perhaps Alec has already arrested him and all our speculations are futile."

"You are feeling better, are you not, Daisy? Discussing it has calmed you, so it is not futile. But now I must be on my way." Sakari rose with her customary majestic grace. "May I offer you a lift, Melanie?"

"No, thanks. The rain seems to be slackening, and I must talk to Daisy about this wretched tennis party. I wish I'd held my tongue!"

"Daisy, may I look in on the twins before I leave?"

"Oh, yes, I'd love to see them, too," said Melanie. "Is Nanny still giving satisfaction?" She had recommended the nurse. "And coping with two babies at once?"

"Yes, but she's making ominous noises about needing a nurserymaid when they start to crawl." Leading the way upstairs, Daisy laughed. "We're hoping for an unexpected legacy, because we're going to have to move to a bigger house."

As Miranda and Oliver were both awake, Nanny permitted a few minutes of cooing and clucking. Then she declared that it was time to change their nappies and the ladies would not care to be present. Her manner made their dismissal more an order than a suggestion.

"English nurses are very fierce," Sakari commented as they returned downstairs. "My ayah would not dare to speak so to me."

"I suppose we've all been brought up on 'Nanny knows best,' " said Daisy. "It carries over into adulthood. Thank you for rushing to succour me, darling. I do feel much better."

Sakari left. Daisy and Melanie returned to the sitting room.

"More coffee?" offered Daisy, who had heard Mrs. Dobson come in and wanted an excuse for biscuits.

"No, thanks. I do wish I could invite Sakari and her husband to the tennis club."

"That *would* set the cat among the pigeons! One would be almost tempted to do it, if only it wouldn't be so unpleasant for the Prasads. Take comfort in the fact that Sakari hasn't the least desire to play tennis. Not to mention its being largely your doing that they've found as much acceptance in St. John's Wood society as they have."

"I hardly did anything."

"That's not what Sakari has told me."

"I'm glad I was able to help, and I've grown very fond of Sakari. But initially, it was Robert's doing," Mel confessed.

Daisy did her best to hide her amusement. To a banker, naturally, what mattered was not the colour of a person's skin but the colour of his money. Still, it was to Robert Germond's credit that he had supported his dutiful wife in introducing the Prasads to their neighbours, not merely entertaining them in the way of business.

Daisy had her own criteria for judging people.

On the whole, she expected to like people she met, and on the whole, she did. It seemed to her a much pleasanter way to live than to go about looking for superficial defects such as the wrong class, or a brown face, thus eliminating a lot of delightful people from one's acquaintance. If she had felt that way, had remained true to her upbringing, she would have let Alec pass out of her life without a second thought. No Alec, no twins: The very idea was unbearable.

"Whoever gets the credit, it was a very good deed," she said to Melanie. "No doubt you want me to come to your tennis party? As long as you don't insist on my playing!"

"I certainly expect you to come and support me. What I wanted to ask you is whether you think it's proper for the Carradine girls to go to a party in the circumstances."

"Why not? It wasn't a death in the family."

"No, but. . . . You said they're under suspicion."

"So am I, Mel, strictly speaking. I don't think it matters a hoot, but if it makes you uncomfortable, just postpone the party. Fay and Brenda shouldn't be too disappointed. They have quite enough excitement in their lives at present."

"They do, don't they?" said Melanie with relief. "How can a mere tennis party compete with a murder case? I do hope you won't get drawn into Alec's investigation."

"There isn't much hope of that." Daisy sighed. "I can't think of any excuse to return to the Tower."

11

*M*elanie left and Daisy returned to her type-writer, determined to finish off her article before lunch. "Finish off " was an unfortunate choice of phrase. Someone had brutally finished off the man she had to write about. Once again unable to con-centrate, she gazed out of the window at the now-sunny day and decided to take the dog out.

Poor Nana had been having a thin time of it since Belinda's departure for boarding school and the twins' subsequent arrival. Now that she was old enough not to chew anything and everything she came across, she was allowed to wander freely in the house. When Daisy was working, she'd lie pa-tiently under the desk, submitting to the occasional use as a footstool, ignoring the chatter of the type-writer keys and the *ping* at the end of each line.

Not that the keys were doing much chattering at present.

Nana's overwhelming joy when she heard her mistress say "Walk!" made Daisy feel frightfully guilty. As they strolled along Prince Albert Road towards

Primrose Hill, she made up her mind to put the Tower entirely out of her mind for the moment, to enjoy the fresh air washed clean by the morning's rain and the capers of the little dog at her heels.

Turning onto a grassy path, she let Nana off the lead. With forays after rabbits, squirrels, and other enticing smells, Nana covered four or five times the crow's-flight distance to the top of the hill, but Daisy's legs were in good shape after all those steps at the Tower and they soon reached the summit.

And she wasn't going to think about the Tower.

She turned about to admire the view. As usual when she came up here, Wordsworth's sonnet floated through her head: "Earth has not anything to show more fair . . ." There was the Crystal Palace, and over there, almost lost in the haze raised by the sun from damp streets and roofs, was the Tower, which she was *not* going to think about.

Nana was making friends with a large shaggy dog of breeding as indeterminate as her own, belonging to an elderly man seated on a bench. Daisy sat down. The big dog, assuming this to be a friendly overture, came over to sniff her fingers.

"Off, Rummy!" He doffed his hat. His dog gave Daisy's hand a lick and went back to Nana. "Sorry about that. Beautiful day."

"Lovely," Daisy replied, but her attention was drifting. "Nice dog."

Rummy. Rumford. Somehow he was the key. At first sight, or on a foggy night, it would be easy to mistake Crabtree for Rumford, both red-cloaked and bushy-bearded. But surely anyone with a deadly grudge against Rumford would know they looked alike and make jolly sure he got the right man.

The murderer must have expected Rumford to

be there at the top of the steps at whatever time
Crabtree had been killed—which suggested an appointment.

Why had Crabtree been there instead? Had he
for some reason kept the appointment in Rumford's
place? Or had the two arranged to meet there for
some inscrutable purpose, something that could not
be carried out indoors, in their next-door houses?
What had Rumford said to Crabtree earlier, when
he waited for him at the top of those same steps? If
only Daisy had overheard, she would probably know
now exactly what had happened later, and why!

Or if they had not met by appointment, then
one knew the other would be there, for whatever
equally inscrutable purpose, and sought him out.
Perhaps Rumford had deliberately set out to kill
Crabtree. Perhaps they had quarrelled and Rumford had accidentally pushed Crabtree down the
steps—though that didn't explain the partizan. Or
perhaps Crabtree had set out to kill Rumford and
Rumford had fought back.

There was a whiff of blackmail about Rumford,
the man who could see through walls. How many
Tower residents might he be blackmailing?

Daisy wondered whether she ought to telephone
Alec to suggest he take a close look at Rumford.
But even if she could get hold of him, when he
might be anywhere in the Tower, he would only say
she was speculating wildly.

She sighed.

"Troubles?" said the old man sympathetically.
"A pretty young lady like you shouldn't ought to
have troubles. Now when you get to my age . . ."
He proceeded to tell her all about his grandson,
who had been killed in the War, his difficult

daughter-in-law, who didn't want the dog in the house, and his rheumatism.

When he began on his hernia operation, Daisy excused herself, called Nana, and headed for home. She wasn't quite sure what a hernia was, but she was quite sure she didn't want to hear about his. Being the sort of person complete strangers chose to confide in was often interesting and even useful, but it had its drawbacks.

It was a pity Mrs. Tebbit had not felt that urge to confide, Daisy thought, walking down the path towards the street. What little the old lady had said suggested she knew Rumford was blackmailing General Carradine. As Resident Governor, the general could presumably send his yeomen hither and yon as he wished, as long as he didn't contravene the traditions of the Tower. He could easily have ordered the Yeoman Gaoler to perform some task that would have taken him to the steps at a certain time.

Yet Crabtree had turned up instead. Of course, any blackmailer worth his salt would be suspicious of being sent on a midnight errand by one of his victims. Had he found some excuse to persuade the Chief Warder to take his place?

Daisy found herself at the bottom of the hill with no Nana frisking around her ankles. She put two fingers in her mouth and uttered a piercing whistle.

Instantly horrified at her own disgraceful behaviour, she watched with mingled pride and dismay as half a dozen dogs raced towards her. Gervaise had taught her to whistle, but she had never made the attempt in anyone's company but his. Having grown up into a rather proper young man—at least where his sisters were concerned—he would probably have been as shocked by her exploit as anyone. A lady simply did not whistle in public. She hadn't really expected to remember how.

But as the unknown dogs veered off and the truant came to sit at her mistress's feet, panting and wagging, Daisy was on the whole almost as pleased with herself as Nana. She sent a silent "Thank you" heavenward, whither she hoped Gervaise had proceeded from the Flanders trenches.

Lead attached, they set off along Prince Albert Street.

All the same, it was very naughty of her, and she hoped no one she knew had witnessed her performance. How could she presume to teach Brenda and Fay proper behaviour when she, at her advanced age, was still at heart a tomboy?

The Carradine girls would be devastated if their father was arrested for murder. Daisy's case against him was very tenuous, not worth mentioning to Alec.

On the other hand, if General Carradine was the murderer and Daisy hadn't mentioned her suspicion, Alec would rightly accuse her of sheltering Fay and Brenda. One way or t'other, she couldn't win.

When Alec reached Colonel Duggan's office, he found that the commander of the garrison had foreseen his needs and mustered all the Guardsmen who had taken sentry duty during the night.

"Thank you, sir, that's a great help. My sergeant will be along shortly to deal with them. Meanwhile, I'd like to have your recollections of last night."

Duggan's account agreed exactly with his wife's. Like his counterpart at the King's House, the sentry at the front door of the Officers' Quarters could hardly have helped seeing anyone who went in or out. Presumably, there was at least one other exit, for servants and deliveries and so on. Checking on that would be another job for Tom. However, Alec was inclined to believe the Duggans.

One last personal question remained. "I gather you transferred to the Hotspur Guards from another regiment. Was that during Crabtree's tenure as RSM or after he left?"

"A year or so before he came to the Tower. He was a damn good soldier and a pleasant fellow. He could have made life sticky for me, me not being one of the 'Gentlemen's Sons' who are supposed to officer the Guards, but he was always most cooperative, even positively smoothed my way. I'm damn sorry he came to such a nasty end, after managing to survive the War."

"My wife gave me the impression there was a certain amount of strife between the garrison and the yeomen."

Duggan laughed heartily. "Between the Resident Governor and myself, perhaps, though it was mostly in his mind. I married his sister-in-law, and not for what she inherited, whatever people say, though I'll admit we couldn't have married without it. But there's nothing Carradine can do about it. Otherwise, I suppose there's always some friction between the members of a temporary garrison and the permanent residents, but remember, the yeomen were all once serving soldiers, and NCOs at that. It's not like being quartered in a civilian area."

"So you'd reject the possibility of the murder being the result of some sort of feud between Hotspurs and Yeoman Warders?"

"Absolutely! I'd wager Mrs. Fletcher got her impression from Christina's nieces. Nice girls, but given to dramatic embellishment. As for the personal matter with the general, that splendid old lady Mrs. Tebbit seems to be bent on putting an end to that, which I'm heartily grateful for. It was making my poor Christina damn uncomfortable."

"Mrs. Tebbit is a force to be reckoned with," Alec agreed. "All right, I won't take that feud too seriously. What about any personal disagreements between members of your battalion and the yeomen? Since Crabtree was the Regimental Sergeant Major, it's not unlikely that he had a few enemies."

"Not many, I shouldn't think. He was a disciplinarian, or he wouldn't have got as far as he did, but always fair, no tyrant."

"There are always some who take discipline as a personal affront."

"True. But I wouldn't necessarily know about it. Sergeants are perfectly capable of dealing with such matters—as I should know, having been one—except for the odd exception that goes to court martial, in which case the man concerned would no longer be among us. I don't know of any festering resentments among the men."

"And among your officers?"

The colonel's lips thinned. "You're putting me in a damn difficult position, you know. Half of them, the half who didn't go through the War, still think they're Public School boys and believe the only unforgivable sin is to snitch on their fellows."

"I can't help that," Alec said impatiently. "They're

not schoolboys any longer, and I'm dealing with murder here. And loath though I am to remind you of the fact, you never were—"

"A Public School boy," Duggan ruefully finished the sentence.

"No more was I. Not that snitches are exactly popular among their peers anywhere, but we're not talking about swiping sweets from a tuck box or cribbing in an exam. A man has been murdered, and with or without your help, I'm going to find out who did it. I have evidence that at least two officers were out and about last night."

Duggan hesitated. "I won't ask you who."

"I wouldn't tell you if you did."

"I suppose not." He paused in thought. "As far as I'm aware, none of my officers was on bad terms with Crabtree."

Alec heard the merest hint of a stress on the name Crabtree. Though at present his sole concern was the unfortunate Chief Warder, he made a mental note of the possibility that one or more of the Hotspurs officers was on bad terms with one or more of the Yeoman Warders.

He asked a few more questions, about the general procedures of the garrison. Except for the Keys Ceremony and certain shared guard duties, the garrison's activities didn't seem to have much to do with the yeomen's, so there were few opportunities for disputes to arise. The motive for the murder probably lay in the past. That kind of case was almost always the most difficult for the poor hardworking policeman, especially when means and opportunity were available to so many and motive might be the only clue he had to rely on.

An orderly came in and, with a smart salute, announced, "There's a couple of detectives outside, sir, asking for DCI Fletcher, and they've brung a swarm of Beef . . . of Yeoman Warders with them."

The colonel looked startled.

"All the warders are Special Constables," Alec explained, "sworn officers of the Metropolitan Police. I assume these are the ones whose alibis my men have accepted. I'm hoping their assistance will help to clear things up more quickly. Is there a room we can use to question your sentries?"

"The room where I've had them gathered will be easiest." Duggan rang for his adjutant.

Alec went out to the anteroom, where DCs Piper and Ross awaited him. The door to the outside was open, and through it Alec saw a couple of dozen Yeoman Warders in full fig. Standing in a grim-faced group, they were an impressive sight, even without their partizans.

"Out for blood, Chief," said Piper, following his gaze. "Aside from the deceased being a popular bloke, they don't take it kindly that someone would attack one of their own. Most of the rest'll join in soon as we've cleared 'em with the sentries, leaving just the ones that live inside the inner wall."

"Excellent. I don't know how many sentries there are, but with so much help, it shouldn't take long to get some answers."

"One-on-one, I shouldn't wonder," said Ross.

"I've explained to them what we need to know, Chief, what questions to ask."

Alec nodded to the adjutant, a stout major, as he came out of the inner room. "This gentleman will introduce you to the sentries and give them their orders. Just a minute, Piper. How much police training do the warders have?"

"Just the standard Special Constable stuff, Chief,

but at least it's recent. Our own chaps were posted here till the beginning of last year."

"Right-oh. Remind them they're in the police, not the army, now. I don't want any complaints. I'd like a word with you, Major, when you're free."

Alec and his men met in the late Chief Warder's sanctum for a late lunch. There had been some competition for the honour of feeding the detectives, with several of the Yeoman Warders bearing offers from their wives.

"Nice to be so popular for once," said Tom, removing the cover from his plate and contemplating with satisfaction a generous helping of steak and kidney pudding and buttered broad beans. "Though no one else's pud ever measures up to the missus's."

"No one makes steak and kidney pud like Mrs. Tring's," agreed Ernie Piper, who had more than once profited from invitations to supper at the Trings'.

"Not half bad, though." Ross had already dived in.

"Enjoy the fleshpots while you can, Ross," Alec advised, listening to the murmur from outside, where a score of yeomen lingered in muttering clusters. As many more were in the Warders' Hall opposite, just waiting to be called upon. "With so many willing helpers, I can't justify keeping you. It's back to the Yard for you as soon as you and Piper have given me your reports."

"Aw, sir!"

"Sorry. Others have greater need of your services. Tom, I'll let you eat in peace, but just tell me, have you cleared the residents of the King's House?"

His mouth full, Tom nodded. He swallowed. "The

evidence proves Mrs. Fletcher did not murder Crabtree," he said gravely.

"Sarge!" Piper was indignant. "That's not something to joke about."

"Wrong, laddie. If there was the slightest chance she might've, *then* it'd be nothing to joke about."

"As it is," Alec cut in, seeing Daisy's champion not entirely mollified, "if she couldn't have done it, neither could General Carradine or his daughters, for which I am profoundly grateful."

"In a manner of speaking, Chief," said Tom, and took another mouthful.

Alec took the hint and refrained from further discussion until they had finished eating. He observed that, however superior Mrs. Tring's pudding, Tom's plate was clean. Nor did he disdain the apple charlotte and biscuits and cheese that followed. His bulk took a good deal of keeping up.

Piper and Ross cleared the plates from Crabtree's desk, where they had eaten, a sight to distress the Chief Warder had his ghost watched, for among his other virtues, he'd been an orderly man. As Alec had noticed earlier, the desktop was clear of everything except the Wait Book and the inkstand.

Alec opened the Wait Book. In a crabbed, painstaking hand was written out a timetable of duties for the week for the warders.

"Ernie, when we're all up-to-date with one another's reports, you'll examine this and any other papers here, and then move over to his house and go through that thoroughly. Pick a yeoman to give you a hand. All right, Tom, let's hear about the King's House."

Tom started explaining about keys and bolts, squeaking hinges, the cook who slept downstairs because the stairs were too much for her these days, and the housemaid who got up even earlier than Daisy to make up the fires. Alec stopped him.

"Never mind. If you say no one could have left by the side door unnoticed, I'm prepared to believe you and to assume you can write it up so that the Super can follow your reasoning, if necessary."

Tom's moustache twitched as he grinned. "Can do. There's just one thing: You know that sort of balcony affair, Chief? It'd be easy to get out there with no one seeing or hearing, and not too hard to lower yourself to the ground. I can't see Mrs. Fletcher doing it."

"She's not athletically inclined," Alec agreed. "Nor is Mr. Webster, let alone the Tebbits. The general or his daughters—it's conceivable but seems to me highly unlikely. What about the servants?"

"The batman could, and one or two of the maids, perhaps. But seems to me the general's the only one'd find it comparatively easy to get hold of one of those pikes and keep it hidden somewhere."

"The general will have to stay on the list, especially if we come across a motive. Did the servants have anything interesting to say about Crabtree? Or any other Tower resident, come to that?"

"Not really. They all seem to have liked what little they knew of Crabtree. The general's a fair-enough employer, as employers go. The young ladies are a scream, a bloody nuisance, or a pair of flighty flibbertigibbets, depending on who you're talking to. Mr. Webster keeps himself to himself. Miss Tebbit's a hapless old maid, and they don't none of them know what to make of Mrs. Tebbit."

Alec laughed. "They're not the first and they won't be the last to be baffled by Mrs. Tebbit. I find Webster still more inscrutable, and not just because he hides behind his spectacles."

"Ah," said Tom. "I didn't meet Mr. Webster."

"He was very helpful to me in explaining the organisation of the Tower community. Which explanation I shall pass on to the rest of you only if it seems absolutely vital. He lives—sleeps—in the King's House?"

"Yes. So he's out of the picture."

"Anything else?"

Tom frowned. "It seemed to me one or two of 'em were holding something back. The batman, for one, who's butler and valet and chauffeur to the general, and maybe the parlour maid. Holding back's not exactly it, neither. They answered all my questions fair enough. But I got a feeling they had something on their minds they were glad I didn't ask about. Maybe nothing to do with the case. You know how people are about their little secrets when us coppers come knocking."

"Not much we can do about that, not knowing what to ask, but keep the pair of them in mind. That's it? Piper, what did you learn from the sentries?"

"We split 'em into groups, Chief, according to where they were posted last night. After the business with the keys at ten o'clock, the Chief Yeoman Warder was seen going off in the direction of his house, as per usual. He wasn't seen to arrive there, on account of the fog."

"Have we any reason to suppose he didn't get home all right?"

"Not that I know of, Chief. But his pals say he always made himself a little supper of toasted cheese after the key business, so I reckon when I go through his house, I ought to be able to tell whether he did that last night. If he didn't, chances are he didn't go home, which'd give us something to think about. And if he did, it'll help the pathologist fix the time of death, won't it?"

"Good thinking. Go on."

"The fog was never so bad the sentries at the King's House couldn't see the front door, and no one came out that way all night, not till Mrs. Fletcher in the morning. But it was bad enough that they couldn't see in the other direction past the next door along, the funny little house jammed in between. By the sound of it, a couple of men came along about eleven, told each other good night, and went into two of the other houses in the row. Two doors heard closing."

"I got confirmation of that from the sentries at the Bloody Tower arch," said Ross.

"And from the men themselves," said Piper, "a couple of yeomen who live there. Liston and Edgemoor. Edgemoor's the Yeoman Raven Master."

"The what? You're having us on!" Tom exclaimed.

"No, Sarge, that's what he's called. He takes care of the Tower ravens. Didn't they teach you the kingdom will fall if the ravens ever leave the Tower?"

Tom snorted, his moustache puffing out. "What I learnt at school, laddie, was history, not fairy tales."

Piper looked as if he was ready to take up arms on behalf of the ravens. Alec said calmingly, "Be that as it may, there are ravens at the Tower and a yeoman responsible for them. Daisy was telling me about them. The Raven Master lives in one of the houses near the steps, does he?"

"Yes, the nearest, him and his wife. The yeomen with special titles get quarters in the Inner Ward, being that it's nicer than the casemates. That's the outer walls, Sarge. Some of the poor buggers live right inside the walls, like mice, and that's no fairy tale."

"Enough!" said Alec. "I suppose he says his wife will give him an alibi?"

"He hopes so." Piper grinned. "Seems she wasn't too happy because he left her to cope with a poorly raven while he went to the Hall for a drink, and it pecked her. When he got home, he had to calm 'em both down and persuade the bird—Huw, its name is, spelt the Welsh way because it's from Wales— persuade it to eat its dinner and go to sleep. Which took a long time, and Huw complained loudly throughout. The chap next door could hear them swearing at each other—"

"Literally?" asked Alec.

"No, Chief." Piper was regretful. "It does say a few words, but he has to be careful what he teaches it, 'cause if there are complaints from visitors, it'll be dismissed from the King's service 'for unsatisfactory conduct.' "

"Are you serious?" Tom wanted to know.

"That's what Mr. Edgemoor said, Sarge. That's what goes down in the Governor's Daily Orders. Anyways, the neighbour looked at the time when the racket stopped, around twenty-five to one. So they're neither one completely in the clear, but they don't seem likely to me."

Alec made a note. "Anyone else?"

"Yes, Chief." Piper spoke with studied nonchalance. "Just before midnight, a Beefeater in his fancy dress comes along from the direction Crabtree went off before. Seems the fog was thinning a bit by then, just enough so the sentry saw this chap had a big beard."

"Crabtree! Midnight, he said?"

"Five, maybe ten minutes before he was relieved. Crabtree went on in the direction of the steps, but it was still too foggy to see that far."

"He didn't hear anything? Running footsteps, a cry, a thud . . ."

"Nope. He did one of those stamp-abouts and couldn't hear nothing but his own boots."

"I doubt he'd be able to hear the victim landing at the bottom, Chief," Tom commented. "That wall is pretty solid and backed by solid earth."

"I wonder where he was going? And whether he got there and was hit on the way back. . . . No, that's unlikely. He landed face down."

Ross spoke up. "He didn't leave the Inner Ward, at any rate, sir. No one did except the relief sentries with the watch sergeant, and an officer doing the rounds. And that's odd, because as a rule the Yeoman Gaoler goes along at midnight to check that all's well with the yeoman on guard right here at the Byward Tower."

"What does the Yeoman Gaoler have to say about his dereliction of duty?"

"We don't know, Chief. He seems to have disappeared."

12

"So Rumford did it," Tom Tring rumbled. "He lived here. He probably knows a hundred places to hide—secret dungeons and who knows what."

"He probably knows ways to get out without being seen," said Alec. "There have been numerous successful escapes from the Tower by those who were locked up and closely guarded. It must be even easier since the moat was drained. But the only motive we're aware of for Rumford is the desire to step into Crabtree's shoes."

"By hiding or escaping, he's shot himself in the foot as far as that's concerned," said DC Ross, keen to contribute.

"Exactly. There could be another motive. Or Rumford could be another victim."

Piper groaned. "If no one's seen him, alive or dead, I s'pose we're going to have to search the whole bloody Tower. At least we have plenty of searchers, and they know the place."

Tom shook his head. "I dunno about that. If there's ways out, there's ways in. As you say, all your Special Constables know the place, and they're all active men, or have been. You don't get to be a sergeant in the army by sitting on your backside. That cuts the searchers to those with real alibis, not all those who live in the Outer Ward, or bailey, or whatever it's called, and didn't go in or out the inner gates."

"A search will be the last resort," said Alec. "Ross, go and present my compliments to Colonel Duggan and say I want soldiers patrolling the moat. It may be locking the stable door after the horse has been stolen, but I'd hate someone to get away over the walls while I'm in charge."

Ross departed, reluctantly.

"In order to avoid searching the place for secret dungeons," said Alec, "we're going to have to use our brains. I, for one, don't know much about Rumford. He lived next door to Crabtree. He is, or was—but I'll use the present tense until we find a body—Yeoman Gaoler, second in command of the Yeoman Warders. Daisy seems to believe he is generally disliked, but I don't think she mentioned why."

"He's a snooper," Piper declared. "I didn't ask about him, seeing it was Crabtree we were interested in, but I got an earful anyways. Rumford has to know everybody's business, always poking and prying about. If anyone knows about secret dungeons, he will."

"Ah," said Tom. "We all know where sticking your nose into other people's business leads, if you're not too particular, don't we."

"Blackmail," said Piper with relish.

"Blackmailers are more likely to be murdered than to murder," Alec pointed out. "I wonder if Crabtree could have tried to kill him and had the tables turned on him."

"Or maybe he saw someone else do Rumford in, Chief," Piper suggested.

"Why would the murderer hide one body and not the other?" Tom pondered aloud. "He had half the night to do it, a nice foggy night. You know what, Chief, if I was you, I'd ring up Mrs. Fletcher and see what she can tell you about our missing Yeoman Gaoler."

"Daisy—"

"Darling, I was just wondering whether *I* ought to ring *you*!"

"Oh?" said Alec guardedly. "What about?"

"You first."

"No, I don't want to waste time asking questions that you may answer before I ask them. At least, if it is the case? Not the babies?"

"Darling, I wouldn't call you at work about the babies unless it was a serious emergency, and if it was a serious emergency, I wouldn't stop to wonder whether—"

"Daisy!"

"The babies are blooming. I was just thinking— I told you about Rumford?"

"Yes?"

How expressive a monosyllable could be, even over the wire. Daisy could tell Alec was pricking up his ears. "You suspect him, too."

"There have been developments. . . ."

"What's happened?"

"You know I can't tell you that, especially on the telephone. But yes, we're interested in him. You've remembered something else about him?"

"Not so much remembered as worked out. I

don't know if it has anything to do with the murder, but I think he might be a blackmailer."

"Great minds think alike. Who are his victims?"

"I can't be sure, of course. No one likes him."

"But?"

"The people I noticed who particularly disliked him . . . I hate this bit."

"I know, love. I can only remind you, as you've heard before, that he who kills once very often kills again."

"Yes. Right-oh, let me think. When Rumford was giving me the full tour of the Tower, I noticed—"

"Wait a bit. Rumford was your guide? Why him? Who decided on him?"

"General Carradine told me he was very knowledgeable."

"The general favours him?"

"I wouldn't exactly say that," Daisy said cautiously. Should she relay to him Mrs. Tebbit's comment about the Resident Governor and the Yeoman Gaoler? "He chose him because of his knowledge. He's also a good raconteur, especially in contrast to Crabtree. He made the stories come alive."

"Was he paid extra to give the tour?"

"Not exactly. The general told me he'd expect a tip, and I already knew the yeomen are supposed to pass gratuities on to the chapel—Darling, what does *ad vincula* mean?"

"Is this relevant?"

"No. Sorry. One of the girls suggested that Rumford pockets his tips, and her father blew her up. He said she mustn't say such a thing even as a joke, because a man can be dismissed for it."

"The Carradine girls dislike Rumford?"

"They don't care for him much."

"Hmm. Perhaps Carradine knows that Rumford pockets the cash, and pays him off in part by giving him assignments that will earn him tips."

"Darling, that's the wildest speculation!" Daisy objected, although the possibility had crossed her own mind.

Alec laughed. "True. What was it you noticed during your tour?"

"How everyone seemed to try to avoid Rumford. It was most noticeable in the Wakefield Tower, where they keep the Crown Jewels."

"Who was there?"

"A couple of warders on guard duty, the Keeper, who was condescending to show off the collection to me, and Webster. As soon as Rumford turned up, Sir Patrick and Webster and one of the warders hopped it. The other guard acted as if Rumford was a bad smell it was his duty to put up with."

"I don't suppose you know those warders' names."

"'Fraid not. Wouldn't they be on some duty roster?"

"I expect so. What day and time?"

Daisy gave him the details, then went on, "When we left and were walking about the place, the other warders kept their distance, and some actively went out of their way to avoid coming face-to-face with us. I don't *think* they were dodging *me*. The ones I met when I was with Crabtree were very friendly."

"Crabtree showed you round as well?" Alec asked sharply.

"At first. He said Rumford was busy elsewhere but would meet me later. Darling, do you suppose Rumford blackmailed him into doing his job for him?"

"It's worth considering. The other warders appeared friendly to Crabtree, you say?"

"Definitely. I'm sure they're all rushing to say how much they liked him. I'd believe it. We didn't meet all that many, but they all seemed genuinely pleased to see him."

"No names?"

"Sorry. I do know the names of a couple of the officers."

"Officers?"

"Hotspurs. Some of them seemed anxious not to meet Rumford, too, including two I'd met who really ought in common courtesy to have acknowledged my presence with more than a distant wave."

"Shocking!" Alec's voice conveyed a grin at her indignation. "Who were they?"

"Captain Devereux and Lieutenant Jardyne. They're friends of the Carradine girls. That is, Jardyne is dotty about Fay, and Brenda makes a nuisance of herself to Devereux."

"I've met Devereux. I wouldn't have thought he'd put up with being mooned over by a would-be flapper."

"Better than Dr. Macleod puts up with Fay, on the whole. Devereux finds it amusing. He's—"

"Macleod? The Hotspurs' doctor?"

"He's not one of the Guards. He's a captain in the Medical Corps and he runs the hospital for the whole Tower."

"Does he, now! And Rumford was coughing last night?"

"Like billy-oh. Crabtree said he'd been gassed in the trenches, not badly, but enough for lasting effects. Alec, what do you—?"

"I'll tell you later. Perhaps. I must go, love."

"But what did you telephone for?"

"To ask you what you've told me."

"Oh! That's lucky. I'm glad you rang me before

I rang you, or we'd be paying for this telephone call."

"I'm at the King's House. I imagine it will go on the King's account. 'Bye, love."

"Cheerio, darling. Glad I could help."

She was reaching for the hook to cut off the connection when Alec said, "Daisy? It means 'in chains.' "

"What? Oh, *ad vincula*? St. Peter in chains: very appropriate for the Tower. Thanks, darling. It might make a rather good last line."

Alec hung up. He would have thought of the hospital sooner or later, he assured himself, even if Tom had not prompted him to talk to Daisy. She hadn't really told him anything new. But he had to acknowledge, strictly to himself, that once she had got herself mixed up in an investigation, it was generally a mistake not to let her have her say.

There was something she wasn't saying, though. Something about General Carradine, he thought, probably some sort of confirmation that Rumford had his hooks into the unfortunate man. The Resident Governor wasn't at all the sort of suspect she tended to take under her wing, but she might well feel an urge to protect his daughters. He'd worry about that later. Time now to see if Rumford actually was under the doctor's care.

Outside Carradine's study, Webster waited impatiently.

"Are you finished?" he asked as Alec emerged. "I have several extremely important telephone calls to place, including one to the Constable and one to the Palace."

"You haven't notified them yet?"

"The Governor hoped to be able to report that you had found the regrettable incident to be an accident after all, or at least that the villain is about to be arrested, but he can delay no longer."

"My apologies," Alec said dryly. Aware that a door behind Webster, on the opposite side of the landing, had inched open, he was pretty sure he could guess who was listening. "We prefer not to be too hasty and find we have arrested the wrong person. Apologies also for keeping you from the telephone. Had anyone thought to arrange for the GPO men to be admitted, we'd have had a line to the Warders' Room by now."

Webster flushed, which, while not in itself an attractive sight, had the merit of reducing his likeness to Jeremy Fisher. "We had other things on our minds," he muttered.

"Great Scott, I'm not blaming you. I ought to have thought of it myself, but I've never worked in such a well-guarded place before. My sergeant noticed that there's a telephone wire to the Guard House. It's more central than the Warders' Room, so he's going to ask Colonel Duggan to find space for us there, and run us in a field telephone if necessary."

"I dare say that will be more convenient for you."

"I expect so. I'm off to the hospital now. That's . . ." He consulted the guidebook plan. "This building next to the Officer's Quarters?" He pointed to the spot. Within the inner walls, he noted.

"We'll show you the way, Mr. Fletcher!" The door swung open and the Carradine girls burst forth.

"Thank you, but I think I can probably—"

"It's no trouble at all, honestly."

"We're going to see Aunt Christina anyway."

It wouldn't hurt to have another chat with them.

What was it Daisy had said about one of the pair and the doctor? Fay was keen on Macleod, who didn't reciprocate?

They were athletic young women, bounding down the stairs ahead of him. As they all went out of the front door, he cast a surreptitious glance at the balcony Tom had mentioned. He doubted Fay or Brenda would have much trouble descending thence to the ground. Suppose Rumford had seen one of them kissing an officer, in one of the corners with which the Tower was so copiously endowed, and threatened to tell her father.

But according to Alec's observation and Daisy's comments, though Carradine was presumably authoritative in a military setting, he was not the sort of authoritarian father whose daughters trembled at his frown. Indeed, they probably paid little heed to the poor man's strictures.

Alec simply couldn't see them as killers, either to keep their own secrets or to protect their father's. They were more like bumbling puppies, sometimes a nuisance, even unintentionally destructive (of young men's hearts), but irresistible.

"Why are you going to the hospital, Mr. Fletcher?"

"You don't suspect Dr. Macleod, do you?" The anxious question came from Fay, younger than her sister but taller.

"You have to suspect everyone, don't you?"

"But doctors swear to do no harm."

"Crippen," said Brenda.

"Sam is nothing like that horrible man!"

"Ethel Le Neve fell in love with Crippen."

Alec intervened. "I have no reason to suspect Dr. Macleod more than anyone else."

"No more than our father?"

"Or us?"

"Or Aunt Alice and Aunt Myrtle?"

The idea of the Tebbit ladies as murderers made both of them giggle. They sobered as they reached the top of the fatal stairs, still guarded by Hotspur sentries.

"He's not still down there, is he?"

"No, the body was removed hours ago," Alec reassured them.

"Poor old Crabtree."

"I shall never go that way again."

"You don't really think we might have done it, do you?"

"You're near the bottom of my list."

"Ooh!"

"We're really on it?"

"Too thrilling!"

Volatile was the word, Alec decided.

As they turned the corner at the end of the wall, a large young officer came towards them. He cast a hostile glance at Alec, who, had he been ten years younger, would have guessed the youth was jealous.

Turning to Fay, he said eagerly, "I was just coming to make sure you're all right."

"Of course, I'm all right."

"There would have been more point in asking several hours ago."

The young man glared at Brenda with a sulky look that was almost a pout. "If you want to know, I was on duty."

"Hard lines," said Brenda ironically.

"Mr. Fletcher, this is Lieutenant Jardyne. Detective Chief Inspector Fletcher, Ray. It's simply spiffing—he's Mrs. Fletcher's husband!"

Jardyne looked a bit happier on hearing Alec was married. He turned to go with them as they went on across the Parade Ground, and he and Fay fell a little behind. What Alec heard sounded more like squabbling children than a lovers' tiff.

13

"*T*ell me about this doctor your sister is so concerned for," Alec invited Brenda.

"He gambles."

"How do you know?"

"The others tease him about it."

Not a secret, then, so of doubtful interest for the investigation. "That's a pity."

"And I sometimes wonder . . ." She lowered her voice. "Mr. Fletcher, I don't know much about dope, just what I've heard people say, but I know doctors can get hold of all sorts of stuff. I sometimes wonder if Sam—Dr. Macleod—is a *dope fiend*."

"What makes you suspect that?"

"He's so moody. Sometimes he's frightfully bright and energetic, but sort of not naturally, if you know what I mean?"

Alec nodded encouragement. Drug use was a natural for blackmail.

"Sometimes he's lethargic," she continued earnestly, "and his tennis game absolutely falls to pieces, and sometimes he's bitter and cynical and says really brutal things to my sister. Does that sound like a dope fiend?"

"It's possible."

"I thought so. It may be because he saw such horrible things in the War, as Fay says, but I don't think that's any excuse to take it out on her. She thinks it's frightfully romantic, and she'll be able to reform him if he'll only marry her."

"Oh dear!"

"Fay is a bit young for her age," said Brenda from the sage eminence of her year's advantage. "Luckily, I don't believe there's the least chance of his ever asking her to marry him."

"A fortunate escape. What about you? Have you a favourite among the officers?"

"Of course. I can't let my little sister steal a march on me, can I? I pretend to mope after Dev, but it's not serious. In fact, he never takes anything seriously. I think it may be another way to cope with the War. If you ask me, the War was a dreadful mistake."

"You're not the first to come to that conclusion. Dev?"

"Captain Devereux. I suppose you suspect him, too?"

"Naturally."

"Oh well, I don't suppose he'll care. He'll make a joke of it. He can be frightfully amusing and lots of fun. He'll even cheat at croquet to let Fay and me win. It makes Ray Jardyne squirm."

"Which, I take it, is the captain's aim."

"Of course. He wouldn't do it just to please us. The thing is, Ray's frightfully stuffy about playing by the rules, but he can't make a fuss, as he'd like to, because of wanting to please Fay."

He was not succeeding, to judge by the way Fay

now hurried to rejoin them, leaving the disconsolate Jardyne behind. A backward glance showed the lieutenant red-faced, his mouth a tight line, his fists clenched.

An officer and a gentleman who was "stuffy" about playing by the rules was unlikely to push an old man downstairs, Alec thought. On the other hand, someone who had trouble containing his temper might find he'd done it before recollecting his principles. He'd have to be interviewed, as would all the other officers, and they could not be left to Tom.

With luck, Tom would be finding out a bit about the officers from the noncoms he was presently talking to.

They came to the northeast corner of the White Tower. Fay pointed to an unprepossessing building to the right of the Officers' Quarters.

"That's the hospital block."

"It's rather large for a thousand or so residents," Alec observed. "Are you a sickly lot?"

"The upper floors are married men's quarters," Brenda explained.

"Garrison, not Yeoman Warders."

"They're a bit cramped."

"But no worse than the casemates."

"Where most of the yeomen live."

Alec realized he had not yet considered the possibility that Crabtree might have been murdered by the wife of one of the residents. The downstairs shove was a method a woman might employ, but the use of the partizan argued against it, and few women would willingly hang about outside on a foggy night. What about a woman as motive—an irate husband as murderer? Men inclined towards excessive study of the Bible sometimes developed peculiar ideas about women. They were usually bachelors, not widowers, and Alec hadn't come across any suggestion that Crabtree was so unbalanced, but it would have to be borne in mind.

"Thank you for your escort, ladies," he said.

"If there's anything else we can do . . ."

"Just call on us."

"We liked Crabtree."

"And this whole business is upsetting Daddy dreadfully."

A natural dislike of trouble on his command, or something more significant?

"Besides, we really, really like Mrs. Fletcher."

"She's awfully nice, isn't she?"

"*I* think so," said Alec.

With a wave, they headed for the Officers' Quarters. Alec turned his steps towards the hospital and his mind towards his first impressions of Dr. Macleod.

At the time, he had known too little about the murder to form any useful judgement of those he met. Macleod had seemed competent, and his report on the body agreed with that of the police surgeon. He had also seemed restless, even nervy. Illicit drug use could explain that, but it was not the first time Alec had come across RAMC doctors who were badly disturbed by civilian mayhem in spite of—perhaps because of—the horrific conditions they had dealt with in war.

Poor chap! If morphia was the only way he could deal with the memories, Alec was not about to harass him, as long as he was not selling the stuff to finance his gambling, or to pay blackmail.

In the foyer of the hospital, an orderly was whistling as he pared his nails with a pocketknife. A swift glance at Alec's RFC tie and he dropped the knife, jumped to attention, and saluted. "Chief Inspector, sir! What can I do for you, sir?"

Alec's fame had preceded him. "I hope you can give me some information. A Yeoman Warder was admitted last night, I believe?" It was less belief than guesswork—and hope. He didn't want to have to tell Superintendent Crane he'd mislaid the man who could be either the murderer or the intended victim.

"Yessir." The orderly consulted a large ledger. "That'd be the Yeoman Gaoler hisself, Sergeant Major Rumford."

Alec breathed again. "Is there by any chance a note of the time?"

"Ten-fifteen P.M., it says here, sir."

Quarter past ten. The fact baffled Alec. It fitted with Daisy's memory of Rumford going off along the wall at a minute or so before ten, and he must have been the yeoman who followed the Carradine girls and Mrs. Duggan past the White Tower. But the police surgeon was pretty clear that Crabtree hadn't been killed before eleven. Could Rumford have reported to the hospital to establish an alibi and sneaked out later? Or were they going to have to abandon the hypothesis of Rumford as murderer?

"Is Dr. Macleod available?"

"Dunno 'bout that, sir. He's taking surgery, but there wasn't many came to sick call today. I don't think he's got more'n a couple left. They leave by the back door, so I don't see 'em. I'll go check."

"Thanks. If he won't finish for a quarter of an hour or longer, I'd appreciate his fitting me in sooner. Detective Chief Inspector Fletcher."

"Yessir!"

The orderly departed, to return moments later with an invitation to follow him.

Macleod's office faced west and was flooded with sunlight. Its untidiness was no worse than many another doctor's office-cum-examination room. He jumped up from his desk when Alec entered and shook his hand vigorously.

"How can I help you, Chief Inspector? Sit down, do." His eyes were bright, too bright, the pupils pinpoints smaller than could be accounted for by the bright light.

Brenda Carradine was a perceptive young lady. Dr. Macleod was almost certainly taking morphia, a "dope fiend" as she had put it, or, as some would say, a morphinomaniac.

"First, I thought you'd like to know that the police surgeon's preliminary findings agree with yours."

"How encouraging! Perhaps I should join the police."

Ignoring the mockery in his tone, Alec said stolidly, "Police surgeon is not a full-time job, I'm afraid. We use GPs in private practice with some specialized knowledge of forensic pathology. Doctor, I understand you admitted the Yeoman Gaoler, Rumford, to the hospital last evening. We've been looking for him."

"Don't blame me for not mentioning his whereabouts. I was asked about poor old Crabtree, and his whereabouts were all too well known."

"Rumford is still here?"

"Unless someone has spirited him away."

"His name was entered in your book at tenfifteen. I assume that's not the time he stepped through the door."

"No, he'd have arrived a few minutes earlier. It didn't take long to realize that he needed in-patient treatment. An interesting case, in its way. He was gassed in France, just a light dose, not sufficient to kill or severely incapacitate. Most of the time, he's able to function perfectly normally. Then a pea-souper crawls out of the river and he's hacking away again."

"Like last night."

"Like last night. He had a bad go of bronchitis last winter, with a touch of pneumonia, and I advised him to retire right away, to move as far away from London and the river as he could get. But the old sod said he wasn't ready to go yet, much as some people would like to see the back of him."

"What do you think he meant by that?"

Macleod gave him the blankest of blank stares. "I haven't the foggiest—pun intended. Rumford said he didn't intend to 'die a Yeoman Warder' and he wasn't ready to turn up his toes yet, thank you."

" 'Die a Yeoman Warder'? That's an odd way to put it."

"Not at all. It's a quote from the Chief Yeoman's toast to all new recruits: 'May you never die a Yeoman Warder.' " Brimming with nervous energy, the doctor explained. "Once upon a time, the fee for appointment to the post of Yeoman Warder was two hundred and fifty guineas. Two hundred and fifty pounds was returned on retirement, the Constable bagging the odd shillings. If the man died before retirement, the Constable got the lot. You'll never put your finger on the pulse of this bloody place unless you understand that it's ruled by tradition."

"I had gathered as much."

"The Constable, by the way, is not one of your lowly bobbies. He is to the Resident Governor as is the Mikado to the Lord High Everything Else. Are you fond of Gilbert and Sullivan?"

"My wife and I have taken my daughter to several performances."

"Ah, yes, I have made the acquaintance of Mrs. Fletcher. A remarkable lady."

Alec would put up with a lot of flapdoodle in the hope of obtaining useful information, but he was reaching his limit. He suspected Macleod was aware of it. Before he could say anything, the doctor reverted to the Constable of the Tower.

"The Constable holds a sinecure, of course. The only time he turns up here is when he's installed. The Lord Chancellor hands over the keys, symbolic golden keys. The Constable promptly hands them on to the Resident Governor and washes his hands of the place. Very wise. The Keeper of the Regalia, on the other hand, has his London pied-à-terre in St. Thomas's Tower, and the present holder of the position makes considerable use of it. Have you met General Sir Patrick Heald?"

"Not yet." St. Thomas's Tower was in the Outer Ward, so Alec had no pressing need to speak to its inhabitant.

"You don't want to. Supercilious bastard. Carradine's not a bad bloke, though, if only he'd rein in those two redcoat-chasers of his. As for Duggan—"

"Could we get back to Rumford? Is it possible he left and returned unobserved after you admitted him?"

Before he finished speaking, Macleod broke into convulsive, febrile laughter. At last, he recovered enough to gasp out, "No, my dear chap, it's not possible. I gave him a hefty dose of morphia to stop the coughing, to relieve his chest pain, and to put him to sleep. 'Sleep that knits up the ravelled sleeve of care,' you know. 'To sleep, perchance to dream,'" he added savagely. "I wonder what the bloody hell the bastard dreams of."

"Bastard?"

"Our Yeoman Gaoler is not a prepossessing character," the doctor said with an airy wave of the hand, but Alec was certain he had some more specific villainy in mind. Blackmail, for instance.

The trouble was, Dr. Macleod was the one person who couldn't possibly have mistaken Crabtree for Rumford. Worse, he'd just given an apparently unassailable alibi to the most promising suspect to date.

The dosage of morphia he'd given Rumford would have to be gone into, and checked with the police surgeon. However, it looked as if the Yeoman Gaoler had been dead to the world by the time the Chief Yeoman Warder was killed. All the same, he might very well have useful information, if only a reason for Crabtree's going out so late last night.

"I'd like to speak to him, if it won't exacerbate his condition."

"You can speak to him all you like. It's not going to affect him one way or another. When he came round, I decided his condition warranted another dose of the same. He's in the arms of Morpheus."

"Pun intended?" said Alec dryly. "When do you expect him to surface?"

"You can probably have a go at him tomorrow morning."

"You're keeping him under for another night? Is that the usual treatment?"

"Not usual, perhaps, but it's been tried with some success. There's not much else one can do. I want to be sure the attack is over and he's in good shape before I bring him round."

"I'll be back in the morning. Incidentally, where were you at midnight last night? Watching your patient?"

"I left an orderly to do that, and a nurse with instructions for another dose as needed. I was tucked up tight in my beddy-byes." Macleod was suddenly depressed, the morphia-induced animation beginning to wear off. "I don't mingle more than I have to with those hidebound, narrow-minded. . . . Oh, don't get me started on the godforsaken army! I was asleep."

"In fact, in the arms of Morpheus," Alec said grimly.

Macleod stared at him, then dropped his eyes. "You might say so. I'll get off it soon, though, I swear it!"

"I hope so. Did you ever treat Crabtree?"

"Not for so much as an ingrowing toenail. I knew him only to pass the time of day with, but by all accounts, he was one of those clean-living old men who ought by rights to have lived to a hundred. It's a bloody world."

"You don't know of anyone who might have had it in for him?"

"No. Again, it's hearsay, but I believe he was generally liked." In a dull voice, he added, "I hope you get the bastard who killed him."

"That seems to be the common desire. We'll do our best. Thank you for your time, Doctor. Please give orders that if the patient should come round, he's not to be told about the murder."

"I already did. He'd be in no condition to have his colleague's death broken to him."

"Very good. I'll see you tomorrow—if not before."

Macleod didn't react to this promise, or threat. He sat with bowed head, staring blankly at the top of his desk.

In the lobby, the orderly was now reading *The Pink Un*. He laid it down, not bothering to hide it, and came to attention with somewhat less alacrity than before.

"Dull job?" Alec observed with sympathy. "You don't have many patients?"

"That about hits the nail on the head, sir. Stands to reason, you get a few hundred strapping young blokes and don't throw bullets at 'em, they ain't going to need a doctor too often."

"No doubt."

"What's more, them Beefeaters is a hale and hearty lot, on the whole. I tell you, sir, some days, if it wasn't for the odd kiddie falling off his bike and the like, we wouldn't see no one here. We're not in business just for the garrison, you see, sir, and with all them that lives in the Tower, we get a bit of everything. The doctor's that good with the kiddies, you wouldn't believe. Ought to be in one of them children's hospitals." He lowered his voice to a confidential tone. "I heard he tried for a job but they didn't want to hire a doctor as had been in the army ever since he got the letters after his name. Like he could've done aught else in '14. Their loss!"

"And his."

"A truer word was never spoke. He's not happy, sir, but he does his job right enough and I ain't heard no complaints."

"Thank you." With that information, Alec felt himself absolved from having to act on Macleod's addiction, unless he found evidence of the doctor's unlawfully selling the drug. What was more, Alec hadn't even hinted at the misuse of morphine. The orderly's testimonial to Macleod's competence was unsolicited.

He took the man's name for the record. As he closed his notebook, his gaze fell upon the *Sport-*

ing Times, lying open on the desktop. The visible page was heavily annotated. "Follow the horses, do you?"

"I has a little flutter now and then, sir. It's the doctor as knows all about form and odds and that. He makes notes, and when he's done, he let's us have his *Pink Un.* I won't say he's always right, but going by what he says, I win more'n I lose. Can't ask better'n that, can you?"

"It sounds good to me," said Alec, who ventured a half-crown each way on the Derby every year and expected to lose it.

He went to find Colonel Duggan at the barracks.

"Your sergeant's made a big hit with my NCOs," the colonel greeted him, grinning. "Some were inclined to take umbrage at being interrogated by a chap who didn't fight. There are few stickier wickets than an uncooperative noncom! But he's been telling them stories about policing in London during the War, chasing spies and black marketeers and pulling civilians out of collapsing houses after air raids. I hope he's getting some useful stuff from them in exchange."

"I expect so. DS Tring isn't my right-hand man for nothing."

"He passed on your request for a room with a 'phone in the Guard House. My adjutant just reported that it's all set up for you."

"Thank you, sir, that's very kind of you."

"I assume you'll want to use it to ask my officers a few questions." Duggan was no fool, Alec reminded himself. He had risen to his present position without the aid of family influence and connections. "I've given orders that they're to make themselves available. Is there anything else I can do for you?"

"Not at present, thanks. I must go and let the Governor know how the investigation is progressing, which, in confidence, is not very fast. Then I'll send someone over to fetch your chaps, one at a time. I assume it's best to start at the top?"

"Definitely. Can't keep majors waiting while lieutenants have their say."

"I'll try not to keep anyone waiting about too long. I greatly appreciate your cooperation, sir."

"I'm certain none of my people are involved. You'll find it's an internal affair, some quarrel among the Beefeaters. But the sooner it's cleared up, the better for all of us. Good luck!"

"I wish I could say I don't need it," Alec responded, "but every time I think I've found a lead, it slips away."

14

Alec returned to the King's House. He walked by way of the fatal stairs, not that he expected to learn anything new, but to refresh in his mind the lie of the land. At the top, he turned and looked down.

Even in the now-bright sunshine, the steep, narrow flight of eighteen or so steps looked dangerous. If it weren't for the partizan, Crabtree's death would surely have passed as an accident. So why use the damn thing? The only possible reason that suggested itself was an attempt to throw suspicion on the victim's fellow warders, which, in turn, suggested that the murderer was not a warder.

He went on. Before knocking on the front door, he stopped to contemplate the balcony, the flat roof of a single-story excrescence filling the angle between the south and west wings of the Tudor building. It appeared to be an afterthought, adding a little extra space to the ground floor. The railing and the drop, though Daisy might balk at tackling them, would present no great challenge to anyone of moderate athletic ability.

On the other hand, climbing back in would be difficult without a ladder or assistance from above. He couldn't imagine the Resident Governor taking anyone into his confidence on such an errand, but had he dismissed the Carradine sisters too quickly?

The front door opened. Webster came out, taking two or three steps before he noticed Alec.

"Oh, there you are," he said irritably. "The Governor sent me to find you. I got through to the Constable at last and he wanted a full report on your investigation. What little we were able to tell him did not satisfy him, so now General Carradine wants a report he can pass on."

Alec took the wind out of his sails. "That's exactly why I was on my way to you. I thought it was about time I brought General Carradine up-to-date." Not that he had the slightest intention of providing a "full" report, given that members of the household were still under suspicion. However, all senior police officers had to be expert at giving little away while making people—especially nosy reporters and self-important members of the upper classes—believe they'd heard a great deal.

They went into the house and up to the study. Carradine was sitting at his desk, staring morosely through the window at the site of the scaffold on the far side of the Green. He turned his head as Webster ushered Alec in.

"Oh, there you are, Fletcher. I hope you've some progress to report."

"Only of a negative kind, I'm afraid, sir." He explained that a fairly large number of people had been eliminated from their enquiries. "Your Special Constables have been of invaluable assistance," he added.

Carradine's temperament was naturally sanguine. "They're a good lot, on the whole," he said, brightening. "They wouldn't be here otherwise. I'm glad they've been helpful. But negative progress—that doesn't sound promising."

"Come now, sir, '*Reculer pour mieux sauter*'? In your profession, you have the strategic retreat. In mine, we often have to clear away a lot of deadwood before we can see the trees for the forest, if you see what I mean."

"Yes, I think so. Yes, of course."

"Every suspect we eliminate makes it easier for us to concentrate our attentions on those remaining." No need to mention that the most promising suspect was out of the picture. Nor that, with Rumford cleared of murder, the likelihood was very much increased that he was the intended victim, thus propelling the Resident Governor and his daughters to positions near the head of the list.

"Ah, yes, that sounds like progress, doesn't it, Jeremy?"

"Indeed, sir." Webster's gaze, as always difficult to read because of his glasses, seemed to Alec to be tinged with scepticism.

Alec hoped the secretary wouldn't feel obliged to point out to his employer just how little had actually been said.

The general started to ask, "Who—?" He frowned as a heavy tread on the stairs interrupted him, then asked again, but with a different object: "Who—?"

A short, plump gentleman burst in without announcement or invitation. "Carradine, I really must protest. . . . Oh, who's this?"

"Our sleuth from Scotland Yard, Sir Patrick." Carradine seemed more amused than annoyed. "Allow me to introduce Detective Chief Inspector

Fletcher. You met his wife here the other evening. Mr. Fletcher, Sir Patrick Heald, the Keeper of the Regalia."

Sir Patrick scowled at Alec and said irately, "So you're the one responsible for . . . Mrs. Fletcher? She's married to a policeman?" He glanced back at the general. "But didn't you say . . . ? Sorry, old chap, no offence. Charming little lady."

Alec managed to preserve the impassive face proper to a policeman, but behind it his thoughts echoed Macleod's words: *Supercilious bastard.* "My wife is a very well-respected journalist," he said in a tone that suggested agreement, although he knew perfectly well that what Sir Patrick referred to was not Daisy's writing ability, but her noble birth.

"Yes, well, I showed her the Regalia myself, didn't I, Webster?"

"You did, sir." Webster didn't appear to care for the Keeper any better than Macleod did.

"Which I don't for your everyday scribbler, I assure you. But what's all this about not being allowed to leave the Tower, my dear fellow? Carradine tells me it was on your advice that he closed the gates."

"That is correct, sir. In a murder case, it's usual to request that all possible witnesses remain within reach until we have had time to make the necessary enquiries."

"I can see that's appropriate for the rank and file, but—"

"I'd have thought, sir, in your official capacity, you'd wish to set an example to others who might find it inconvenient or distasteful to have their movements restricted."

"I suppose, if you put it like that. . . . Oh, very well! But I have an engagement at my country place tomorrow evening that I don't care to miss."

"I expect we'll have everything cleared up in good time, sir," Alec said untruthfully.

"Very well. Carry on. You'll keep me informed, Carradine?"

"Of course, Sir Patrick. I can't apologise enough for the misunderstanding this morning."

With a disgruntled grunt, the Keeper departed.

"To be fair," said Carradine, "he's been quite patient and forbearing. My chaps at the Byward Tower told me he drove along to the gate at the usual time of opening and was quite put out to find it locked. He's not involved in the administration of the Tower, of course, and no one had thought to inform him of Crabtree's unfortunate demise. My fault entirely."

"At that time, sir," Webster pointed out, "we were scarcely beginning to comprehend the fact ourselves."

"True. I can't think why he had to leave so early, today of all days! I suppose he had an engagement in the country—golf, luncheon, who knows. Well, one must expect to be inconvenienced by murder."

"In any case," said the secretary doggedly, "I was not aware that Sir Patrick was in residence last night."

"Nor I, nor I."

"Are you aware, general," said Alec, "that your Yeoman Gaoler is in the hospital?"

"Good gad, no! Was he attacked, too?"

"Only in the lungs, by the fog."

"Poor chap." Carradine's commiseration was perfunctory. "Did you know, Jeremy?"

"Dr. Macleod sent over the regulation chit this morning. I put it on your desk, but you haven't had much opportunity to deal with everyday business today." Webster was soothing without being sycophantic.

He was probably a good secretary in spite of his peculiarities, Alec decided. But if he was more competent than first appearances suggested, might he not also be more athletic than his thick glasses implied? Consider the prodigious leaps performed by fat little goggle-eyed frogs. Back on the list went Mr. Jeremy Fisher.

Carradine was regarding his paper-strewn desk with aversion, which metamorphosed unexpectedly into thankfulness. "I usually visit any of our men who land in sick bay, but in the circumstances, I hardly think . . ."

"You won't be missed, sir," Alec assured him. "The doctor has Rumford under heavy sedation."

"Excellent, excellent."

"You'll want to speak to the Constable, sir, to bring him up-to-date on Mr. Fletcher's 'progress.' "

Webster's sarcasm was obvious to Alec, but the general ignored or failed to notice it. "Yes, the sooner the better," he said. "See if you can get hold of him, Jeremy."

Alec slipped out quickly before that inconvenient "Who . . . ?" question could raise its head again. That had been much easier than his report to Superintendent Crane was going to be.

He met Tom and Ernie at the Guard House.

Tom had nothing useful to report from questioning the Hotspur NCOs. Several had known Crabtree before he retired from the regiment, and they were unanimous that he wasn't the sort who made enemies.

Ernie had obtained the key to the Yeoman Gaoler's House from Webster and searched it, as well as Crabtree's. In the latter, he had found signs of the making and clearing up of toasted cheese. Assuming he had eaten it immediately after the

Keys ceremony, the autopsy should be able to time his death pretty accurately.

"And at Rumford's?" Alec asked. "A nice list of names? An account book or bankbook with unexplained deposits?"

"No such luck, Chief."

"Ah," said Tom. "That don't really surprise me. These noncoms, they aren't writers. I mean, they're literate, but it's not automatic to write everything down like it is in the force. On the other hand, they have a phenomenal memory for names and faces. They're in charge of keeping all those privates in order, and they don't want to have to stop and think 'What's that bloke's name?' before they yell at him. I reckon Rumford'd rely on his memory for who he had his hooks into."

"Not even a nice hoard of banknotes, I suppose?" Alec said unhopefully.

"Three quid and change, in a tobacco jar on the mantelpiece. If he's been extorting cash, he must've hidden it in one of those secret dungeons."

"Darling!" Daisy stopped shaking the rattle as she looked up from the nursery floor, where she was sitting. "I'm so glad you're home in time to see how clever our babies are."

"Should they be on the floor with the dog, Daisy? My mother would have forty fits."

"That's what I told Nanny. That's what persuaded her to permit it. We always had a dog or two wandering in and out of the nursery when I was little. I'm sure it's good for them. They won't grow up afraid of dogs, and by the time they're old enough to pester her, she'll be used to them."

Alec sank wearily into a chair. "All right, if you

say so. Show me what brilliant things our offspring are doing."

"Watch. They both raise their heads and gurgle when I shake the rattle. Miranda keeps her eyes on it when I move it across in front of her, and Oliver grabs at it."

"I wonder if that's a prognostication of their future attitudes to life. Miranda will be contemplative and Oliver will be grasping."

"He won't!" Daisy said indignantly. "It could just as well mean he's going to be good at sports. Oh dear, Nana's sniffing his little bottom. I expect his nappy needs changing. Nanny's having her supper—that's why she let me play with them—but she'll be up in a minute, thank heaven. I'm glad you're home in time for dinner, darling."

"So am I, but I'm going to change out of these shoes first."

"There's an awful lot of walking at the Tower, isn't there? Though I don't suppose you had to go up and down all those winding stairs. Put on your slippers—I'm not expecting anyone to drop in this evening."

"Good. Nana, come! We appreciate the alert, but excessive interest is unwholesome and unbecoming. Perhaps I can teach you to bring me my slippers. You know, Daisy, I think we're going to have to start calling either Nana or Nanny something else before the twins begin to talk, or we'll have the most unholy confusion."

Daisy let Alec finish his soup before she said, slightly reproachfully, "I assume you'd have told me if you'd arrested anyone. I expected you to come home really late if you were still baffled."

"Not so much baffled as frustrated. We've interviewed just about every inhabitant of the Inner Ward, except the rank and file Guardsmen not on sentry duty, whose whereabouts are pretty well attested to by their NCOs. Tom and Ernie and I spent hours going over our notes of the interviews, and where do you think it all leads?"

"Rumford," Daisy said at once. "Won't he talk?"

Alec shook his head, but he waited until Mrs. Dobson had cleared the soup plates and brought in the veal cutlets before he said, "Not so much won't as can't."

"Whatever do you mean? Don't tell me he's been murdered, too!"

"No, no, nor died of his chest complaint. I'd still be afraid he'd managed to get away somehow if you hadn't told me about his coughing. In the end, I put two and two together and ran him to earth in the hospital."

"Heavens, I never thought of that. That must have been where he was making for when Crabtree and I met him at the top of the steps. Oh, darling, does that mean he got there before Crabtree was killed?"

"Officially signed in at quarter past ten," Alec said gloomily. "The police surgeon puts the murder at around midnight, certainly not before eleven."

"What a nuisance! Rumford would have been the perfect murderer. He really couldn't . . . ?"

"He really couldn't. Dr. Macleod is trying some new kind of treatment that involves knocking him out with drugs."

"Not permanently?"

" 'Permanently'?"

"I mean, an experimental treatment would be a

good way for a doctor to do away with a black-mailer."

"Great Scott, Daisy . . ." Alec flung down his nap-kin and started to stand up. Then he calmed down. "No. If he was going to do it, he's had plenty of op-portunity. He knows I'm aware of why he's being blackmailed, if such is the case."

"Why?"

"I can't tell you that. But in spite of Macleod's failings, he's an intelligent man. He knows that if Rumford dies under his care, I wouldn't let it pass as a natural death. Another thing: Rumford put himself into Macleod's hands. He wouldn't have done that if he wasn't sure he could trust the doc-tor, which probably means he's not blackmailing him, in spite of knowing his secret. After all, it's never difficult for a doctor to do away with a patient, and I'm sure for the few we catch, there must be others we never even suspect. All the same, I ought to have considered the possibility, and I didn't."

"You can't think of everything, darling. Eat your dinner before it gets cold."

"Yes, Mother." He forked in veal, potatoes, and Brussels sprouts.

"You're right: Rumford would be a fool to black-mail the doctor who treats him for a chronic con-dition. Even if Macleod wouldn't go so far as to kill him, he could easily mess up his treatment on pur-pose, without anyone guessing."

"Leaving him in even worse health."

"If Rumford's not the murderer," Daisy contin-ued, ruminating aloud, "then Crabtree must have been killed because someone mistook him for Rumford. Have you found out what he was doing at the steps at midnight? If Rumford was on the way to the hospital, he wouldn't have made an appointment to meet him. I bet you anything you like he asked him—Rumford asked Crabtree, that is—to do some job for him, something he was supposed to do at midnight. It must have been something official, because of both of them wearing their fancy dress."

Alec stopped with knife and fork poised and stared at her. "Yes, of course. Something that Rumford normally did every night at midnight. Now why does that ring a bell?"

"I can't imagine. I think you're drowning in a sea of information. But whatever he was supposed to do, he can't have done it, and someone ought to have noticed. Not that it really matters where he was going. What matters is that he took over Rumford's routine without anyone knowing, so the murderer thought he was killing Rumford."

"That's still pure speculation." He resumed eating. "In fact, it sounds to me suspiciously like one of your circular arguments."

"No, darling, is it? How disappointing. It all fits together so nicely."

"That is the nature of circles. For one thing, it all depends on Rumford being a blackmailer, which is sheer guesswork."

"Well, never mind, you'll find out tomorrow when you talk to him."

"I hardly think he's likely to admit to it. Ernie didn't find any proof in his house, no list of names and amounts or anything of the sort. I'm going to need some evidence before I can tackle his supposed victims. And failing that, I have absolutely no other theory to fall back on!"

15

*H*alf an hour after Alec left the house next morning, the telephone rang. Daisy was crossing the hall, on her way to the nursery from the kitchen and her daily consultation with Mrs. Dobson about the day's menus.

Given Alec's irregular hours, they were limited to meals that would either cook quickly or keep hot without spoiling. Cutlets and stews were staples, but since becoming friendly with Sakari's chauffeur, Kesin, Mrs. Dobson sometimes daringly branched out into curries. Tonight, at whatever hour Alec arrived home, curried lamb would await him.

Brring-brring. Daisy unhooked the receiver, pressed it to her ear, and spoke the telephone number into the mouthpiece.

"Mrs. Fletcher?" came a breathless whisper.

"Speaking. Who is this?"

"Brenda. Brenda Carradine. Is Mr. Fletcher there?"

"No, I'm afraid he's already left for the Tower. He should get there any minute."

"Oh, good." She continued to whisper. Fortunately, they had a good connection. "I mean, it's not him we need to talk to, but we didn't want him to overhear what you're saying."

"And you don't want anyone at that end to overhear what *you're* saying?"

"We knew you'd understand."

"So far," said Daisy, "I understand nothing. What's wrong?"

"I can't tell you on the telephone. Someone might overhear. Could you possibly *possibly* come here? We know it's a great imposition, only everything is so dreadful and we don't know what to do, and you're the only person we can turn to."

"What about your aunt Christina?"

"Oh *no!* She might tell the colonel, and that would be too awful for words."

"Brenda, whatever it is, there's a chance I might have to tell Alec."

"That's just it. You'll know if he absolutely has to know, and if not, you might be able to. . . . Oh, I can't explain over the 'phone. *Please* come!"

"Right-oh," Daisy said with a silent sigh. "It'll take me awhile to get there. I don't want to get caught up in the morning rush."

"Oh. Can you hold on a minute?"

Daisy heard a muffled sound of anxious consultation.

Brenda returned. "Mrs. Fletcher? We still have most of our quarter's allowance. We'll pay for a taxi. We'll meet you at the Middle Tower, all right? We'll wait there till you arrive."

Heavens above, they must be really worried! Daisy agreed, and rang off.

What on earth was Alec going to say when she turned up at the Tower? She had better think up something she needed to tell him both urgently and privately, something that couldn't be passed on in a telephone message. Of course, what the Carradine girls had to tell her might qualify.

Urgent or not, she had to change into clothes more appropriate for going into the city—her grey costume, she thought, in view of the distressing events at the Tower—and she absolutely refused to sacrifice a visit to the nursery for at least a few minutes with the babies.

When Alec reached the Middle Tower, a huddle of early-rising reporters lay in wait for him. He managed to escape making a statement by reminding them that the Tower of London was a royal palace.

"It's as much as my job's worth to pass on any information," he told them, wondering whether it was true. "You'd better apply to Buckingham Palace, or perhaps Downing Street." They all groaned. "Or, come to think of it, the Constable of the Tower, who's the King's representative. . . . No, I can't give you his address or telephone number, but I'm sure gentlemen as resourceful as yourselves won't have any difficulty finding out."

They swarmed away towards the nearest public telephone booths.

"Neatly done, sir," said one of the two Yeoman Warders on duty, backed up by a couple of Hotspur sentries. "We was wondering what to do about them pestiferous newshounds. I've a coupla messages for you. DS Tring and DC Piper got here a few minutes ago. They'll be waiting for you in the Guard House. And the Governor gave orders not to let anyone leave, but he said to ask you if that's what you want, sir."

"Yes, I'd prefer to keep everyone within easy reach for the moment."

"Right you are, sir. The Governor'd be glad to see you soon as you can spare a moment."

Alec noted with interest the conciliatory wording of this request. Not only did a general outrank a chief inspector by any measure, but the Resident Governor was the Tower's CO and, as such, surely entitled to demand a meeting at his own convenience. To the mind of a detective, such uncalled-for politeness had a slightly fishy odour.

Carradine had changed his tune since yesterday. Why? He had had time to reflect on Alec's interest in Rumford, and there were hints that his relationship with the Yeoman Gaoler was not all sweetness and light.

"If you don't mind me saying so, sir," the other yeoman interrupted his thoughts, "we're all hoping you'll need us to give a hand again today. We want to have a hand in collaring the bastard that did in Mr. Crabtree."

"I'll bear it in mind. You've already helped enormously."

Walking across the bridge, he noted more shakoed Guards spaced at intervals along the moat. They faced inward towards the outer walls, a reminder that the Tower had functioned as a prison for many centuries. Under a grey sky, it looked the part.

At the Byward gate, a sentry challenged Alec. He was fumbling for his identification card when a yeoman appeared from under the arch.

"It's all right, laddie," he told the sentry in patronizing tones. "This here's the head detective. Glad to see you, sir. Your chaps just arrived. Think you'll catch him today?"

"I hope so."

"So do we all," the yeoman said fervently. "Seeing no one had any call for wishing Mr. Crabtree ill, some of us is thinking it must be a madman, and we're worried he may go for someone else. I've got a wife here, sir, and kiddies."

A murmur of agreement arose from a group of men who had drifted out of the Warders' Hall while their colleague was speaking. Some wore yeoman's blue-and-red tunics, others civilian clothes, as if they weren't sure how to dress with no tourists to impress. Alec addressed them all.

"I don't believe it was a madman. But you're all sworn police officers, and quite capable, I'm sure, of preventing anything of the sort. Not, however, while you're gathered together here. If you have no other orders, I suggest you patrol all areas not directly overseen by Guardsmen. I'm sure you can work out among yourselves where you're most needed."

Sheepishly they dispersed, except two. The man who had first spoken to Alec took up a position to one side of the arch, with the other opposite. They were both armed with partizans and both looked ready to use them if given half a chance. As he continued along Water Street, Alec wondered whether the yeomen actually had training in using their mediaeval weapons.

The vivid green leaves of the flourishing creeper growing against the inner wall caught his eye. Would it be possible to climb up or down it? At the far end, where there were no houses backing onto the wall, it reached nearly to the top of the parapet of Ralegh's Walk.

He went over to take a closer look. The stems seemed sturdy enough to support a climber, but a quick look showed none of the damage that would have been inevitable. Tom had better examine it carefully, though, he decided. If someone from the Outer Ward could have murdered Crabtree and then gone up the steps to Ralegh's Walk and climbed down. . . . Well, half of yesterday's work would go up in smoke.

The feat could not have been accomplished soundlessly, however, and the sentries at the Bloody Tower gate were only a few yards away. But someone—the Carradine girls, he thought—had mentioned noise from the river, the usual hoots and whistles of fog-bound shipping. It might have been enough to cover the rustles and thuds of a climber, especially taking into account the deadening effect of fog. Yes, Tom must take a look.

Unchallenged by the two Hotspur sentries, Alec passed through the arch under the Bloody Tower and headed up the slope towards the entrance to the modern, ugly Guard House.

A burly yeoman appeared from the narrow passage between the Guard House and the Bloody Tower. "Chief Inspector, sir!"

"Yes?"

He saluted. "Parkinson, sir. I was on duty in the Wakefield Tower this week, sir. Left my partizan there evening afore last. I know I didn't ought to've, but everyone does it. And I know that's no excuse, sir—"

"I'm not responsible for your conduct as Yeoman Warder, and your partizan has nothing to do with your conduct as Special Constable."

"But that's it, sir. I want it for patrolling, like you said, sir, so I went along just to see could I get it, but the door's locked up all right and tight. So I wondered, could you . . ." His voice trailed away as Alec shook his head.

"Sorry. Partizans are outside my purview. If you want to go and ask whoever has the key—the Governor's secretary?—that's up to you, but you can patrol perfectly well without it. It's not as if there's a shortage of able-bodied men around." In fact, he'd only suggested patrolling to keep them happily occupied. A murderer who waited for a foggy night to ambush a blackmailer wasn't likely to attack at random in broad daylight.

"Sir," said Parkinson gloomily.

Alec went on into the Guard House. The sergeant on duty saluted and informed him yet again that Tring and Piper had preceded him. He did not, however, remark upon the urgency of laying hands on Crabtree's killer. Hotspur Guards and Yeoman Warders lived in the same space but inhabited different worlds.

Tom was already leafing through a report and Ernie was diligently making notes. They both looked up as Alec came in and said in chorus, "How's Mrs. Fletcher?"

Alec assured them that Daisy was her usual cheerful self.

"Resilient lady," Tom commented. He paused, then said to Piper, "Aren't you going to congratulate me on my extensive vocabulary, laddie?"

"Not likely, Sarge. I've been studying the dictionary, and that thesaurus you gave me. I know what *resilient* means. Didn't know how to say it, though, till just this minute."

"It sounds as if you've undercut your own advantage, Tom," said Alec with a grin.

"Ah." Tom's moustache twitched in a matching grin.

"Resilient." Piper savoured the word. "Just right for Mrs. Fletcher. She solved the case yet, Chief?"

"No. And, thank heaven, for once she has no excuse to get mixed up in it any further. Like us, she suspects Rumford was the intended victim, but she's as baffled as we are as to who did it. I'll go and see if I can talk to him in a couple of minutes. In the meantime: Ernie, what do we know about a yeoman by the name of Parkinson?"

"Married, three kids." With his head for detail, Piper spoke even as he went straight to the appropriate page of his notes. "Lives in Mint Lane. That's what they call the casemates where you turn left just after the Byward Tower. In the Outer Ward. Why, Chief?"

"He's mislaid his partizan. It may—or may not—be locked up safe in the Wakefield Tower. But if he lives in the Outer Ward, he didn't use it, unless . . . Tom, I want you to check whether it's possible to climb down that vine on the wall below Ralegh's Walk, and if so, whether there are any signs that someone did."

"I couldn't do it, Chief, that's for sure." Tom patted his own vast midriff. Much of it was muscle, but it tended to mislead villains, who didn't realize in time that the big man was as quick on his feet as any sprinter. His size would be an insurmountable handicap for climbing down a vine, though. "Ernie might manage it, if you want a practical demonstration. I don't mind standing below to catch him."

"Hey, Sarge!"

"I'll go give it a dekko, Chief. What else?"

"You can put your mind to devising unobtrusive tests of athletic ability for the inhabitants of the King's House. I don't want to have to ask them all to attempt the climb from that balcony." He gave them each some details to clear up. "We'll meet here in an hour. If I'm not back and haven't sent a message, come to the hospital and rescue me from the clutches of an unmasked blackmailer and/or a morphinomaniac."

"Sure you don't want us to go with you, Chief?" Piper asked anxiously. "How'd we explain it to Mrs. Fletcher if you got hurt?"

"I'm sure Daisy would appreciate the thought, Ernie, but there are orderlies about, and nurses. On the other hand, come to think of it, it may be important to have a competent witness other than myself to anything he says. Let's leave Tom to get on with the rest and you come along. I'll explain on the way how I intend to tackle him." Straight-faced, he added, "Bring your notebook and several well-sharpened pencils."

Piper gave him a reproachful look. "As if I ever go anywhere without 'em, Chief!"

Tom chuckled. "You've wounded him to the heart, Chief. Right, I'll get on with this lot, and if you're not back when I'm done, I'll go and rescue the both of you."

Dr. Macleod had not yet put in an appearance. A disapproving Sister admitted that he had left orders to let the police speak to Rumford.

"I'm sure I don't know why you'd want to." She sniffed. "Any nurse—any hospital orderly even—knows you can't believe a word they say when they're coming out from morphine."

"Is he still very dopey, Sister?"

"Not really," she said grudgingly. "The last dose wore off a few hours ago, and he was left to sleep it off. He's drunk about a gallon of tea since he woke up, so he should be able to talk to you. But don't take his word for anything."

She showed them into a small, rather dreary ward with north-facing windows. Only one bed was in use, the occupant lying down, staring at the ceiling. At first glance, he could have been Crabtree's twin.

"Wait here while I make sure he's comfortable." Starches rustling, the nurse went over to the bed and announced in the loud voice even nurses often use to the sick, "Gentlemen to see you, Mr. Rumford. Do we want the bedpan first?"

"Nay!" growled the patient.

Waiting at the door, Piper whispered, "Chief, why's she so keen we shouldn't believe him?"

"Protecting Macleod," Alec guessed. "Come on. Thank you, Sister."

They went over to the bed. Rumford was flat on his back. Indeed, he had little choice, since, in typical hospital fashion, the sheet was tucked down so tightly over his chest as to allow no activity but breathing. He turned his head on the pillow to look at them, and scowled.

Alec saw that his pupils were smaller than seemed normal for the dull grey light. Presumably he was still under the influence of morphine to some extent, and no doubt the Sister's warning about not taking his word as gospel was justified.

"Good morning, Mr. Rumford. I hope you're feeling up to a short interview."

"Who'rt tha?"

"Detective Chief Inspector Fletcher of the Metropolitan Police. Of which you are a sworn Special Constable."

"That's right," Rumford said grudgingly. "Sir."

"I'm afraid I bring bad news. The Chief Warder, Mr. Crabtree, was attacked the night before last."

"Night before . . .?" He sounded confused.

"The night you were admitted to hospital. Mr. Crabtree was pushed down the steps by the Bloody Tower at midnight. I'm afraid he did not survive the attack."

Rumford blinked. It took him a moment to assimilate the information. Then he sat up straight, bursting the bonds of the bedclothes, and roared, "Some bastard tried to kill me!"

Alec couldn't have hoped for a more useful reaction. As planned, he postponed "Why?"—which could lead to the need for a caution—and went straight to "Who?"

Rumford started spitting out names. Piper's shorthand pencil flicked across the page.

"What's going on in here?" The nurse's sharp voice made no impression on her patient, who continued to reel out his list. Alec moved to head her off. "Chief Inspector, I can't allow—"

"Is it dangerous for him to sit up?" he asked. "If not, I'll have to ask you to leave, Sister. This is important police business. You may recall that we're investigating a murder."

"But—"

"You might also consider that anything Mr. Rumford says in answer to our questions is confidential and for our ears only."

She bridled. "I'm sure nurses are every bit as good at keeping confidences as policemen," she snapped.

"Good." Behind him, he heard Rumford running down. He smiled at the nurse. "We're nearly done. Your patient isn't coughing. I think you'll find he's come to no harm."

"No thanks to you." She hovered in the doorway but didn't follow as he rejoined Piper.

Rumford had stopped. Alec decided against pressing him. However unpleasant, the man had been ill. Anything he said was unlikely to be admitted in evidence, in view of the lingering effects of morphine. "Why" could wait. It might never have to be asked, now that they had the names of those he believed had cause to wish him dead.

They left the Sister fussing over him.

"You handled her a treat, Chief. Interfering old witch."

"It's her job to take care of her patients, Ernie. You got everything down?"

"Got the lot," Piper said with satisfaction. "Mostly Beefeaters, I think, but would you believe—"

"Not here, Ernie," Alec said grimly. "I heard the first couple. We don't want to start any rumours. We'd better have them notify us when he's released. Someone might have another go at him."

16

Brenda and Fay were waiting at the Middle Tower, as promised, when Daisy stepped out of the motorcab. They greeted her with one anxious eye on the taximeter and when, on reading the amount, they each uttered a sigh of relief, so did Daisy. She didn't want to bankrupt them, but she did feel that having offered to pay, they should do so.

The matter of a tip caused a minor argument between the sisters, the cabbie listening in with a grin. When they gave him a shilling, he touched his hat and said it was a pleasure doing business with such generous young ladies. He drove off, still grinning.

"We gave him too much, didn't we?" said Fay.

"The usual is sixpence," said Daisy, "or even threepence for a short distance."

"That's what I said."

"But it was a long way," Brenda reminded her.

Forestalling further disagreement, Daisy said, "Never mind, he's happy."

"We're not."

"Everything is too dreadful."

"We were—"

"Don't you think you'd better wait till we're alone to tell me?"

They were passing through the arch, with a pair of Hotspurs and a pair of yeomen within earshot. Abashed, the girls fell silent.

As they crossed the moat, Fay started talking again, but Brenda said, "Not here. We'll only have to stop again at the Byward Tower."

"Let's go up to Ralegh's Walk."

"Good idea."

"The Tower's closed to the public."

"So no one will go up there."

"If you don't mind standing, Mrs. Fletcher?"

"Couldn't we sit on one of those benches on Tower Green? We'd see anyone who came near."

"Yes, but everyone would see us."

"And someone would be bound to come and join us."

"No one looks up at Ralegh's Walk."

"Except tourists and Rumford."

"And Rumford's in hospital."

"Right-oh," sighed Daisy. "As long as it doesn't start to rain." She had brought her umbrella, but she didn't fancy standing about on the wall under it. The clouds looked more and more threatening.

The sentries had been taken off the shortcut stairs. Fay, accustomed to going that way, turned under the arch without a second thought. Bracing herself to follow, Daisy made an effort to blank from her mind the vision of the red-cloaked figure lying on the flagstones Fay so heedlessly trod.

Just behind Daisy, as Brenda set foot on the bottom step of the long, steep flight, she uttered a wail. Daisy nearly jumped out of her skin.

"Fay, we shouldn't have come this way!"

Fay turned, face aghast. "I forgot!"

"So did I."

"How could we?"

"Poor Mr. Crabtree!"

"Too late now," said Daisy, recovering her sang-froid. "Go on, Fay."

Fay scampered up the rest of the flight. Daisy continued at her own pace, with Brenda crowding at her heels.

At the top, Brenda said, "Isn't it awful: I suppose in a few months—"

"Or a few weeks—"

"Or even a few days—"

"We'll go up and down without thinking of him."

This was one of those odd instances Daisy had noted before, and Alec had commented on, when the sisters almost seemed to be reading each other's minds. It was going to be interesting to see if the twins developed the same ability to finish each other's sentences.

"Sorry, Mrs. Fletcher," said Fay.

"It must be worse for you."

"Because you saw him."

"Let's not talk about it," Daisy said determinedly. "I hope you didn't bring me here to ask for details."

"Oh no!"

"We may be a bit gauche . . ."

"But we're not *totally* insensitive."

"I beg your pardon."

"What we want to tell you about is much worse."

"For us. Not for . . . for . . ."

"For society in general."

"And Mr. Crabtree in particular. Oh, botheration!"

This latter exclamation was caused by the sight

of a large man, a *very* large man, up on Ralegh's Walk, standing on tiptoe to peer over the parapet.

Daisy instantly recognized the suit, maroon-and-green check, one of Tom's less obtrusive. In fact, amid the glories of the yeomen's Tudor costume and the Hotspurs' red and white, it wouldn't be in the least conspicuous.

"It's Detective Sergeant Tring, my husband's right-hand man. You haven't met him?"

"No."

"We couldn't forget him if we had!"

"What on earth is he doing?"

"I've no idea. Perhaps he'll tell us."

She led the way up the steps. Tom turned and saw her. After a moment's startlement, he grinned so broadly, his moustache couldn't hide it. In fact, he seemed to be shaking with silent laughter, an impressive sight.

"Good morning, Mrs. Fletcher."

"Good morning, Tom."

"We weren't expecting you here today."

"I wasn't intending to come," Daisy retorted. "I was invited. Girls, Mr. Tring. Tom, this is Miss Brenda Carradine, and Miss Fay Carradine."

Brenda said, "How do you do?"

Fay was much too curious to bother with the formalities. "What on earth were you peering over the wall for, Mr. Tring?"

"Ah." He regarded the pair with bright, considering eyes. "That would be telling. On the other hand, maybe one of you young ladies could help me."

Fay's eyes widened. "With your investigation? I will. How?"

"You see, there's something I need to check just

the other side of this wall, and it's too high to see over properly."

"I don't think even all three of us could lift you," Brenda said dubiously.

"Bless your heart, I don't imagine you could. But I could lift one of you. You see, I've spread a newspaper. . . ." As he spoke, a sudden gust of wind threatened to fly away with his newspaper. One large hand clamped it in place. "So you wouldn't dirty your clothes. Now, suppose I was to brace my knee against the wall, like so." He raised a leg like a tree trunk and pressed his knee to the stone so that his thigh was horizontal. "Do you think you could climb up, Miss Fay, and look over?"

"Of course." She took his hand and placed one foot on the step formed by his leg.

"Brenda, hold her ankles!" Daisy ordered.

Balanced on high, Fay looked back down at them. "What am I to look for, Mr. Tring?"

"That there vine, miss, growing up t'other side of the wall. What I want to know is, is it sturdy enough up here for someone to use it to climb down?"

Fay leant against the wall and craned over the top.

"Be careful!" Brenda begged.

"No," said Fay. "That is, Mr. Tring, the stems aren't anywhere near strong enough to bear a climber. They're not much more than tendrils, for several feet down."

"That's what I thought." He helped her down. "Thank you very much, miss. I'm much obliged."

"Why do you need to know?"

"Ah," said Tom, "now that's what I can't tell you."

"Can't or won't?" asked Fay pertly.

"Didn't ought. The Chief Inspector'd have my guts for garters."

The girls hooted with laughter at this expression, which hadn't previously come their way. Tom smiled indulgently.

"I bet, if we weren't here, you'd tell Mrs. Fletcher," said Brenda.

"I might. Then again, I might not. And now I must be on my way. Does the Chief know you're here, Mrs. Fletcher?"

"No. I suppose you'll have to tell him."

"I might. Then again, I might not."

"Thanks, Tom, but it doesn't really matter. He's sure to find out one way or another."

Tom went off. At the bottom of the steps, he looked up, and the Carradine girls waved to him.

"Is he a friend of yours, Mrs. Fletcher?" Fay asked.

"A very good friend."

"But he's not . . . you know . . ."

"His suit!" Brenda giggled.

"He's a dear, and my son's godfather," Daisy said firmly. She didn't want to get involved in a protracted discussion. The gust that had tried to steal Tom's newspaper now proved to be the forerunner of a cold, persistent wind. "Now let's please get on with whatever it is you wanted to tell me, before I freeze to death."

"Oh dear, are you cold?"

"I can't think of anywhere both indoors and private."

"How about the Bloody Tower?"

"Won't it be locked?" asked Daisy.

"It might not be. There's not much in there worth pinching."

"Just Ralegh's *History,* and who'd want that?"

"People pay to go in just because the Little Princes were murdered there."

"Ghouls!"

As they talked, they moved along the wall towards the Bloody Tower. Brenda tried the door, and a moment later they entered the room where the princes were said to have been smothered by Sir James Tyrell, on the orders of Richard the Third. Though draughty, it was considerably warmer than out on the wall. If the ghosts of the boys were about, they didn't make themselves evident. Daisy wondered how long it would be before reports of a Yeoman Warder haunting the steps where Crabtree died started to circulate.

"Right-oh, tell me all."

Between the two of them, Daisy could practically see the scene at the King's House breakfast table that morning.

When Brenda and Fay went down to breakfast, their father and Mr. Webster were ensconced behind their newspapers, the *Morning Post* and the *Times*, respectively. Both grunted in response to the girls' greetings. They were undismayed. The general was always grumpy at breakfast, and Mr. Webster was always grumpy, full stop.

Having filled their plates at the buffet, they sat down.

"Is there anything about our murder in the paper, Daddy?" Fay asked.

"*Our* murder! It's not *our* murder."

"I'm afraid, sir," Webster remarked in his bland way, "in a sense it is ours. The Tower is your domain, the victim—"

"I won't have another word about it at the breakfast table!" the general shouted.

Miss Tebbit arrived in time to receive the full force of the shout, without having any notion what it was about. "I'm so sorry, Cousin Arthur," she said in a tremulous voice. "I didn't mean to . . . I'm not certain just what . . ."

"My dear cousin," said General Carradine irritably, "I beg your pardon for raising my voice. It was in no way your fault."

"Oh dear, I can't help feeling . . . I do apologize. . . ."

Webster, who had stood up to hold a chair for her, said in a soothing tone, "The general was disturbed by something I said, dear lady. Won't you sit down and let me get you something to eat?"

"Thank you so much, Mr. Webster. That's very kind of you. Just tea and toast, thank you. Weak tea, if it's not too much trouble, with just a dash of milk. Cousin Arthur, I hope—"

"My dear lady, I was just saying that I don't want to hear another word about . . . about the police investigation at the breakfast table."

"Oh dear, I'm sure I can't stop her. Mother is so very determined once she's made up her mind."

"But Aunt Alice never comes down to breakfast," Brenda pointed out.

"So Daddy may eat in peace," added Fay.

"Oh, but . . . well, she says she's been thinking," Miss Tebbit quavered, "and she's coming down this morning."

In tight-lipped silence, the general folded his newspaper, folded his napkin, and stood up. "I hope you'll excuse me, Cousin Myrtle. I have work to do."

He'd left his escape too late. Mrs. Tebbit marched into the room, took her place at the other end of the table, fixed him with a gimlet eye, and said, "Sit down, Arthur. I've been thinking."

Meekly, the general sat.

"It's plain as a pikestaff," the terrible old lady continued—the very word made her cousin wince— "that the murderer's intended target was Rumford. Dreadful man! I advise you to 'come clean,' Arthur, as the modern expression would have it, I believe would it not, Brenda?"

"Yes, Aunt Alice." She exchanged a glance with her sister, both agog and aghast.

"Otherwise you, Major General and Resident Governor of the Tower of London, will be impeding the law. Obstructing the police in the course of their duties is the technical term, I understand. I don't for a moment suppose that you potted the unfortunate Crabtree, but how will Mr. Fletcher ever find out who did if those who could set him right as to the intended victim remain silent? And if the murderer is not caught, I daresay he may have another go at Rumford, in which case you will have that man's death on your conscience. Extortionist though he be, I can hardly suppose—"

"And then Daddy made us leave the room," said Brenda.

"So we don't know if he agreed to come clean."

"Or if Aunt Alice will tell Mr. Fletcher if Daddy doesn't."

"Or what it is he has to come clean about!"

"We're not even sure if she thinks he killed Mr. Crabtree."

"Which he didn't, of course."

"But it does sound as if he did something he shouldn't have."

"And we don't know if it was something truly awful."

"Or just embarrassing if people found out."

"So we don't know what to do."

Two pairs of eyes as blue as Daisy's own fixed her with an appealing gaze.

"Oh dear," said Daisy. "You really don't have any idea what the secret might be?"

"We think it must have happened in Mesopotamia."

"Because he won't talk about Mesopotamia."

"Though he tells us stories about India and his other campaigns."

"Did Rumford serve in Mesopotamia? Under your father?"

"He was in the Service Corps."

"They went all over the place."

"Do you know," Daisy said thoughtfully, "I can't see why it much matters what Rumford was blackmailing General Carradine about. Alec doesn't really need to know. What he needs is evidence that Rumford is in fact a blackmailer. He might not be able to do anything about him, but at least he can be fairly certain that the murderer was after him, not Crabtree. With that, instead of trying to find out who might have had it in for Crabtree, he can concentrate on looking for evidence against Rumford's victims."

"Such as Daddy!" Fay wailed.

"It's only fair to tell you," said Daisy, "I'm pretty sure Alec already suspects your father—"

"Of murder?" Brenda gasped.

"No, no, of being blackmailed by Rumford."

"How did he find out?" Fay asked.

"He's a detective," Brenda pointed out. "That's his job."

Fay accepted this rationale, to Daisy's relief. She didn't want to admit to having passed on

Mrs. Tebbit's comment about Rumford making a nuisance of himself to the general.

"Mrs. Fletcher," Brenda went on, "I was just wondering, if Daddy owned up to Mr. Fletcher about Rumford before he was asked, would it count in his favour?"

"I expect so. Alec couldn't cross him off the list of suspects, but obviously he's bound to look with more favour on someone who's not trying to conceal a secret."

Brenda and Fay consulted each other with a glance.

"We'd better get back to the house quickly."

"Before Mr. Fletcher arrives."

"And tell Daddy to come clean."

"Aunt Alice was right."

"Will you come with us, Mrs. Fletcher?"

"Yes, please do."

"Daddy's more likely to take us seriously—"

"If you're there, too."

What Alec would say if he found her at the King's House didn't bear thinking of. But she couldn't let the girls down by backing out now, even if she wanted to, which, to be honest, she did not. She wasn't meddling, she assured herself. It was just that having reluctantly accepted the rôle of mentor to the Carradine sisters, she simply couldn't abandon them at such a critical moment.

As they left the Bloody Tower, she glanced out of the slit window overlooking Water Street. Opposite was Traitors' Gate, with St. Thomas's Tower above. Sir Patrick Heald was coming out from his lodgings in the tower. Daisy shivered. Somehow Traitors' Gate held more sinister significance than any other part of the Tower, even the site of the block. She felt that those who had arrived by water,

including Princess Elizabeth, must have found it
even more terrifying than being driven through the
streets and across the moat. What was it the young
Elizabeth had said to her gaolers? Poor Crabtree
had told her, in his flat voice:

" 'Oh Lord, I never thought to have come in
here as a prisoner. I pray you all, good friends and
fellows, bear me witness that I come in no trai-
tor. . . . ' "

Queen Mary had imprisoned her. How could anyone treat her own sister so? Daisy wondered, thinking of her own sister, Violet, as she watched Brenda
and Fay emerge onto Ralegh's Walk ahead of her,
their blond bobbed heads close together. Yet Elizabeth had long outlived Bloody Mary and gone on
to reign for glorious decades.

Outside, the sharp wind was blowing harder than
ever, but it was driving the clouds from the sky. In
the west, enough blue was visible to make a sailor a
pair of trousers. Perhaps the day would turn out
fine in the end.

Daisy remembered Fay bringing her up here
the day she and Melanie had come to lunch at
Mrs. Tebbit's invitation. She turned to Fay.

"You know, if you think your father ought to admit
to Alec that Rumford's blackmailing him, then it's
only fair for you to tell Alec that Rumford had his
eye on your smoking."

Fay stared at her in horror. "But he never asked
me for money!"

"You gave him cigarettes," said Brenda.

"Only because he. . . . Well, all right, he said things
like 'Does the Governor know you smoke?' And
I'd make a sort of joke of it and tell him I was giving it up so he could have my gaspers. And I'd give
him what was left of the packet. I didn't get nasty

little notes threatening to tell, or anything like that. He never even *said* he'd tell."

"Does that count as blackmail?" Brenda asked Daisy.

Daisy had been half-joking, but now she decided it was a serious matter. "I think so. It'd be practically impossible to prove, just your word against his, but if that's the way he works, if he doesn't write letters, just makes sly hints, then the more people willing to testify against him, the better. In any case, I do think you should tell Alec he extorted cigarettes from you. Even if it only gives him a hint as to Rumford's methods, it would be worth it."

"Worth it for Mr. Fletcher, but what about me?"

"You're not going to be arrested for smoking."

"No," said Brenda, "but she still doesn't want Daddy to know she smokes. The poor man already puts up with so much from us, it really would be the last straw. And on the whole, he's actually quite a decent old stick."

"I expect I could arrange for you to talk to Alec without your father present."

"I knew it was a good idea to ask you to come," said Brenda.

They went on down the steps from the wall and round the corner to Tower Green. Just before they reached the King's House sentry, Fay glanced back.

"Oh bother! Here comes Sir Patrick."

"Oh no! We won't be able to talk to Daddy."

"He may be going somewhere else," Daisy suggested. She looked round, prepared to greet the Keeper of the Regalia should she find him close at their heels. He was still some distance behind them, coming slowly along the wall, having obviously taken the long way round rather than ascend the fatal steps.

"There isn't anywhere else for him to go."

"Not that he'd consider worthy of his attention."

"You don't like him?"

"He's smarmy," said Fay decidedly.

"But he's a knighted general and a member of the King's Household," Daisy reminded her, "and very well dressed."

"I don't care, he's smarmy."

"Mr. Tring is much nicer," said Brenda, quicker than her sister to grasp Daisy's point. "Bother, I suppose we can't very well go in and close the door in his face."

"Can't we, Mrs. Fletcher?" Fay appealed.

"Certainly not, however smarmy he is. It would be a direct snub. He's given you no cause for that, and your father has to work with him, remember. Turn round and smile politely."

So all three turned, smiled politely, and said "Good morning."

Sir Patrick looked unwell. His usually rosy face was pale, with patches of hectic red on the cheekbones and dark smudges beneath his eyes, as if he'd slept badly. Even generals were entitled to be upset by the proximity of murder, Daisy thought, trying to be charitable. After all, some generals managed to stay far away from the slaughter at the front lines.

"Good morning, ladies," he said with a smile as unconvincing as theirs. "Do you happen to know whether the Resident Governor is available?"

"We've been out, Sir Patrick."

"So we don't know what our father is doing just now."

"Won't you come in?" invited Brenda, managing to sound gracious. "We'll ask if he's free to see you."

She rang the doorbell as they entered. The maid who answered its summons was sent to find out if the master would see Sir Patrick. Awaiting her return, they stood awkwardly in the hall, exchanging remarks about the weather. Daisy thought the girls could, without discourtesy, excuse themselves to go upstairs and doff their coats, taking her with them, but she couldn't very well prompt them.

And when the maid returned to show Sir Patrick up to the study, she found Brenda and Fay determined to go with him. As he followed the maid, they followed him, and Daisy followed them.

Fay whispered an explanation: "We don't want to give Daddy a chance to say he hasn't time to talk to us."

Daisy nearly pointed out that Sir Patrick might have private business to discuss, but if she was going to attend their confrontation with their father, she was in no position to throw stones.

Actually, she wasn't at all sure that she wanted to be present when the girls advised the general to confess to having committed some blackmailable misdeed. Carradine was liable to be not only embarrassed but astounded by their effrontery, and still more astounded by hers, especially given her relationship with the police. She had no business in the middle of what, if it occurred at all, should be a private family affair.

As if reading Daisy's mind as easily as her sister's, Fay linked her arm through Daisy's and squeezed it. "We're so glad you're backing us up," she murmured.

Too late to escape! Ah well, however furious, the

Resident Governor couldn't order the Yeoman Gaoler to take his axe and chop off her head. The question was, had the Resident Governor taken someone else's partizan and made a bungled attempt to chop off the Yeoman Gaoler's head?

17

General Carradine looked surprised at the mass invasion of his study, but not very. No doubt he was resigned to possessing two insubordinate daughters. To Daisy's surprise, though, he appeared to be relieved to see her. She couldn't imagine why.

Webster presented his usual impassive mask to the invaders. He'd probably look just the same if a troop of Prussian cavalry trotted up the stairs.

If anyone was made uneasy by the ladies crowding into the room, it was General Sir Patrick Heald. Daisy couldn't blame him. But he braced up and bit the bullet. "Carradine," he said, "I told you, did I not, that I must get away to Kent for my wife's do this evening? I find the gates are still locked. Is there to be no end to our incarceration? Have you no word on when we shall be released?"

"My dear fellow," said Carradine, "I'm as anxious to hear as you can possibly be. I've had the Constable on the telephone wanting to know when the public can be admitted again. At this moment, I'm waiting for Chief Inspector Fletcher to come and give me some answers, but whether he'll provide the answers we want, I can't tell you. It's all up to Scotland Yard, you know. You're very welcome to wait here with me until Mr. Fletcher brings the latest report."

Brenda and Fay exchanged a glance of dismay, but they needn't have worried.

Sir Patrick muttered something about letters to write. "You will let me know as soon as you have word?"

"Certainly, Sir Patrick. You'd better send a telegram to Lady Julia, however, to warn her you may be unavoidably delayed in town."

"I suppose I'd better. It really is most inconvenient."

Daisy waited until the door closed behind him before she said, "Alec can't actually prevent Sir Patrick's leaving if he insists, general."

"It won't hurt him to be put to some inconvenience for once in exchange for his free residence in town." Carradine sounded slightly malicious. He worked for *his* residence.

"He seems very anxious to go."

"Doesn't want to upset his wife. She's the one with the money. Keeps him firmly under her thumb, too, which is why he's so glad of his 'pied-à-terre,' as he insists on calling it. You're not to repeat that, girls," he added sternly.

Brenda and Fay stifled their giggles. "We won't, Daddy."

"We wanted to talk to you."

"Before Mr. Fletcher comes."

"About what Aunt Alice said this morning."

"There's no need for you to trouble your heads about that." Carradine frowned at Daisy. "You haven't been bothering Mrs. Fletcher on the subject, have you?"

"We needed advice."

"And she did offer to teach us modern etiquette."

The Governor sank his head in his hands. "You told her all about it."

"We don't *know* all about it, Daddy."

"Only what Aunt Alice said."

"Recollect, sir," said Webster, "even I don't know the subject of Rumford's unfortunate insinuations."

"No, that's true." Clutching at this straw, Carradine raised his head.

"But we think Aunt Alice is right."

"You should tell Mr. Fletcher."

"Not *everything*."

"Just that he was blackmailing you."

"And Mrs. Fletcher agrees."

"She says he probably doesn't need to know more than that."

"And if you tell—"

"The police are less likely to believe you murdered Crabtree," said Brenda encouragingly.

Carradine surged to his feet, leant on the desk with his fists, and roared, "I did not murder Crabtree!"

"Oh, we know that, Daddy."

Subsiding, the Governor looked at Daisy.

"I shan't tell Alec what the girls told me. He'd only object that it's nothing but hearsay. However, I should warn you that he already has a fair notion of Rumford's doings, and that you're one of his victims."

"If I admit to your husband that Rumford is blackmailing me, is it true he won't ask what about?"

"I can't guarantee anything," she admitted, "but I do know that the police abhor blackmailers almost as much as murderers, and they do their best to keep their revelations quiet."

"Yes, that's all very well, but if Rumford is arrested for extortion, what's to stop him blowing the gaff?"

"Daddy, did you do something truly awful in Mesopotamia?" Fay asked apprehensively.

"I don't know where you got that idea, my girl," Carradine said, his face grim, "and it's none of your business anyway. Off with the pair of you. I want to talk to Mrs. Fletcher."

For once, the girls obeyed without argument. As they left, Fay cast a look of appeal at Daisy.

"I'll come and find you in a little while," Daisy promised. Once again, she wished fervently that she hadn't come. What on earth could the Governor want to ask her that she hadn't already told him?

"Why the deuce did I invite Alice to come and live with us?" he groaned.

Neither Daisy nor Webster attempted to reply to this rhetorical question. Before the beleaguered general could say another word, the door opened again.

"Oh, sir, here's the Chief Detective. He wouldn't wait downstairs. . . ."

Alec walked in. His policeman's imperturbability failed to withstand the shock of seeing his wife. "Great Scott, what the deuce are you doing here, Daisy? I beg your pardon, sir. Good morning."

"Is it still morning? I feel as if I've aged several years since the sun rose. Good morning, Mr. Fletcher."

"You wanted a report, sir, but I'm afraid—"

"I know, I know, you want to ask some questions. Sit down, do. But before you start, I have something to tell you."

"I'm sure you'd prefer Daisy to leave."

"No, no, she already knows everything—everything I'm going to tell you, that is—thanks to those dashed girls of mine. The plain fact is, Rumford's been blackmailing me. If, as I assume to be the case, you have come to the conclusion that Crabtree was killed by mistake because he was taken for Rumford—"

"Why, exactly, do you assume that?"

"My elderly but shrewd cousin, Mrs. Tebbit, worked it out," said Carradine dryly. "I'd be very surprised if you hadn't. Mrs. Fletcher made the acquaintance of both men and no doubt passed on her equally shrewd judgement of their characters."

Alec's dark look forbade her commenting on Carradine's assumption that she had set him on the right track. She wondered whether she ought to take notes of his interview with the Resident Governor. Better not unless he asked her to.

"Before we get to your involvement, sir, I'd like to clear up one or two points. First, as I approached, a gentleman was hurrying away from your house. He ducked down the side steps—I was coming round the other way, from the hospital—and his hat hid his face, but I think it was Sir Patrick Heald?"

"I expect so. He was here just before you, wanting to know when he'd be permitted to leave the Tower. I'm surprised he didn't stop to ask you. He has some engagement in Kent this evening that he's anxious not to miss. May I send to tell him he's free to go?"

"No, I'd better talk to Sir Patrick before he goes. I don't want to have to chase after him down to the wilds of Kent, which would probably embarrass him, besides."

"I hope you'll see him next, then, or I'll have him coming round to pester me again, though I keep telling him it's not for me to decide."

"We'll see. Now, Mr. Webster was kind enough to provide a good deal of helpful information about the organisation of the Tower. Am I correct in thinking that Crabtree took orders only from you, sir, and from Mr. Webster acting in your name?"

"Yes, that's right." Carradine looked at Webster, who nodded. "You want to know whether either of us sent him on an errand that would have taken him to the steps in the middle of the night. I did not, and Jeremy has no authority to give orders except those passed on directly from me. The last time I saw the poor fellow was when he handed me the Keys, as usual, precisely at ten. Mrs. Fletcher was present and, I'm sure, will confirm that I gave him no instructions."

"Not that I recall," said Daisy. "I remember you were anxious about Brenda and Fay because they hadn't returned with me. Otherwise, I might have mentioned—" She stopped as Alec sent her a warning glance, then went on without mentioning what she hadn't mentioned. "But as it was, I didn't say anything about it." Alec would guess she was talking about the meeting with Rumford.

"You're certain?" Alec asked.

"Quite certain."

"Well," said the mystified Governor, "I have no idea what you didn't tell me, but I suppose you understand each other. Have you found out what time poor Crabtree died, Mr. Fletcher?"

"Midnight," intoned Webster. The others stared at him, and he went slightly pink. "Wasn't it, Chief Inspector? It's the only time that makes sense. Since you told us that Rumford is in the hospital—"

"Of course!" said Carradine. "Rumford and Dixon, the Chapel Clerk, take it in turns to pop down at midnight and check that all's well with the Byward watchman and in the Warders' Hall. That night must have been Rumford's turn."

"It was, sir," Webster confirmed. "I checked the schedule as soon as the Chief Inspector said Rumford was ill, and I also checked what time he was admitted to the hospital, which was shortly after the Keys were handed over. My theory is—"

"I see you've been doing my sleuthing for me, Mr. Webster," said Alec, torn between amusement and dismay. "You're right so far, and I may want to get back to you later for your theory, but at present I must get on with the subject of blackmail. Have you by any chance kept any of Rumford's demands, general?"

" 'Kept'? Oh, letters, you mean. He didn't write any."

"None? Not even the first time?"

"What need, when he lives so close? We see each other practically every day. Not that he was next door when I first came here. His first demand, couched as a request, was that whenever there might be a vacancy for any of the special positions, he should be considered. They all draw extra pay, you know, Chief Warder, Yeoman Gaoler, Raven Master, Chapel Clerk."

"Chapel Clerk!" Daisy exclaimed, drawing a heavy frown from Alec.

"Just so, Mrs. Fletcher. I couldn't in good conscience have made Rumford Chapel Clerk, so it's fortunate that Dixon is a healthy chap. Not that I should, in the normal way of things, have considered Rumford for any distinction. He's not at all popular among the men, you know. But when, not long after, the previous Yeoman Gaoler retired, he came to me privately and threatened to . . . er . . . to make public a certain matter if he didn't get the post." Carradine took out a silk handkerchief and mopped his forehead. "A matter that is no one's business but my own."

His loyal secretary sprang to the rescue. "I wonder now whether perhaps Rumford was responsible for Abercrombie's retirement. He was fit and not so very old, and he hadn't a great deal to look forward to, just going to live with a sister and her husband. I remember he seemed uneasy when he asked me for an appointment with you, sir."

"It wouldn't surprise me. That's water under the bridge. What I wonder is whether he'd have pulled up short and dropped the whole idea if I'd stood firm. I take it he had victims other than myself, Mr. Fletcher?"

"So we believe," Alec said cautiously. "My people are talking to some of the others now."

"He was damned—dashed—clever about it, you know. He never asked for more than I could easily afford, and as often as not, it was some favour he wanted, something that cost me nothing, such as giving guided tours to visitors who looked as if they might tip well." He noticed Daisy's nod. "Ah, Mrs. Fletcher, you guessed. No journalist could overlook my daughter's comment."

"Luckily, I'm just writing a story for travellers and would-be travellers, not looking for scandal."

"I'm afraid I'm pretty sure Rumford does skim something off the top before handing on gratuities to the chapel fund."

"But otherwise, he's an excellent guide," Daisy assured him.

This earned yet another repressive frown from

Alec, who said, "I'm surprised he hasn't used his . . . influence to get out of the midnight assignment."

"Oh no, darling, it gives him the perfect opportunity for snooping."

"Daisy!"

"Sorry! I shan't say another word."

"Insofar as regulations allow, he does pick and choose his duties," Carradine confirmed, "but he's never asked to avoid that one, so Mrs. Fletcher may be right."

"You're quite sure you've never received a written demand?"

"Never."

"Has he ever told you exactly what he knows?"

"Nothing but hints," Carradine said curtly.

"So he may, in fact, not know any particulars."

"Put about in the wrong quarters, hints would be bad enough. If he'd demanded enormous sums, I might have chanced it, but for a little here and there, the price of a bottle of scotch—it wasn't worth the risk, let alone murder."

"And this has been going on for years?"

"Four years. It looks as though he must suddenly have got greedy, doesn't it? Pushed someone too hard."

"It's possible." Alec was noncommittal. He stood up. "Thank you for your cooperation, sir. I hope I shan't have to ask for . . . more explicit candour, shall we say, but there will very likely be further questions."

"I have one for you." Carradine mopped his forehead again, but his tense shoulders had relaxed somewhat. "What am I to report to the Constable?"

Alec smiled. "You may tell him that the police are making definite progress. Coming, Daisy?"

It was less an enquiry than an order. With a

graceful apology to the Governor for barging in, Daisy meekly followed Alec out.

"I should have known better than to hope you would stay away," he said resignedly, "but just what do you think you're doing here?"

"I didn't *want* to come, darling."

"Pull the other one; it has bells on."

"I'm serious! I had no intention of coming, but—"

"It was our fault, Mr. Fletcher." Carradine's daughters appeared from nowhere.

"We telephoned."

"We were in despair."

"Mrs. Fletcher was our only hope."

"Aunt Alice made this tremendous pronouncement."

"She told our father to confess."

"We were afraid she might tell you he killed Mr. Crabtree."

"And then you'd arrest him."

"You haven't, have you?"

"No, I haven't. I must talk to Mrs. Tebbit, though. Do you know if she's available now?"

"I expect so."

"But we have something to tell you first."

"At least Fay does."

"Fay, I don't think it's really necessary," said Daisy. "After what the general has told Alec—"

"But I want to," said Fay.

"It might help," her sister said, supporting her. "You never know."

Alec sighed. "Very well, then. Can you tell me right here?"

Fay cast a look at the door of her father's study. "Oh no, not here."

"The aunts are in the Council Chamber."

"Would you mind coming into our sitting room?"

"It's a bit of a mess, but the chairs are quite comfy."

"You'll come too, won't you, Mrs. Fletcher?" Fay begged.

A large gramophone cabinet dominated the small sitting room. Decorated in bright, jazzy colours, the room was awash in gramophone records, magazines, scarves flung over the backs of chairs, and an open, half-eaten box of chocolates. Fay hastily removed a laddered stocking from one seat.

The window opened onto the balcony. Alec went over to look out. "A nice spot to sit in summer," he said.

"We're not allowed out."

"It's not safe."

"Daddy put his foot through."

"They patched it up."

"But some of the beams need replacing."

"The railing's rickety, too."

"It takes forever to get things done here."

"Daddy says there are dozens of layers of bureaucracy between him and the roofers."

"I wouldn't doubt it."

"Do sit down," Brenda invited.

"We're not supposed to have men in here."

"But it's all right—"

"Because you're a policeman—"

"And Mrs. Fletcher is here, too."

"Would you like coffee?"

"It must be just about time for elevenses."

"Not for me, thank you," Alec said with a touch of impatience.

"Later perhaps," said Daisy. Just visible from the corner of her eye, the box of chocs tantalized her. On her own strict instructions, Alec never bought her chocolates, because she tended to scoff the lot.

She'd never have a boyish figure to suit the mod-ish straight up and down look (surely the tide of fashion would bring back curves soon?), but there was no need to supply unnecessary temptation.

Brenda cleared a slew of magazines off the seat of the last of the three armchairs and sat down, and Fay perched on the arm. "Fire away," she said.

"I take it Rumford is our subject. Has he been pestering you, or someone you know of, other than the general?"

"Just me," Fay said regretfully, as though she'd have liked to present him with a long list of Rum-ford's victims. She told the tale of Rumford's extort-ing cigarettes. To Daisy's surprise, Alec seemed genuinely interested.

"He never asked for money?"

"Not a penny."

"Did you tell anyone other than your sister?"

"I mentioned it to Ray—Lieutenant Jardyne—just joking about it. He was furious, but I made him promise not to confront Mr. Rumford, be-cause it would only get back to Daddy."

"Ah." The way Alec uttered Tom Tring's favourite monosyllable told Daisy he thought the informa-tion might be useful.

Alec asked both girls a couple more questions without learning anything else, but he considered himself well repaid for giving Fay his time. Thank-ing them, he said, "Would you mind going to ask Mrs. Tebbit if she can see me now?"

"She'll be thrilled."

"You don't still think Daddy killed Mr. Crabtree, do you, Mr. Fletcher?"

"It's my job to keep an open mind, but I can tell you he's moved down a few places on my list."

"Oh, do you have a little list?"

"Like in the *Mikado*?"

" 'They'd none of them be missed,' " Fay carolled.

"But Daddy *would* be missed."

"Off you go, girls," said Daisy. "The sooner Alec clears up this case, the sooner you can stop worrying about your father."

They scampered out. Alec turned to Daisy to send her home as peremptorily as she had dismissed Brenda and Fay, but she got her word in first. "Darling, how lucky you didn't take my word for it that Fay had nothing useful to add."

"What do you mean?"

"Well, for a start, I saw you prick up your ears when they told you about the balcony."

"I did not prick up my ears!" he said, revolted.

"That's what it looked like to me, though I don't suppose they noticed. My guess is, you thought someone might have climbed down that way, but they'd hardly try it at the risk of going through the roof or knocking over the railing. Doesn't that mean the Governor couldn't have done it?"

"Probably, assuming the girls are telling the truth. It's easily checked."

"And I've worked out why you were interested in Rumford cadging cigarettes. If he'd bother to blackmail for such a minor return, it's more likely that the Governor was telling the truth about never being asked for more than he could easily afford. But perhaps Rumford suddenly got greedy. Perhaps he's decided he wants to retire."

Alec recalled Macleod telling him Rumford had rejected his advice to retire and move far away from the river for his health. Suppose he had actually intended merely to postpone retirement for a few months while he built up his nest egg. But did he have a nest egg? Piper had found no cash and no bankbooks. And if he'd spent his ill-gotten gains as he received them, what had he spent them on?

"That," Daisy was saying, "would explain why someone was driven to murder him now, not earlier in his iniquitous career."

"Yes, you're right. I should have considered that possibility."

"Never mind, you can consider it now. Now tell me about Lieutenant Jardyne."

"He's not on the list of blackmail victims." Alec's mind was still on the question of a nest egg, or he wouldn't have given so much away.

"You have a list? Darling, how helpful. Don't tell me Rumford gave it to you?"

"Not exactly. Or perhaps I should say not deliberately. I asked him who might want to kill him."

"Sneaky! Jardyne wasn't on the list?"

"No."

"But he has a motive of sorts, in protecting Fay from Rumford's clutches."

"I don't know that I'd call pocketing the odd packet of cigarettes 'clutches.'"

"But Jardyne might. He was out and about, earlier at least. He's a silly boy, and he has a crush on Fay and a precarious hold on his temper. Suppose he just intended to tell Rumford to stop victimizing her. Rumford would have been sure to make some nasty comment—he has a nasty tongue—so Jardyne lost his temper."

"And found a partizan?"

"Oh! Well," said Daisy optimistically, "you never know where you'll find one lying about."

Alec laughed. "However, he could hardly have had words with Rumford that night, as the man on the steps was Crabtree."

"Hmm, yes, that does rather spoil that particular theory, doesn't it?"

"Jardyne stays on my list, though. Young men in love have done stupider deeds to win a fair maiden's heart."

Fay Carradine came in with a message that Mrs. Tebbit would be delighted to see the Chief Inspector.

"Thank you. You're off home, Daisy?"

"Heavens no," said Daisy with an air of triumph. "Mrs. Tebbit is the lady of the house. I can't possibly leave without making my bow to her."

"Oh yes, Mrs. Fletcher, Aunt Alice wants to see you, too."

So Daisy followed Fay upstairs, and Alec, silently fuming, followed Daisy.

18

Fay chattered all the way up the stairs. As they entered the Council Chamber, Daisy turned back to Alec and whispered urgently, "I've just thought of something. Did you know—"

"My dear Mrs. Fletcher," Mrs. Tebbit interrupted, "how nice to see you *again*."

"Bother!" she whispered. "Tell you later." Raising her voice, she went on. "It's not exactly a visit of condolence, Mrs. Tebbit, but I felt I simply had to come and see how you're all doing. Not to mention thanking you for reviving me with tea and sympathy."

"What a terrible shock you had!" Miss Tebbit twittered. "A terrible shock for all of us."

"I still think brandy would have worked quicker," Mrs. Tebbit grumbled. "Mr. Fletcher, may I offer you a glass of something? Or are you not permitted to drink on duty?"

"Thank you, Mrs. Tebbit, but it's frowned upon. Especially at this time in the morning."

"Presumably you're allowed coffee. In any case,

I always have coffee at this hour, so you may please yourself. Brenda, you did order coffee and biscuits?"

"Of course, Aunt Alice. As always. You said one should not allow untoward events to interfere with one's regular habits or social obligations."

"Very true, my dear. Ah, here it is."

A maid brought in a tray. Alec waited impatiently while the social niceties ran their course. Seeing it would not delay matters significantly, he accepted a cup and a gingersnap.

As soon as the maid departed, he said, "I gather you have something to tell me, Mrs. Tebbit. No doubt you'd like to speak privately?"

"On the contrary. Secrecy breeds hypocrisy, and a host of other ills. Everything is better out in the open."

Brenda and Fay exchanged one of their looks.

"Not absolutely everything," Daisy protested, injecting—in Alec's view—a note of sanity into the proceedings. What was the alarming old woman up to?

"Not absolutely everything? Well, perhaps you're right, Mrs. Fletcher." She took a sip of coffee, an apparently innocent act, which had the effect, no doubt deliberate, of heightening the tension.

Miss Tebbit was obviously on tenterhooks. "Mother, what is it?" she pleaded.

Mrs. Tebbit ignored her. "Mr. Fletcher, am I correct in believing that man Rumford to be an extortionist?"

"So it would seem."

"Then I must inform you that I believe he is blackmailing Jeremy Webster."

"No, Mother, I'm sure you're mistaken!" Miss Tebbit's cheeks turned pink in agitated outrage. "Mr. Webster would never do anything wicked, anything that couldn't bear the light of day!"

"What's it to you, Myrtle?" enquired her mother with interest.

Alec decided she had started this hare more to tease her daughter than to enlighten the police. However, he couldn't ignore it.

Pinker than ever, Miss Tebbit cried, "I can't let you malign a good man. He's not even here to defend himself."

"You're defending him very nicely."

The girls looked befuddled, Daisy amused.

"Nonetheless," Alec said dryly, "I shall need to hear his own defence, if you have anything more than imagination to go on, ma'am."

"Naughty boy! As a matter of fact, I do. This is a strange old house, as you may have realized. Bear with me—I'm getting to the point. There are any number of small interconnected rooms, which, I gather, were once used to house prisoners of high status or full pockets, and their yeoman guards. Would you believe the Governor of the time used to charge them to dine with him?"

"Mrs. Tebbit, I—"

"I know, I know! You're a busy policeman with no time to listen to the maunderings of an old woman," said Mrs. Tebbit mournfully. "Well, then. I was exploring my cousin's interesting residence, shortly after we first came to live here, when I overheard voices in an adjoining room. I recognized Mr. Webster's voice at once. The other I was not able to identify at the time. However, at a later date, when I came across the Rumford man, I at once realized it was he whom I had heard."

"You're quite certain?"

"Oh yes. Most definitely a northerner, though

with the edges smoothed by rubbing shoulders with all and sundry in the army."

Alec glanced at Daisy, who looked up from scribbling in her notebook and nodded. Rumford's first words in the hospital had certainly been North-country.

He still thought Mrs. Tebbit had her own agenda, which had nothing to do with his, but that didn't mean she had nothing of interest to reveal, even if the decrepitude of the balcony ruled out Webster as murderer. "What was said?" he asked.

"Rumford said something about Mr. Webster being very interested in the Crown Jewels. Anyone would think, he said, that he was plotting how to pinch them."

"Jeremy wouldn't!" Miss Tebbit exclaimed.

"It was his duty to draw the Governor's attention to the danger, Rumford said," Mrs. Tebbit continued remorselessly. "But some piece of good fortune, such as unexpectedly finding a couple of pounds in his pocket, might distract him and make him forget what he ought to report."

"No!"

By now, Alec observed, Daisy had torn the top leaf from her notebook, folded it, printed "Mr. Webster" on the outside, and passed it to Brenda. Brenda read the name, mouthed "*Now?*" at Daisy, and slipped out of the room. Daisy was apparently going along with Mrs. Tebbit's plot. He might as well play his part, though he was pretty sure of what was coming next.

"And what did Mr. Webster say to that?" Alec asked the old lady.

"I didn't stay to listen," she said with unconvincing primness. "In my day, young ladies were taught not to eavesdrop."

"Mother!"

"But as I left, I couldn't help overhearing Mr. Webster's response. He said 'anyone' had better think again, because his only interest in the jewels was scholarly, as the Governor knew very well."

"There, I told you so, Mother. Jer—Mr. Webster would never do anything dishonourable."

" 'Jeremy,' is it? In my day, a young lady didn't address a gentleman by his Christian name unless they were betrothed. Or he was closely related," she added, rather spoiling the effect. "Has Mr. Webster asked you to marry him?"

"Oh no, Mother. And I've never addressed him as anything but Mr. Webster. It was just a slip of the tongue, because Cousin Arthur calls him Jeremy."

"And has he ever addressed you as Myrtle?"

"Oh no, Mother. He's far too much the gentleman."

"Gentleman, pah! He's a slowcoach, that's what he is."

"I expect the poor man's scared to death of you, Aunt Alice," said Fay.

"Slowcoach *and* coward," Mrs. Tebbit said with relish.

"He is not! I won't let you abuse Mr. Webster—"

"Miss Tebbit!" Webster burst into the room.

"Mr. Webster!"

"Myrtle!"

"Jeremy!"

"At last," said Mrs. Tebbit. "Just like the dénouement of a drawing room comedy. Faugh, I'm quite exhausted. Mrs. Fletcher, thank you for your assistance. Very quick-witted! You'll stay to luncheon, I trust? . . . Excellent. And Mr. Fletcher?"

Alec begged off. The charade had been amusing, and he had gained more evidence that Rumford was a blackmailer with modest demands. But he had several actual victims to interview, and it didn't seem necessary to ask Webster to confirm Mrs. Tebbit's story. Besides, if he interrupted the billing and cooing after all Mrs. Tebbit's efforts to bring the pair together, the formidable old lady would turn her tongue on him.

Brenda and Fay were whispering together, their amazed gazes fixed on the couple, now holding hands. Daisy and Mrs. Tebbit had their heads together, both with self-satisfied smiles. Matchmaking instincts prevailed over the maternal today, it seemed. As Alec left the Council Chamber, Daisy gave him a little wave and he waved back.

So much for romance; now back to blackmail and murder.

Leaving Daisy to lunch with her eccentric friends, Alec returned to the Guard House. While waiting for Tom and Piper, he made notes on his interviews with the Resident Governor and Fay, and what Mrs. Tebbit had overheard. He wondered briefly what it was that Daisy had remembered that she wanted to tell him. It was as likely to be about the babies as the investigation, and if the latter, it was probably one of her wild theories. He put it from his mind.

The others came in together.

"Any luck, Chief?" Tom asked.

"Carradine confessed that Rumford's been blackmailing him."

"Blimey, Chief," said Ernie, "and him a major general and Resident Governor of the Tower of London!"

"The higher the tower, the farther to fall," said Tom, "not to mention the greater the pickings for an extortionist."

"Did you find out what Rumford had on him, Chief?"

"No, and I told you not to ask people."

"I didn't, Chief. Just wondered if he happened to spill the beans."

" 'Into the valley of death,' " Tom quoted. "Maybe he gave the wrong order, like in *The Charge of the Light Brigade,* and nobody came back alive to tell on him."

"Then how'd Rumford find out, Sarge?"

"How did Tennyson find out about the Light Brigade? Some little sneak like Rumford was standing by and watching. In the Service Corps, he was. Here today and gone tomorrow."

Alec quashed the discussion. "I have no idea what Carradine did, only that it may have happened in Mesopotamia. It's not relevant, at least at present. But something interesting did emerge. I want to hear about your interviews before I go into that. Let's get yours out of the way first, Ernie. You took the ones living in the Outer Ward, didn't you? None of them could have killed Crabtree."

"That's right, Chief, assuming it's not possible to get over the inner wall. But they were all over the ruddy place today. Just about wore out the soles of my boots hunting 'em down."

"My fault. Rumours were flying, saying whoever attacked Crabtree must have been crazy and might attack anyone, so I told them to patrol the place."

"That's idiotic," Tom said austerely. "The yeomen, of all people, knew it should have been Rumford there."

"But the madman theory is always attractive, Tom,

suggesting as it does that none of the people one knows, who are all manifestly normal, did the deed."

"Ah." Tom sighed. "Human nature. But these chaps have been soldiers for a couple of decades and got to the top of the noncom heap. I'd've thought they'd be able to think straighter than that."

"Murder's different," said Piper. "Since we got here, I've heard that ten times if I've heard it once. They've all been in combat, most in the trenches, but soldiers killing soldiers in battle is one thing; cold-blooded murder's another."

"I don't think this was precisely cold-blooded," said Alec. "I think it was done in desperation. But let's get on with it. Ernie, you ran your quarry to earth in the end?"

Piper had taxed four yeomen with being victims of extortion. Once reassured that he wasn't going to ask for details of their misdeeds, three had sheepishly acknowledged the fact. One adamantly refused, but Piper was pretty certain he was lying.

"The three all said much the same," he reported. "They'd none of them received blackmail letters. Rumford just hinted at what he knew, saying just enough so they were certain he really did know. And he never asked for more than they would have spent on booze and smokes, never enough to put a dent in the housekeeping money. But he's been at it for years, here a bit, there a bit. I reckon it's added up to a nice spot of change over time. So why didn't I find anything in his house? No money, no fancy stuff . . ."

"Didn't look hard enough, laddie," said Tom.

"All right, you go search it, Sarge."

Alec shook his head. "Now he's come round, we'd have to ask his permission or get a search warrant, and I'm not prepared to do either. Not yet anyway. For all we know, he spent the take on booze and smokes, or the geegees, or giving chorus girls a good time on his day off. Tom?"

"I went first to see the Chapel Clerk, Dixon."

"Carradine was just telling me how relieved he was that Rumford didn't demand to be made Chapel Clerk," Alec said with a grin, "given his despicable character. I didn't mention the failings of the present occupant of the post."

"Ah. Well, I didn't ask what his failings are, but he came across Rumford during the War, too, like it seems the general must've done. Otherwise, it's just as the lad says, nothing in writing, never asks for more than can be afforded without real hardship. Dixon's been here at the Tower longer than Rumford. He says it wasn't but a month after Rumford arrived that the blackmail started."

"He didn't say, or you didn't get the impression, that recently Rumford's demanded more? Larger sums or more often?"

"No, Chief. I'm pretty sure it's been slow and steady right up to the present."

"No alibi?"

"Just his wife. They live in the Beauchamp Tower, right by the chapel. He never told her about the blackmail. He says he went as usual to lock up the chapel at ten o'clock and took the keys to the chaplain. She says he came in at quarter past, same as usual, and didn't go out again."

In the meantime, Piper had turned up the notes of Dixon's statement in the initial interviews with the Yeoman Warders. "That's exactly what he told DC Ross, Chief."

"I didn't trouble the Reverend, seeing that was too early to interest us. Seemed to me the Dixons were telling the truth."

"All right. The chaplain wasn't on Rumford's list, but I suppose we'd better have a word with him at some point, see if he has any light to shed on the business. He seems to have been overlooked. Who else, Tom?"

"One of the Hotspur sergeants, name of Willis. Denied everything, but he's got an alibi anyway. Playing snooker in the sergeants' mess. Three more sergeants as witnesses, his opponent and two on-lookers waiting for their turn at the table—and keeping an eye on the clock."

"Would they lie for him? Esprit de corps?"

"Yes, probably, but not in this case, I don't think. After all, Crabtree was one of them not so long ago. They all knew him. The corpse was one of the *corps,* as you might say."

"Great Scott, Tom, if you're going to take up bilingual punning, I'm looking for another right-hand man."

"Not speaking parley-voo, I doubt another chance'll ever come my way, Chief."

"Thank heaven. Whom else did you see?"

"Edgemoor. The Raven Master. No trouble with him. He told me Rumford heard him teaching bad language to Callum—that's the bird that got dismissed for conduct unbecoming a Tower raven. It was when he'd just been promoted to Raven Master. He thought it would be funny, and every-one would assume Callum just picked up the words around the place. He didn't realize it would get the raven chucked out for fear of upsetting visitors."

"But they wouldn't chuck Edgemoor himself out for that, would they?" asked Piper. "If they found out?"

"No, but he'd be busted back to ordinary Yeo-man Warder. Rumford took off him just a little less than the extra he got paid for being Raven Master. Clever bugger! But aside from the pay, Edgemoor got to be fond of the birds."

"Still, Sarge, he wouldn't be in enough trouble if Rumford told to make it worth killing him."

"Very true, laddie. He has a pretty good alibi anyway, doesn't he?"

"Yes, that's right. Up half the night nursing one of his birds, overheard by a neighbour."

"Did Edgemoor receive anything in writing from Rumford?" Alec asked.

"Never, Chief."

"That's the lot, then, Tom? . . . Good, we've established a pattern that holds for the Resident Governor also. Rumford's threats and demands have been verbal, not written, and he's been taking what his victims can afford without hardship. At least till now."

"Ah," said Tom. "Are you thinking the same thing I'm thinking, Chief?"

"I expect so. We'll get to that in a minute. Neither of you took notes of this lot of interviews?"

"You said not to, Chief," Piper reminded him, "so's not to make them nervous, because we wanted their cooperation."

"Quite right. But now, I want it all written down while it's fresh in our minds, before details get forgotten."

They set to work, Piper's pencil racing over the paper, Tom's more laborious. Alec decided to leave out all mention of Fay Carradine's venial sin, but he wrote down what Mrs. Tebbit had reported of Rumford's conversation with Jeremy Webster. Webster had routed the predatory Yeoman Gaoler. However, Alec thought with a frown, that didn't necessarily mean there was no basis for the accusation.

Should he alert Carradine? Awkward, especially as it looked as if the general was going to have Webster as his cousin by marriage. Better, perhaps, to mention the secretary's keen interest in the Crown Jewels to the Keeper of the Regalia. General Sir Patrick Heald was surely the best person—

"One thing I didn't mention, Chief," Tom said, interrupting Alec's thoughts, "Edgemoor said he's getting fed up with paying out. He reckons he's pretty secure in his position, seeing his mistake is long past and the ravens are thriving under his care. He was going to tell Rumford to go to hell next time he asked to be paid off. I told him Rumford wouldn't be coming round anymore. That's right, isn't it?"

"Yes, one way or another, we'll put an end to his racket, even if we can't arrest him. He hasn't yet told Rumford where to get off?"

"No. So I can't see it makes much difference far as we're concerned."

"Probably not. I'll think about it."

19

*P*iper finished his notes first. He sat lost in thought, no doubt trying to work out what conclusion Tom had drawn from Alec's words: "At least not till now." Ernie excelled at taking verbatim notes of interviews, his memory for detail was superlative, and he had a better feeling for numbers than either Alec or Tom. What he lacked was imagination, the ability to look at the mass of details and see where they led. He was getting better at it, though, willing to listen and learn. He was still young, in his mid-twenties. Alec thought that with experience he'd make a good detective and probably rise further in the ranks than Tom had ever aspired to.

With a satisfied sigh, Tom put the final full stop to his scrawl and looked up. "What's next, Chief?"

Alec smiled at him but turned to Ernie. "You've been in a brown study. What have you come up with?"

"It's the motive, Chief. All these little sums here and there—not enough for any one victim to kill for, you'd think. What we've heard about so far prob'ly adds up to a thousand quid or so over the years. A nice little bit to retire on, but even nicer if it was twice as much."

"According to what the doctor told the Chief, Rumford didn't want to retire," Tom pointed out, his tone encouraging.

"He could've meant not right then, Sarge, right when he got out of the hospital that time last winter, couldn't he? Maybe he decided to ask for more, so's he could double his money quickly and get out before anyone got so upset they'd do something about it. Only he got it wrong."

"Good thinking, Ernie," said Alec. "That's more or less my conclusion. To give credit where credit is due, Daisy came up with the idea first."

"Mrs. Fletcher's always right." Ernie was unstinting in his admiration for Daisy.

"Tom?"

"Sound reasonable to me."

"Only it leaves us with more questions. First, has he given notice, or whatever the yeomen do when they retire? Webster's the man to ask. But you'd think he or Carradine would have mentioned it, so, second, did Rumford miscalculate and ask for more than someone could manage, at least on the spot? Perhaps one of the victims needed time to collect the cash."

"Or said he did," Tom put in, "hoping for a chance to put Rumford out of the way before push came to shove, in a manner of speaking."

"Good point. Now it seems to me that if he increased his demands on all his victims, he'd vastly increase the chance that one of them would take exception and act. By all we've learnt so far, he's too shrewd to risk that."

Tom nodded. "More likely he'd go for a big sum from one, but—" He stopped as a knock on the door was followed by the entrance of an orderly with a tray of sandwiches and bottled beer.

"Compliments of the sergeants' mess, sir," he announced. He unloaded the tray and departed.

"Looks like you made a big hit there, Sarge," said Piper, regarding the mountain of food. "Even if Sergeant Willis denied everything."

"Guilt offering, laddie. But I won't say no."

"Let's just hope," said Alec, "that they coordinated with the yeomen. Otherwise, we may find ourselves consuming two lunches to avoid offending anyone."

" 'S all right with me," said Tom.

For a while, the only sounds were those of mastication, beer *glug-glugging* into tankards, and the odd comment: "Could do with more mustard." "Any ham and cheese left?" "A bit heavy-handed with the horseradish."

To this last remark, from Piper, Tom retorted, "Don't look a gift horseradish in the mouth, laddie."

Alec and Ernie groaned.

Tom was still working his way through the last beef with horseradish when Piper sat back with a replete sigh.

"Don't do 'emselves too badly, those Hotspurs, do they, Chief?"

"They have certainly done us well."

"Wonder who'll give us lunch tomorrow."

"With any luck, we shan't be here to find out."

"You think we're going to bag chummy today, Chief?" Tom dabbed at his moustache with one of the napkins thoughtfully provided by the sergeants' mess.

"I hope so. Unless we're on completely the wrong track, which is possible. I want you to go to the King's

House first to ask Mr. Webster whether Rumford has made any official move towards retirement, or even asked how to set the ball rolling, in the past few months. Then go and have a chat with the chaplain, general enquiries, with an emphasis on his views about the people Rumford named, especially his clerk, of course. If he balks at gossiping, tell him. . . . Well, you know how to go about it."

"Don't worry, I'll keep him happy, Chief."

"Then make a tour of the inner wall. I want to know what, if any, possibility there may be of climbing over surreptitiously, in both directions, though from inside is most important. There are plenty of nooks and crannies in the Inner Ward where a man could hide until midnight, but if we're looking for someone who lives in the Outer Ward, he got out without being seen by any sentry."

"Right, Chief."

"You'd better take a yeoman with you. The Raven Master, perhaps. He seems to have taken to you, and he probably knows the place as well as anyone."

"Yes, but having been blackmailed, he might not be too keen on helping catch the man who tried to do Rumford in."

"Remind him it was Crabtree who was actually murdered. I'll leave it to you to choose the best man for the job, though. Ernie, you'll come with me to have a word with the rest of the people Rumford thinks would want to kill him. I want a record of these interviews."

They left the Guard House, Tom going off towards the King's House, Alec and Piper in the opposite direction.

As they went up the steps to the Parade Ground, Alec wondered whether he ought to have another

word with Lieutenant Jardyne. He had told Daisy
the youth was out of the picture, since he could
hardly have quarrelled with Crabtree while under
the impression he was quarrelling with Rumford
over Fay's cigarettes. But a fiery young man in love
was not a rational being. Suppose he had waited in
the fog for Rumford, brooding over his grievances
and Fay's wrongs, eager to prove his gallantry to
the girl who disdained him. Drinking, perhaps? In
the heat of the moment, might he not have attacked without waiting to quarrel first?

Against that were the cold, clammy fog, which
even with the aid of alcohol would have made it
difficult to keep his anger white-hot, and the partizan.

Damn that partizan, Alec thought. The pathologist agreed with Macleod that Crabtree had died
of a broken neck before the weapon transfixed
him. If the murderer had not gilded the lily, the
death would almost certainly have passed as an accident.

"Why the partizan?" he demanded of Piper.

"That pike thing, Chief? To make it look like a
Beefeater did it?"

"Yeoman. So we've been assuming. Or a yeoman
wanted to make us think someone else was trying
to cast suspicion their way. However you look at it,
it doesn't work, and you'd think that must be obvious to anyone not completely naïve."

"I s'pose so."

"So why the partizan?"

"To make sure he was dead?" Piper hazarded.

"That's the obvious answer. But what a risky way
to do it! Because of the angle, we can be almost
certain it was thrown from the top of the steps, a
difficult shot even if he had been able to see clearly.

If Crabtree hadn't already been dead, it might well not have done the job. Not to mention a good chance of the damn unwieldy thing making a clatter that would bring a sentry to investigate."

"Why didn't he at least go down the steps and find out if the victim was dead?"

"Exactly."

"Too nervy?"

"Could be. Throwing the partizan was still a bloody stupid risk to take. That's what bothers me. It has the smell of improvisation, of acting on impulse, but all the rest was apparently well planned. The murderer knew just where Rumford was supposed to be and when. He patiently waited for a foggy night, not unusual at this time of year so close to the river. He got to the steps without being seen and he got clean away without being seen. And then the partizan. It's almost as if a different person suddenly took over."

"You don't think that could be it, Chief? Someone else threw it?"

"Conspiracy or chance? No, we'll have to keep the possibility in mind, but I consider it highly unlikely." Alec stopped at the foot of the steps to the Officers' Quarters. "I'd better have a word with Colonel Duggan before I start on his officers again. With any luck, he came home for lunch and hasn't gone back to his office yet. See if you can find out whether Captain Devereux and Lieutenant Jardyne are in the building, and if not, where they might be found."

"Jardyne, Chief? Rumford didn't give us his name."

"No, but I want to speak to him. You'll find out why."

They went in. An orderly ascertained that the

colonel was in his quarters and available to see Alec. Duggan's batman, awaiting Alec outside the flat, saluted smartly and opened the door.

The colonel's voice came from within. "Of course, the Chief Inspector hasn't come to arrest me, Teenie." His tone surprised Alec—not exasperated but tenderly reassuring. "I haven't done anything felonious, I promise you."

"I know you haven't, dearest, but what if he's made a mistake?"

"My love, whatever people may think, the police are not stupid, at least not those who reach Fletcher's rank. Least of all Fletcher himself."

So much for eavesdroppers hearing nothing but ill of themselves. Alec coughed.

"Here he is, Teenie. You can ask him for yourself."

Mrs. Duggan came to Alec with both hands held out. "Mr. Fletcher, Sidney had nothing to do with that poor man's death."

He took her hands. "I have no reason to suppose he did, Mrs. Duggan."

"There, what did I tell you?" Duggan chuckled, giving Alec a man-to-man wink. "The little woman would have it that you were coming with handcuffs to haul me off to prison."

Daisy would have hit the roof if Alec had called her "the little woman." But then, if she'd thought someone was coming to arrest him, she'd probably manage to smuggle him out of the country. At least Duggan was more affectionate than patronizing. To all appearances, as he had claimed, he hadn't married just for his bride's money.

"All I came for," said Alec, "is to advise the colonel that I'm going to be holding second interviews with a couple of Hotspur officers. I would politely say to ask your permission, sir, but it wouldn't be true."

Duggan frowned. "No, no, quite. You must see whom you will. But I'm not very clear at what point military law might insist on taking over. Court-martials and so on, you know. I'll have to consult my adjutant."

"I hope it won't come to that, but by all means find out your position."

"Which officers, Mr. Fletcher?" asked Mrs. Duggan apprehensively.

"Captain Devereux and Lieutenant Jardyne."

"Dev? Oh dear! Brenda will be so upset."

"I'm not about to arrest him, Mrs. Duggan."

"No, but. . . . If Dev seems rather brash and care-for-nobody, it's because he lost so many friends in the War, and several family members, I believe. You won't take offence at his manner, will you? He's not at all like that underneath."

The colonel muttered "Tosh" or "Pish," or something of the sort.

"I frequently have to deal with far worse manners than I've encountered from Captain Devereux," said Alec. "It's my job not to let such things influence me." He noted that Mrs. Duggan expressed no concern about Jardyne's interrogation.

Belatedly recalling her duties as a hostess, she offered Alec coffee.

"Thanks, but no. I must be on my way."

Duggan accompanied him to the door. "I appreciate your notifying me of which way you're looking. Don't need to tell you, I have absolute confidence in all my officers."

"Naturally. As I told Mrs. Duggan, I'm not on the point of arresting either of them."

"Good. Excellent." The colonel shook Alec's hand

heartily. "When this is all over, I hope you and Mrs. Fletcher will dine with us one evening. Delightful young lady."

"Isn't she?" Alec agreed, wondering whether Daisy had taken herself home to the twins after lunch or was lingering at the Tower to continue meddling in his investigation.

"Lieutenant Jardyne is in the bar, Chief," Piper greeted him. In a low voice, he added, "Two cocktails before lunch, wine with, and several brandies since."

"Good work. How did you get that out of them?"

"One of the mess orderlies is a Private Piper, born and bred in Norfolk, which is where my grandfather came from. So we reckon we're prob'ly some kind of cousins."

"I see." Alec knew perfectly well that Ernie's paternal grandfather had been a born and bred Cockney, a rag and bone man who prospered at his trade and rose to be a costermonger. "How nice to find a long-lost relative."

"Isn't it?" Ernie said straight-faced. "It helped that the lieutenant isn't too popular with the ranks. Apt to go off half-cocked, Cousin Bert says. I don't know what we're going to do with him. Proper sozzled, he is, according to Cousin Bert."

"*In vino veritas,* let's hope. I wonder if he's trying to drown a guilty conscience or merely his sorrows? As long as he's not under the table, we'll manage, but we'll have to get him out of there. One doesn't lightly walk into an officers' mess without an invitation."

"Not to worry, Chief. Cousin Bert's arranged it all. I'll just give him the nod, and we'll go into the orderly room, and a couple of the lieutenant's pals will bring him to us."

"Great Scott, Ernie, how. . . . No, I'd rather not know."

"Least said, soonest mended," said DC Piper smugly, and went to give Private Piper the nod.

A couple of white-jacketed orderlies, forewarned by Cousin Bert, cleared out of their room. It resembled a butler's pantry, with a deal table at which they had been polishing silver and glassware.

Alec had no sooner seated himself than three young Hotspurs entered the room, two hauling between them a drunkenly protesting third. Piper had a chair ready. He pushed it in behind Jardyne's knees so that he involuntarily sat down.

"I say, fellows . . ." he mumbled.

The others guffawed. Alec had met both but couldn't bring to mind their names, one Guards lieutenant being very like another.

The shorter of the two patted Jardyne on the shoulder. "You should be glad she's not here," he said severely. "You wouldn't really want her to see you in this state. All present and correct, Chief Inspector."

The pair saluted and departed.

"Coffee," Alec said to Piper. "Black."

On the sideboard was a coffeepot keeping warm over a spirit lamp. While Piper found a cup and poured, Alec regarded Jardyne in silence.

The lieutenant shifted uneasily, then said in a belligerent voice, "You're the 'tective. Talked t'you yes'day. Where's Fay? Fellows said Fay's here."

"I'm afraid the fellows misunderstood. I want to talk to you about Miss Fay."

Jardyne shook his head, and once started, he seemed unable to stop shaking it. "Mustn't bandy 'bout lady's name in mess. Damn bad form. She doesn' love me."

Piper set the cup of coffee in front of him. His

head stopped moving as he reached for it hungrily and took a gulp. He almost spat it out.

"Coffee! Ordered brandy!"

"You've had enough," Alec said briskly. "More than enough. Drink the coffee and let's see if we can get some sense out of you."

Sullen but obedient, Jardyne drank. Piper refilled the cup, then sat down with his notebook at the ready.

"Tell me again about the night you and Captain Devereux escorted Miss Brenda Carradine and Miss Fay Carradine home to the King's House from here."

"Foggy."

"That's right." Alec switched to an encouraging tone.

"Colonel didn' want the girls t'walk alone, 'cause of fog. Brenda took Dev's arm, but Fay wou'n't take mine. Girls!"

Alec was amazed that Fay had had so much sense. "You left them at their front door. What next?"

"Went for a walk. A'ready told you." He sipped the fresh coffee. "Dunno what Dev did."

"Where did you walk, Lieutenant?"

"Ri' round the bloody walls. Some of it you can walk on top of the walls."

"Starting from the King's House, which direction did you take?"

Jardyne blinked as if he couldn't work out the answer. He took a deep swig of coffee. "Round . . . round the Green? Opp'site way from Captain Dev'reux. Past the scaffold site. Behin' the chapel. Behin'—"

"All right. So you went all the way round and back to the King's House."

The head shaking started again, but this time he managed to stop it. "No. No use. What's the good of throwing gravel at a girl's window if she won't talk to you when she looks out?"

"Where did you end your walk, then?"

"Mess. Here. Officers' Quarters. Went to bed."

Alec glanced at Piper, who nodded. It was the same story Jardyne had told yesterday.

"What time did you get in?"

"No idea. Didn't look." A moment's hard thought produced "After ten. Must've been 'cause the girls watched that Keys business."

"While you were out, did you see anyone?"

"No. Dark. Foggy."

"Miss Fay—"

"Damn it, don't want to talk about her!"

"Miss Fay," Alec persisted, "told you about some dealings she had with the Yeoman Gaoler, Rumford."

Jardyne scowled. "Told her I'd take care of the sod. She wouldn't let me. Said Rumford'd go straight to the general, and if she wanted him to know, she'd tell him herself."

"But with Rumford dead, he couldn't tell tales. White knight slays dragon. Maiden is duly grateful."

"No! Over a few cigarettes? You must be out of your mind!"

"After a few drinks—"

"I'd been drinking cocoa, devil take it! Oooh," Jardyne groaned, turning greenish, "I think I'm going to be sick."

Piper was very prompt with a nice silver soup tureen emblazoned with the emblem of the Hotspur Guards.

Once the worst was over, Alec let the lieutenant go.

"Cigarettes and cocoa," said Piper, "the very

thought of 'em was too much for him. I don't think
he did it, do you?"

"No, I'm inclined to think not. I don't believe
the young idiot would attack without warning, and
he'd only to say a word or two to Crabtree to know
he'd got the wrong man. Where's Devereux?"

"Supposed to be over at the barracks, doing
something military. D'you want to go over there,
Chief, or send for him to come here?"

"We'd better not keep your 'cousin Bert' from
his silver polishing any longer. I leave you to apologize for the tureen."

"Chief!"

"I dare say anyone working in a mess bar has
similar messes to deal with not infrequently. Come
after me when the family reunion is over. You'll
find me if you don't catch up before I get to the
barracks."

20

*A*lec went out. The morning's breeze had cleared the sky of clouds and then dropped, leaving a beautiful afternoon, more like June than April. On the Parade Ground, a squad of scarlet-coated Guardsmen were performing intricate manoeuvres to the rat-a-tat of a drum and occasional shouts from a sergeant. An officer, also in dress uniform, was looking on, tapping with his swagger stick on his shining knee-boot to the rhythm of the drum.

Recognizing Captain Devereux, Alec walked slowly towards him, wondering if accosting him at such a time would be an irreparable breach of military etiquette. Too bad—he was a policeman, not a soldier. If he worried about the professional sensibilities of his suspects, he'd never be able to do his job.

Devereux turned towards him and raised a hand in greeting. "Good afternoon, Chief Inspector. Come to grill me, or merely to admire my company?"

"A bit of each, Captain."

"We're practising for Trooping the Colour. These old ceremonies have a life of their own. You'd think the late 'Great' War would have put paid to anything but the most practical training for the troops, wouldn't you? But spectacle and patriotic fervour go hand in hand, so we put on our red coats and shakos and march about in fancy dress like circus performers. Shall we go in? Carry on, sergeant!"

Piper joined them as they went into the barracks. Devereux stuck his head into the staff office and informed the adjutant that he was "assisting the police with their enquiries," then led them to a small room with several well-worn easy chairs and a drinks cabinet.

"Officers' withdrawing room," he said with his usual sardonic inflection. "Have a seat. Coffee? Smoke?" He took out a slim gold cigarette case stamped with the regimental arms. Snapping it open to display a neat rank of Sobranies, he offered it to Alec.

"Thanks, but I'm a pipe man." He made no move to take out his pipe.

The cigarettes were next offered to Piper, who refused with regret. They were several cuts above his usual Woodbines, but he dutifully followed Alec's lead.

"Coffee would be welcome," said Alec, relenting as Devereux lit his own cigarette and drew deeply.

A perfect smoke ring emerged from the captain's lips as he rang a bell by the fireplace. An orderly appeared, disappeared, then reappeared with coffee. Sipping it and comparing it with Scotland Yard coffee, Alec reflected that the Hotspur officers really didn't do themselves too badly.

He got down to business. "Tell me again about the night of the murder, that foggy night."

"Am I correct in supposing that this second interview means I'm not merely a possible witness but a definite suspect?" Devereux showed no sign of anxiety.

"Not necessarily, sir. We find people often remember details in a second telling that were forgotten or not realized first time round."

"Come off it, Chief Inspector. 'Sirring' me only makes me the more certain you believe you have reason for suspicion. The more so because, if I may be crass, your wife's father outranked mine, a mere baron of a comparatively recent creation. There's some sort of distant connection, though, and I knew Mrs. Fletcher's brother."

Alec was always amazed at how the aristocracy were interconnected. "Let's not go into that, if you please," he said, but he left off the *sir.* "You escorted the Carradine young ladies to their front door, and then . . ."

"I returned to the colonel's quarters to finish my cocoa. I have a fondness for the colonel's lady, which, knowing her, you will not misinterpret. Since Mrs. Duggan wishes her husband's officers to drink cocoa at bedtime, I set a heroic example for the younger gentlemen to follow. It's excellent cocoa, made with the best milk," he added reflectively.

Piper frowned, apparently feeling the captain was not taking his interrogation in the proper spirit.

Remembering Mrs. Duggan's support of Devereux, Alec summoned all his patience. "And after the cocoa?"

"I reported to the Guard House. That should have been at eleven, but you can ask Captain Burney at what time I relieved him. Not more than a minute or two after the hour, or he'd have let me know about it. I went straight to bed. The sergeant on duty deals with the changing of the guard every two hours. More often than not, the officer of the watch sleeps through the night."

"But not you."

With a sudden ferocity quite unlike his usual flippant manner, Devereux snapped, "Sentries need to be kept on their toes."

Somewhere in his past, men had died because of a somnolent sentry, Alec guessed. "So?" was all he said.

"So when I'm on duty I go out twice, sometimes three times a night in between the changes of the guard. I told you, I think, that the cot is damn uncomfortable. That combined with the racket of men tramping in and out wakes me. It's not difficult to stay awake for half an hour. Then I go out just when they've settled down, well before they start smartening up for the arrival of the sergeant with reliefs. I don't take note of what time I go out, but it's not normally as early as midnight. For one thing, the Yeomen Warders are still about and, being ex-army sergeants, would happily report any sentry drowsing at his post."

"You don't use the stairs where Crabtree was killed? It would seem the quickest way between the sentry at the King's House and those at the gate beneath the Bloody Tower."

"To tell the truth, I don't usually go to the King's House. It's out of the way, and it's really more of a ceremonial post than a serious lookout. As you may have gathered, I haven't much time for pomp and circumstance. I must have passed quite close to where Crabtree lay, but I had no reason to look in that direction. I'm sorry I didn't, or I might have spared Mrs. Fletcher the unpleasant discovery."

"How many times did you pass the arch to the steps without glancing in that direction?" Alec asked.

"Only once, as a matter of fact. It was such a foul night, I went out only once. I gather the fog cleared later, but I didn't go and look. I leave the Guard House by a back door, go up between it and the White Tower to the barracks, then round by the mess, the Armoury, out into Water Street, back under the Bloody Tower to the Inner Ward, and in through the front entrance. So as I came up the slope, my attention would have been directed at the sentries in front of the Guard House, the opposite direction from those steps."

Alec didn't have to check his plan of the Tower to realize the truth of this assertion. Devereux's story was reasonable, which didn't prove it was true.

"Tell me about Rumford."

"Rumford! The Yeoman Gaoler? What's he got to do with it?"

"Come now, captain, you're not a beef-witted Hyde Park soldier, and I'm not a beef-witted village bobby."

"Sorry." His wry grin was disarming. "I take it you're working on the theory that Crabtree was killed mistakenly, in lieu of Rumford."

"In the light of what we have learnt, it seems probable."

"And since you're asking me about him, I take it you're aware that I have had dealings with the fellow."

" 'Dealings' is one way to describe it, certainly."

Devereux sighed. "All right, he was blackmailing me. I was not alone, I believe. A thoroughly nasty piece of work is our Yeoman Gaoler. But, even as you and I, Chief Inspector, are not beef-witted. I'd be the last to say there are no stupid officers in the Guards, but I doubt there are many—if any—stupid sergeant majors in the whole British Army."

"In what way did this particular sergeant major demonstrate his cleverness?"

"By never demanding more than I can easily afford."

"He didn't suddenly, recently, ask for a large sum?"

"No. Not from me. What is more, he has never attempted to touch me when the battalion is not on garrison duty here at the Tower. I receive a more than adequate allowance from my father, and the War cured me of any interest in the accumulation of *things*."

Alec thought of the expensive cigarette case, and the expensive cigarettes inside it. He made no comment, leaving an expectant silence waiting to be filled.

After a few moments, Devereux duly filled it. "I should make it plain that the peccadillo Rumford found out about was not a criminal offence, nor anything that would get me cashiered. I did something stupid—beef-witted, if you like—in France, immediately after the Armistice. It would be of interest only to my family. I rather think my father would take it in his stride, but it would severely distress my mother, and to me, her peace of mind is worth paying for."

"I would appreciate more information, captain." Alec put on his best stolid, impassive policeman show. "At the very least, it could help us round out the picture of Rumford's modus operandi. Anything you choose to tell us will remain confidential unless it's needed in a court case, in which case Rumford is liable to make it public anyway."

"Who are you trying to nail, Rumford or the murderer?"

"My job is to nail the murderer, the person who thought he was killing Rumford. I rather doubt Rumford will hang about to see if he has another shot at it. Since his leaving the Tower will put paid to his activities here, and, I trust, the fear of retaliation will prevent his taking them up again elsewhere, I'd say it's unlikely he'll be prosecuted. The police try to deal sensitively with cases of blackmail."

"Right-oh, then. I can't see how it'll help you, but you know your own business best, and Crabtree's killer shouldn't go free. Who knows whom he might go for next? So here's the sorry tale, for what it's worth." Devereux studied his fingernails.

To cover embarrassment—or lies? Alec wondered.

"Towards the end of the War," the captain continued, "I was billeted in the half-ruined château of a charming Frenchwoman. Having had no word of or from her husband since the first German assault on the Marne, she considered herself a widow. She was by no means the only one in what little was left of the village. We became . . . fond of each other. And in that momentary euphoria when the Armistice was declared, we were married. A civil ceremony such as they have in France." He cleared his throat, stubbed out his cigarette, and lit another.

"The husband came back?" Alec prompted.

"Her husband came back. The mayor who had 'married' us was very helpful, swore all records would be expunged. Of course, it was an embarrassment for him, too. . . . What I absolutely cannot fathom is how Rumford found out. I didn't tell anyone in the regiment. Our only witnesses were two friends of hers, local Frenchwomen. But there were troops marching in all directions all over the place, and I suppose the Service Corps was about, busy doing its level best to keep everyone supplied with left boots when what they needed were puttees."

"The Service Corps doubtless had dealings with local people. I imagine French villages are as much hotbeds of gossip as are English villages."

"In other words," Devereux said harshly, "I'm fooling myself believing Rumford's the only one who knows."

"Possibly. Probably. It's been my experience that once two people know a secret, it's no longer a secret."

"No one's said anything."

"So many soldiers coming home from the War with stories to tell. Names get forgotten, or garbled. If any of your acquaintances happen to have heard and remembered, they wouldn't dream of mentioning your . . . misfortune to you. And, fortunately, blackmailers are few and far between. If you hadn't happened to come into contact with Rumford, I doubt he'd have sought you out. He doesn't go in for putting pen to paper."

"Nothing in writing. Sometimes I wonder if it was all a bad dream. Sometimes the whole War seems like a bad dream. Six . . . nearly seven years ago! Surely no one's going to start talking about it now."

"Most likely not. Once I've had a word with Rumford, I'd be very surprised if he starts telling tales." Yet Alec had seen so many lives ruined by secrets and lies supposedly long buried. In vain, he told himself he was a copper, not a parson. It was none of his business to advise anyone of anything but the right to send for a lawyer. He blamed Daisy's influence, she who was always taking lame ducks under her wing, to coin a phrase. "But if it were to come out," he found himself saying, "would you rather Lady Devereux heard it from a stranger, or from you?"

The captain regarded him with a frown for a long moment. "I'll consider the matter," he said at last. With a return to his usual sardonic manner, he went on, "Now you've heard the pathetic tale, you can see why I'd rather it didn't become common knowledge. I don't exactly cut a heroic figure. In fact, I'd be the laughingstock of the regiment."

"I'd say it's highly unlikely we'll need to use it. I appreciate your frankness and cooperation, captain."

"And you believe I had nothing to do with the murder?"

"My belief is neither here nor there. We have to look at the evidence." Alec stood up. "I'm afraid we may well have more questions for you at a later date, but we'll let you go back to your marchers now. Thank you for your time."

"My time is the army's," Devereux said dryly. "Anything I can do to help, Chief Inspector, just let me know."

Alec and Piper left the room. Outside, Lieutenant Jardyne was standing opposite the door, shifting from foot to foot. Alec gave him an enquiring look.

Not meeting Alec's eyes, he mumbled, "Waiting for Captain Devereux. Ah, there you are, sir!" With obvious relief, he pushed forward past the policemen.

From Devereux, Jardyne received exactly the same raised-eyebrow look he had just had from Alec. Jardyne went on past him into the small room. Devereux shrugged his shoulders, raising his eyebrows at Alec with a "What's got into him?" expression. But he followed the young man and closed the door behind him.

Conspirators? Surely not!

Alec and Piper found their way out of the barracks. Emerging into bright sunlight, they stopped to watch the marching and countermarching. Time was kept by the tramp of booted feet now, the drummer giving only an occasional rat-tat.

"Sad story, the captain's," Piper commented.

"Yes."

"You reckon it's true, Chief, or is it a load of cod-swallop?"

"On the whole, I'm inclined to credit the French marriage. I'm not at all convinced he really expects his father to take it calmly if the story comes out. Whether Lord Devereux would be so furious as to cut off his allowance—well, that's pure speculation. I hope we shan't have to delve into his lordship's temperament!"

"Seems to me a bit far-fetched, paying out like that to keep his ma happy."

"I dare say there are a few discreditable details he didn't see fit to pass on to us—which would make his parents' reactions the more to be dreaded. What's more to the point, as he acknowledged eventually, the story would make him the laughingstock of the regiment. He's the sort who likes to deride, not to be derided."

"Aren't we all, Chief!"

"You're right, of course. In any case, you'll have to talk again to the sentries who were on duty when the captain made his inspection, to get a rough idea of the time."

"It's a pity no one saw him leave the Guard House."

"Yes, though even if he did his round long after midnight, it won't prove he didn't go out earlier and shove Crabtree down the steps. I'd say it would be out of character, though."

"It's got to be him, Chief. Unless we can work out how the Governor could've got out of his house, or Sarge finds a way over the wall, Devereux is the only one left with means, motive, and opportunity, and enough money to make it worth Rumford's while to make a push for a big final payment."

"If Tom finds a way over the wall, all bets are off. But remember, it's only a theory that Rumford suddenly asked for more, and if he did, that he went for a big sum from just one person. No one has admitted it. Methinks it's time we had a little chat with the Yeoman Gaoler."

21

*L*unch seemed to Daisy to go on forever. General Carradine was preoccupied. Fay and Brenda's babbling was more inane than ever. Webster and Miss Tebbit gazed into each other's eyes and ate nothing. Mrs. Tebbit, despite her earlier complacency at bringing the couple together, made acerbic comments on the idiocy of lovers, to which they were fortunately oblivious.

And all the time, Daisy had a nagging sense of something she ought to have told Alec, something she couldn't quite pin down, something that would change the shape of everything, or at least open new doors.

Doors?

The beginnings of enlightenment slipped away as Fay said, "Oh, Mrs. Fletcher, Mrs. Germond won't cancel the tennis party because of the mur—" She caught her father's kindling eye. "I mean because of what's happened, will she?"

Daisy wanted to reassure her, but in all honesty, she could not. Melanie was dismayed at the prospect of introducing to her friends the daughters of a man suspected of murder. On the other hand, rescinding invitations once issued was simply not done.

"I doubt she'll cancel it, but you must expect some delay. Once Alec has made an arrest. . . . Sorry, General!"

"Never mind," said Carradine gloomily. "It's on all our minds. Are we to expect an arrest anytime soon?"

"I'm afraid I can't tell you. That is, I don't know. It's not that Alec's forbidden me to say."

Mrs. Tebbit cackled. "A lot of good it does him forbidding you anything if you decide it ought to be done."

Much as Daisy would have liked to deny this statement, she could recall more than one occasion when she had gone against Alec's expressed wishes. Always for excellent reasons, of course, though he didn't always see it that way.

General Carradine didn't look as if he saw it that way, either. His view of her suitability as a model for his daughters was definitely not in the ascendent. But then, he had more than enough causes for disgruntlement, from the disruption to the demesne he ruled as Resident Governor to being suspected of murder, not to mention the revelation that he had a murky secret in his past.

Poor man! Daisy thought. Time to change the subject to something innocuous, but the only thing that sprang to mind was the weather, which had been done to death . . . had been exhausted on her first visit. She almost wished she'd stayed at home with the twins.

Twins—now there was a subject that might bore but could hardly offend. She started talking about a study of twins she had read recently, and how her babies were already so very alike in some ways and so different in others. Fay and Brenda and Mrs. Tebbit all turned out to be interested. Daisy found herself babbling on about her children like a second Cornelia.

Cornelia? Whence did that name pop into her head?

Oh yes, ancient Rome. Though Daisy's school had considered Latin too weighty for female minds, they had read tales of Rome and Greece. Cornelia was the mother of someone or other—the Gracchi brothers, that was it, who had done well in ancient Roman terms. Daisy wasn't sure whether they'd been twins. But Cornelia had spoken memorable words about them. . . .

And something niggled at Daisy's mind, insisting that she needed to know.

Ruthlessly, she broke into love's not-so-young dream. "Mr. Webster, you must have had a classical education, didn't you? Do you recall the story of Cornelia and her children? What was it she said about them?"

The frog who would a-wooing go blinked at her. "Cornelia?"

"The Gracchi?"

"Oh, that Cornelia! There are different versions, but it seems a visitor found her plainly dressed and asked where were her jewels."

"Thoroughly ill-bred," commented Mrs. Tebbit.

Ignoring the interruption, Webster continued. "Cornelia called her children to her and replied, '*Haec ornamenta sunt mea.*' "

" 'These are my jewels,' " Carradine translated, looking happier, whether because he understood the Latin or because he was reminded that his daughters really were rather nice girls on the whole.

"Too sweet!" said Brenda.

"Are we your jewels, Daddy?" Fay asked.

Daisy didn't hear his answer. She remembered what she had been about to tell Alec when Mrs. Tebbit had interrupted. Perhaps he already knew, but if he didn't—

"Don't you agree, Mrs. Fletcher?" asked Mrs. Tebbit.

"Sorry, I was woolgathering." Daisy returned to the conversation, wondering how soon she could politely get away.

She managed to escape without coffee and made straight for the Guard House, taking the shortcut steps in her haste. However, Alec wasn't there, nor Tom, nor Ernie Piper, and no one was certain exactly where they were.

Rather than wander about the Tower, just missing them at every turn, Daisy decided to go and sit on one of the benches at the top of Tower Green. From there, she'd have a good chance of spotting them wherever they went. The sun was warm, and she could do with a bit of peace and quiet to try to think. She might even come up with solutions to all the questions before she found Alec.

Outside the Guard House, she turned up the slope and ascended the wide, shallow steps where she had watched the salute to the Keys only two days ago. It seemed more like two weeks.

To her right, on the Parade Ground, Hotspurs in full dress uniforms were marching to and fro to the beat of a drum. To her left, on one of the benches she was aiming for, a man was sitting. She hoped it was no one she was acquainted with, but as she approached, she saw that it was Dr. Macleod, dressed in khakis except for his white coat. She couldn't very well ignore him.

"Beautiful afternoon," she said. "May I join you?"

"By all means, Mrs. Fletcher." He looked far from well, but he half-rose, tipped his cap, and summoned up a smile. "This is the sort of weather that makes me think I'd like to live somewhere where it's always warm."

"Really? I expect the army would post you to India if you asked, or Egypt."

"Not really. I'm too much a Scot at heart. Besides, I've got to get out of the army." His voice rose. "I can't stand it much longer!"

"Oh?" Daisy said cautiously.

"It's being around soldiers all the time. Do you know how many soldiers' arms and legs I've cut off? How many soldiers' bellies I've sewn up? How many soldiers I've watched die of gangrene? How can I forget when they're all around me all the time? I've got to get out!"

"You were in Flanders? My fiancé drove an ambulance there. He was with the FAU." As always on the rare occasions when she talked about Michael, she was on the defensive. Even seven years after the Armistice, people regarded conscientious objectors as cowards.

"Conshie, was he?" said Macleod. "The Friends' Ambulance Unit did marvellous work. Without them, many of our patients wouldn't have stood a chance. I wonder if I met him?"

"Michael Ramsay." Her heart still tried to skip a beat when she uttered his name. A corner of it would always be his, much as she loved Alec.

"Ramsay—yes, I knew him. A good chap. He

didn't make it, did he? I'm sorry. So many dead. So many dead! Look at them!" He waved his arm wildly at the drilling soldiers. "They go on marching, but they're all dead. They just don't know it yet. All it'll take is a squabble between politicians who never leave their comfortable clubs. They should be the ones in the front lines. I've got to get out!"

Though desperately sorry for him, Daisy was beginning to feel a trifle nervous. "What will you do when you leave the army?" she asked.

"I'm going to buy into a practice somewhere peaceful, somewhere that hasn't heard the sound of bugles in centuries." His voice was dreamy now. The rapid changes of mood were bewildering. "And now I have enough for one big stake, one final chance to escape."

"You're going to use your money to bet with? But you might lose everything."

"Not me. There are ways to hedge one's bets. One is not likely to win a large amount, though, which is why I have to start with a decent stake. At last I have it. The end is in sight."

His feverish intensity sounded hardly rational. Daisy could only hope he knew what he was talking about.

Absorbed in Macleod's dreams and nightmares and her own memories, she hadn't been watching for Alec. "Have you by any chance seen my husband?" she asked, glancing around.

"No, not today."

The Guards were still marching back and forth, passing through one another's ranks, wheeling and turning. Here and there, a Yeoman Warder patrolled with partizan in hand. The King's House could have been uninhabited, for all the signs of life it showed. From the house next door to the right, another yeoman emerged, staff in hand.

The Yeoman Gaoler, Daisy thought. That was his house. He must be out of hospital and ready to take up his duties, in spite of the threat of prosecution for blackmail hanging over him.

He stood there, his stance bearlike, with shoulders hunched, turning his head back and forth as if bewildered by the familiar scene.

"Are you sure Mr. Rumford is well enough to leave the hospital?" Daisy asked.

"Good Lord no!" Macleod jumped up. "I gave no order for his release."

The sudden movement caught Rumford's attention. He peered at them, and then set off at a lumbering run towards them, using his fearsome axe-topped pike to boost and balance his strides, like a mountaineer. As he ran, he roared out something incoherent.

Macleod took a couple of steps backwards, hands held out in front of him as if to calm the Yeoman Gaoler—or to ward off a blow. "Don't be a fool, man!" he shouted. "You're not well."

His obvious alarm infected Daisy. Feeling a bit silly, she got up and moved round onto the grass behind the bench.

Rumford rushed onward up the slope. He came close enough for Daisy to make out his slurred words: "You took it, you sodding son of a bitch! You had my keys!"

He made a wild swipe with the axe at the doctor, who wheeled round and fled. Turning the end of the wall, he started down the steps and out of Daisy's view, Rumford in hot pursuit.

Daisy screamed. "Help! Stop him! *Help!*"

The King's House sentry raced across Tower Green, jumped up on a bench standing against the wall, and aimed his rifle down the other side.

Daisy closed her eyes.

A shot rang out, immediately followed by two or three more.

When Alec and Piper left the barracks, they had turned right and walked along between the building and the marching soldiers.

"Who's next, Chief?" Piper asked.

"General Sir Patrick Heald." Alec acknowledged to himself that he had been postponing the Keeper of the Regalia. Though he was perfectly capable of dealing with chief constables and generals and earls and countesses, even an occasional marquis, he'd never before had to tackle a member of the Royal Household.

Putting off Sir Patrick had probably been a mistake. The man must be fuming by now over his evening engagement, for which he'd be late, if he didn't miss it altogether. On the other hand, the fact that he hadn't departed suggested he had a healthy respect for Scotland Yard, so perhaps the interview wouldn't be too bad.

"On Rumford's list, but outside the walls," said Piper. "So it's just to confirm Rumford's methods. Unless Mr. Tring's found a way to fly over the walls. Here he comes now."

DS Tring emerged from between the chapel and the end of the barracks, accompanied by a yeoman with a raven on his shoulder. Spotting Alec and Piper, he exchanged a few words with the Raven Master, then came towards them, leaving man and bird patiently waiting.

"Any luck, Chief?"

Quickly, Alec brought him up-to-date on Jardyne and Devereux. "And you?" he asked.

"Mr. Webster says Rumford *has* asked about retirement procedures but hasn't yet completed any of the formalities. The chaplain couldn't or wouldn't say anything helpful about his flock. He's certain sure Crabtree's death must somehow have been an accident. The walls—we haven't quite finished going round inside, but from what I've seen, anyplace with the slightest possibility—" He stopped, looking beyond Alec.

Alec turned. Devereux was approaching.

"Thought I'd better just come and tell you that young fool Jardyne begged me to assure you of his— Good God, what the deuce?"

Above the tramp of feet sounded a shrill scream. All three detectives swung round.

"It's Mrs. Fletcher!" Tom cried.

They all started running.

Daisy stood near the scaffold site, yelling for help. Past her ran a yeoman with a huge axe, chasing a man in a white coat down the steps.

Alec recognized Dr. Macleod even as he saw him stumble. He saw the gleaming axe rise and fall, saw the bright blood spurt, heard the rattle of rifle fire.

"Captain, go to my wife," he shouted. "Police! Hold your fire!"

22

*D*aisy had her eyes shut and her fingers in her ears. She had stopped screaming, but her own screams still echoed in her ears.

An urgent voice close beside her penetrated: "Mrs. Fletcher, it's Devereux. Your husband asked me to help you." She lowered her hands as the captain continued. "You can't see anything from here, but you needn't open your eyes. I'm taking you to the King's House."

She produced a sort of gulp, hoping he'd interpret it as thanks and consent. He put his arm around her waist and led her forward.

Their footsteps crunched on gravel, and then they were on grass again. Sure now that whatever had happened on the steps was out of sight, Daisy opened her eyes. The sun still shone down on the green and pigeons in iridescent spring finery bowed and cooed to one another under the sceptical gaze of a pair of ravens.

"I'm all right," she said. "I think."

He took his arm away but offered it for her to

lean on. After a couple of wobbly steps, she was grateful to accept.

By the time they reached the King's House, the front door was open. Fay and Brenda surged out.

"Mrs. Fletcher, you're pale as a ghost."

"What's going on?"

"Don't ask," said the captain grimly. "Take Mrs. Fletcher into the house, and don't bombard her with questions. She's had a ghastly shock. I must go and see what I can do to help the police."

"We thought we heard gunfire."

"Daddy's having fits."

"You will come back, won't you, Dev?"

"And tell us all about it?"

"No. The Chief Inspector will no doubt report to General Carradine." He turned on his heel and strode off before Daisy could thank him.

The girls supported her into the house, their solicitude expressed by their unprecedented silence. After the captain's command, they didn't dare ask the questions that were hovering on their lips, and they simply couldn't think of anything else to say. In no time, Daisy was once again reclining on a sofa, swathed in a rug, and being swamped with hot, sweet tea.

This time, she gladly accepted Mrs. Tebbit's prescription of a glass of brandy. It was midafternoon, not dawn, and she had had an even worse shock, she suspected, only she didn't want to think about it.

"I don't want to cause any difficulties," she said, her voice tremulous despite her effort to speak firmly, "but I'd like to go home."

"I don't think you should be alone," Miss Tebbit suggested with a questioning glance at her mother.

"Certainly not. But I do believe you'll feel better,

my dear Mrs. Fletcher, if you get clear away from this unhappy place. Myrtle, telephone Mrs. Germond at once and enquire whether she would be so kind as to go to the Fletchers' house and await Mrs. Fletcher's arrival."

Miss Tebbit scurried off and Mrs. Tebbit turned to the girls. "If Mrs. Germond is available, you two must go to your father and requisition—I believe that is the proper military term, though it sounds more like a noun than a verb to me—yes, you must requisition the motor-car."

"We will, Aunt Alice."

"And we'll go with you, Mrs. Fletcher."

"To keep you company on the way home."

"Unless you'd rather not."

"I will say this for Arthur: He's not mean about the use of the motor-car. Or his wine. Do have another brandy, my dear."

Sip by sip, the whole generous tot had disappeared. Daisy decided she felt much the better for it, but, recalling a certain disgraceful episode in her past, she didn't care to risk another. Though that had been whisky she'd drunk by mistake, and perhaps brandy. . . . No, better not.

A few minutes later, Miss Tebbit trotted back, looking flustered.

"Well?" her mother demanded. "Don't tell me Melanie Germond refused. She's a kind soul, even if her husband is a bank manager."

"So was Alec's father." Quite irrelevant, Daisy thought. It must be the brandy speaking. She'd never known Alec's father, but his mother certainly couldn't be described as a kind soul.

"I wonder if that's why I have in general a low opinion of bank managers' wives," said Mrs. Tebbit outrageously. "Come, Myrtle, what did she say?"

"Oh dear! Mrs. Prasad was taking tea with her when she was called to the telephone. She told her all about it—"

"*She? Her? It?*"

"Mrs. Germond asked me to hold the line while she told Mrs. Prasad about Mrs. Fletcher. And Mrs. Prasad insists on coming to fetch Mrs. Fletcher. I couldn't stop her, Mother."

"Ninny," Mrs. Tebbit said dispassionately. "Mrs. Prasad is a close friend of yours, is she not, Mrs. Fletcher?"

"Oh yes! Is she on her way? I must go out to the Middle Tower."

"In your condition? Most inadvisable. Brenda, Fay, you will go to your father and tell him I say he's to give instructions that Mrs. Prasad's motor-car is to be admitted to the Tower and to leave again with Mrs. Fletcher aboard."

A few minutes later, the front doorbell rang and a maid came in to announce that Detective Sergeant Tring would like a word with Mrs. Fletcher.

"Certainly not!" said Mrs. Tebbit. "How can he think to trouble you at such a time!"

"Oh, but I must see him." Daisy started to struggle up from the sofa. "I ought to have thought. . . . They'll need to know what I . . ." Her voice faded, but she knew she had to tell what she had seen and heard. Which meant thinking about it—

"Stay there," the old lady commanded. "If you must, you must. The sergeant may come in." The Tebbits sat up straighter and looked at the door with interest. When Tom's bulk appeared in the doorway, Mrs. Tebbit said firmly, "Sergeant, I will not have you bullying Mrs. Fletcher."

Brenda and Fay returned just in time to overhear her and intervene.

"It's all right, Aunt Alice," said Brenda.

"Mr. Tring is a friend of Mrs. Fletcher's," Fay explained.

"Will you tell us what's happening, Mr. Tring?"

"Please!"

"I'm afraid not, ladies. No doubt you'll find out in due course. I must speak to Mrs. Fletcher alone."

"Oh Tom!" Daisy said, holding out both hands, and she burst into tears.

He crossed the room with his swift, surprisingly light tread, engulfed her hands in his, and pressed them gently.

"You'd better stay here, then, I suppose," grumbled Mrs. Tebbit, levering herself out of her chair. She led the way out.

Tom checked that the door was shut, then pulled up a chair beside Daisy and handed her a handkerchief. Like Alec, he always carried a spare for weeping witnesses and sobbing suspects. "The Chief said to tell you he's sorry he can't come right now, but he's got his hands full."

"I'm sure he has." Daisy blew her nose. "I don't want to know—not yet—what happened after . . . after I closed my eyes, but I'll tell you what I can."

"Can't ask for more, Mrs. Fletcher." He took out his notebook.

"I was sitting on a bench there at the top of Tower Green with Dr. Macleod. He was talking quite wildly—I gathered he'd been having nightmares about doctoring in Flanders. He was desperate to escape from the army. I was so sorry for him, though he was a bit unnerving, too."

"Ah," said Tom inscrutably.

"He said he had put together a stake big enough for a winning bet to let him buy a practice. And there was something about hedging his bets. It was about then that I noticed Rumford coming out of his house. He looked around, seeming somehow confused, I thought. I don't know if he recognized the doctor at that distance, but anyway, he saw us and started up the slope towards us at a sort of clumsy jog-trot." Daisy tried to put off the bit she didn't want to remember. "So I suppose he must have recognized Dr. Macleod, or he would have walked, wouldn't he?"

"I dare say."

"He was carrying his . . . his axe. The ceremonial one, like the yeomen's partizans. And he was bellowing as he came. He looked like a bear, but he sounded more like a bull. When he got closer, I heard him shout. . . ." She frowned, trying to recall the exact words. "He shouted, 'You took it, you . . . something something. . . . You had my keys!' "

"Ah!" said Tom, this time with an air of enlightenment. Daisy was glad to have helped, though she hadn't the foggiest idea how. "Those are Rumford's exact words?"

"I think so. Except for the 'something something,' " Daisy said primly. The occasional *blast* might pass her lips, or even, under extreme stress, a *damn*, but she wasn't prepared to utter Rumford's expletives, even under the influence of brandy, even to Tom.

"Ah well, I expect we can do without them." His eyes twinkled and his moustache failed to hide his grin, but it was momentary. "Did you get the impression Macleod had been saving up bit by bit till he had enough for his stake?"

"Umm . . . not really. Everyone said he was a gambler, so I assumed he'd recently won a lot. It wasn't anything he said, more the way he said it, the excitement of a sudden win, not the reward of patience, if you see what I mean?"

"I think so. I'm afraid I have to ask you what came next."

Shutting her eyes only made the picture more vivid, so she opened them again. "Rumford swung at Dr. Macleod with the axe, and the doctor ran away. Rumford ran after him. I . . . I didn't see how I could stop him—"

"Thank God you didn't try!"

"So I just yelled for help for all I was worth. I saw the sentry, the one from the King's House, run across to the wall. After that, I stopped watching. I heard . . . he fired, didn't he?"

"Both he and the Guard House sentry."

"And?"

"They stopped Rumford in his tracks." Tom pocketed his notebook and took her hand. "It was too late for the doctor."

Daisy forced back tears. "Poor man. He was so unhappy, but so hopeful for the future."

"Mrs. Fletcher, I'm going to tell you something because I think it'll maybe make it a bit easier to come to terms with what's happened. I didn't ought to tell, and I'd appreciate it if you'd keep quiet about it."

"The Chief shall never know you told me, I promise. Or anyone else." He'd already helped alleviate the ghastliness by whetting her curiosity. "What is it?"

"Dr. Macleod was a morphia addict."

"Oh. Does that explain his extravagant manner?"

Tom nodded. "Most likely he started taking it to deaden the memories of the War, but the stuff doesn't help in the end, just makes the nightmares more vivid. And chances are he'd never have got off it. I've seen plenty of 'em, and when they're that far gone. . . . Well, maybe he'd've doubled his money and bought a practice, but whether it'd've done him any good is another matter."

"Oh, that *poor* man!"

"Very unfortunate. Only thing is, from what you've said, Mrs. Fletcher—and this is pure speculation, mind—"

"Such as the Chief constantly exhorts me to avoid?"

"Not quite that pure. I'd be pretty surprised, I own, if it didn't turn out to be true. What I reckon is, Dr. Macleod's sudden big stake and the proceeds of Rumford's blackmailing activities are one and the same pot of money."

And the more Daisy thought about it, the more it made a dreadful kind of sense. While Rumford lay helpless in the hospital, Macleod had had every opportunity to borrow his keys.

"We've been wondering where his takings went," Tom continued. "We've plenty of evidence that he was extorting money from a number of people, yet young Piper found nor hide nor hair of it when he searched the house, and he's a pretty good searcher, though I say it as him who trained him. So it looks to me like the doctor stole it."

"Yes, that would explain what Rumford meant. Macleod couldn't resist the temptation of easy access to his keys while he was in hospital."

"That's how I see it. The one thing that puzzles me is why the doctor would be sitting there in the sun chatting, in full view, while Rumford went into his house and discovered the theft. Wouldn't you think he'd've made himself scarce? I suppose, fuddled with the morphia, he might not've expected Rumford to put two and two together."

"Oh, I almost forgot. When Rumford came out of his house looking sort of bewildered, I asked the doctor whether he was really well enough to leave the hospital. And Macleod said he hadn't ordered his release."

"You're sure of that? Evidence, not speculation?" Tom took out his notebook again to write down their exact words, as near as Daisy could recall. "Thank you. This clears up that question nicely. I'd better be getting along to tell the Chief. You going to be all right, Mrs. Fletcher?"

"Yes, thank you, Tom. They're very kind to me here, and a friend is coming to fetch me, take me home. Alec can ring me up there if he needs to ask anything else. Oh, I've just thought—I'll have to meet Sakari at the Bloody Tower. The steps . . ."

"Not much I can do about the layout of the Tower, but if you can bring yourself to go down the shortcut steps, the others are all screened off. I could walk you down there if it'd help."

"You're a perfect dear, but I know the Chief needs you. I don't want to keep you waiting while I say my good-byes, and I really must say my good-byes properly this time. Especially as I don't think I'll ever want to come back to the Tower. When the twins are old enough, you'll have to do your godfatherly duty and bring them."

"I'll look forward to it." Tom patted her shoulder and went off.

Daisy powdered her nose. As she put on her hat, removed by Fay to allow her to lie back on the cushions, Fay and Brenda burst into the room.

"We were watching."

"From the stairs."

"Can't you tell us what's happened?"

"We're not allowed to leave the house."

"We'll find out soon anyway," Fay coaxed.

That was true. Perhaps Tom had refused to enlighten them simply to avoid the ensuing brouhaha. Why shouldn't she tell them, rather than let them learn from a servant?

Just in time, she remembered Fay's crush on Dr. Macleod. Someone else could break the news, she decided.

"Sorry, as Mr. Tring wouldn't, I'd better not."

They all went upstairs to the Council Chamber.

"So Rumford's the murderer," Mrs. Tebbit greeted them.

"Aunt Alice, how do you know?"

"Mrs. Fletcher wouldn't tell us!"

"While you two were sitting on the stairs, I went into your father's study and asked him. Naturally, he had been informed, over the telephone. I always knew he was a bad lot."

"And now he's killed the doctor," said Miss Tebbit, eyes wide with horror.

"Really, Myrtle, have you no tact?"

"Not Dr. Macleod?" Brenda exclaimed.

Fay said faintly, "Oh!" and sat down suddenly.

"Fiddlesticks!" said Mrs. Tebbit. "It's a shock, I don't doubt, but nothing will persuade me you had a genuine affection for the man."

Brenda sank on her knees at her sister's side, patting her hands, while Miss Tebbit fluttered about apologizing.

At that moment, the maid came in. Gazing at Fay as she addressed Mrs. Tebbit, she said, "Madam, there's a yeoman at the door says a lady's come in a motor to pick up Mrs. Fletcher. A foreign lady."

"Escape while you can," advised Mrs. Tebbit. "You mustn't keep Mrs. Prasad waiting."

Cravenly, Daisy obeyed. So once again she departed from the King's House without a proper leave-taking.

—————— 13 ——————

*T*he robust yeoman waiting for Daisy was clad in Tudor blouse and bonnet but carried no partizan. "Parkinson, madam," he introduced himself. "Terrible business this. Mr. Rumford wasn't the most popular bloke in the world, but who'd've thought he'd go berserk and start doing people in? It's a disgrace to us all, that's what it is."

"I shouldn't worry about that. No one's going to blame the Yeoman Warders as a body for the misdeeds of one."

"You'd be surprised, madam," he said darkly. "I'm afraid we'll have to go down these steps here, though I'll never tread them again but what I'll think of poor Mr. Crabtree, foully done to death. Did you know his ghost's been seen already?"

"No," said Daisy, "but it doesn't surprise me a bit." Obviously, Crabtree was destined to join the legion of haunting spirits for the edification of visitors to the Tower. He would be a kindly ghost, she didn't doubt, as he had been a kindly man.

"Only after dark. We won't be seeing him this time of day."

Stepping out from under the arch at the foot of the steps, Daisy kept her face resolutely turned from those other steps. She tried not to wonder how long it would be before Dr. Macleod's ghost was spotted there. Still, it couldn't be expected to haunt in broad daylight, and perhaps the nightly Ceremony of the Keys would drive it thence.

An addict and a thief! Still, she thought of him with pity.

They went down the cobbled slope and under the Bloody Tower, passing beneath the vicious-toothed portcullis. The Hotspur sentries, backs turned to Wellington's Armchairs, stood as rigid and blank-faced as if nothing out of the ordinary had happened that afternoon.

"Here comes the motor-car," said Parkinson, pointing along Water Street to their left. "The chauffeur went to turn it while I was fetching you."

Daisy saw brass headlamps gleam in the sun as the familiar dark red Sunbeam tourer emerged from under the bridge between St. Thomas's and the Wakefield towers. The hood was folded down and from the backseat Sakari waved madly, her round, dark, beaming face encircled with a diaphanous gold-embroidered scarf. Beyond her sat Melanie, peering anxiously from beneath the brim of a conventional brown cloche.

Lost in thought, Daisy hardly noticed. People kept saying Rumford was the murderer. He was *a* murderer, to be sure, but according to Alec, he had been in the hospital when Crabtree was killed. Surely Crabtree's murderer was still at large!

The Indian chauffeur, Kesin, pulled up so that the back door of the car was precisely opposite Daisy. Parkinson escorted her across Water Street, opened the door, and handed her in.

As the car set off at a stately pace, Sakari enveloped her in a scented embrace. "Daisy dear, you do lead an adventurous life!"

"Whatever's happened now?" asked Mel. "Miss Tebbit didn't say, only that you'd had a shock. Another shock."

All the odds and ends that had been teasing Daisy came together in her mind. "I'll tell you in a minute." She pulled her notebook from her handbag. "There's something I've been meaning to tell Alec for simply hours, and we're always interrupted. I'll have to leave him a note. Sakari, tell Kesin to stop at the next gateway, please."

She wrote as she spoke, then tore out the leaf, folded it in three and then in three again, tucked the ends into each other, and printed "DCI Fletcher" on the outside. She wished she had some way to seal it, but just because one yeoman was a murderous blackmailer, it didn't mean the rest couldn't be trusted to deliver a letter unread, especially one addressed to a police officer.

The Byward Tower gate had been shut again after Sakari's car passed through on arrival. Two yeomen opened it as they approached, and when the car didn't move on, one came over.

"What can I do for you, madam?"

Daisy handed him the note. "Please see that this is delivered to Chief Inspector Fletcher at once. It's urgent."

"I'll see to it, madam, never fear."

Saluting, he stepped back, and Kesin drove on over the moat.

"Now . . ." said Sakari.

"Wait till we're past the Middle Tower," said Daisy. "All I want is to get outside this terrible place."

* * *

Alec, Tom, and Piper spent several hours dealing with the immediate aftermath of the murder of Dr. Macleod. At last, Alec sent the others to the Guard House to write up their reports while he went to make verbal reports to Lieutenant Colonel Duggan and the Resident Governor.

He went first to the barracks, only to find that Duggan had just gone home. Wearily, he trudged over to the Officers' Quarters. Mrs. Duggan greeted him with much clucking and tutting, asked after Daisy, and pressed him to take the most comfortable chair while she called her husband and made tea.

"Mr. Fletcher'll want a whisky, my dear," said Duggan, coming in. "I'll hear no nonsense about not drinking on duty."

Alec gratefully accepted. Mrs. Duggan tactfully removed herself. Duggan poured a good-size tot, handed it over, and poured himself another.

"Well, now," he said, sitting down, "I hope my lads haven't rendered themselves liable to civil prosecution?"

"That's for the coroner to say, sir, but I doubt it. They were attempting to prevent a murder, after all."

"I'm sorry they didn't succeed."

"It wasn't a failure of marksmanship. Damn good shots. One in the leg, one in the shoulder, and one furrowed his scalp. He'll live to hang. But even if they'd killed him instantly, the axe would have done for Macleod." Alec suppressed a shudder. It was one of the most gruesome scenes he'd ever had to witness. But at least there was no question about who was responsible, no dearth of eyewitnesses.

"Damn shame about the medic. Speak no ill of the dead, but I can tell you now, he's been worrying me. Not under my command, I'm thankful to say. He answers—answered to the Resident Governor and the RAMC."

"His troubles are over. I hope your niece by marriage doesn't take his death too hard."

"That's right, potty about him, wasn't she? I expect the wife'll have young Fay weeping on her shoulder. It was all a lot of nonsense, if you ask me. A spot more?"

"Thank you, sir, but I'd better go and let General Carradine know what's going on. My superintendent will no doubt send you a copy of my report, or at least such parts of it as pertain to your men. I appreciate your cooperation throughout."

"Anything more we can do for you, just let me know."

They shook hands, and Duggan showed Alec out.

Devereux, no longer in dress uniform, was lounging on the steps, smoking. "Good evening, Chief Inspector," he said.

"Good evening, captain. I must thank you for removing my wife from the scene."

"A remarkable lady. To tell the truth, I was happy to remove myself. I'd thought I was hardened to anything, but time passes. . . . I was honoured to be entrusted with Mrs. Fletcher's care. Dare I hope that I have been removed from your list of suspects for the Chief Warder's murder?"

"I wish I could say so. The best I can say is, it would seem my instinct is to trust you in an emergency. Congratulations, by the way, on recognizing that the second murder doesn't solve the first."

"People do jump to conclusions."

"They do. I sincerely hope General Carradine is

not so deluded, or I'm going to have to disabuse him of the notion."

Alec went on his way. The air was growing chilly, but the evening light of the sun shone golden on the ancient walls of the White Tower, belying their bloody history. The steps had been washed clean. Only the huddled groups of Yeoman Warders, no longer patrolling singly, suggested the horror of the past two days. One of their own had been murdered, and one of their own had committed murder.

The Resident Governor was in his study. When the maid ushered Alec in, he was on the telephone, saying, "Yes, I expect to be able to tell you more very shortly. The Chief Inspector has just arrived. . . . Yes, I'll ring you back immediately. . . . Of course, my lord." He hung up the receiver and handed the apparatus to his secretary to set on a side table. "The Constable of the Tower," he said gloomily. "I hope you have *some* good news, Fletcher, however little. You'd better take notes, Jeremy."

"Well, we know who killed whom and how, which in some investigations is a big step forward."

"I doubt if I can make much of that, since half the population of the Tower seems to have witnessed the murder. Sit down, man. Whisky?"

Alec accepted a seat but refused the drink. "We also know *why* Rumford killed the doctor."

"That's good going. It's usually the other way round, isn't it? The victim kills the blackmailer."

"Yes, as in the mistaken murder of Crabtree. But Macleod appears not to have been a victim of extortion. Our theory is that Rumford had the sense not to blackmail the doctor who held his life in his hands every time he was ill."

"Macleod did a good job, kept him going, so why kill him?"

"Acting on information received—from my wife, as a matter of fact—my DC searched Macleod's quarters. He found a satchel stuffed to bursting with banknotes, Treasury notes, and silver. We believe it to be the proceeds of Rumford's blackmailing, taken from the Yeoman Gaoler's House while he was in hospital, under sedation."

"Good Lord, you're saying Macleod stole Rumford's hoard? But how the devil did he know it was there?"

"The nurses at the hospital say Rumford used to talk about it under the influence of morphia. They're trained to take no notice of what patients say under the influence of drugs, which is nonsense more often than not. But Macleod obviously thought it was worth a try, since he had free access to Rumford's keys and was able to keep him out of the way for as long as he wished."

"Not quite long enough," put in Webster. "Dr. Macleod was due to go on leave tomorrow."

"Thank you, that's another piece of the puzzle. Macleod told my wife he hadn't given the order for Rumford's release from the hospital, which the Sister confirmed. He could hardly have kept him in bed indefinitely. We assume he intended him to stay another day, but Rumford left under his own steam."

"With disastrous result," said Carradine. "If you ask me, Duggan's men are a trifle overeager."

"They did hope to prevent murder," Alec pointed out.

"How many shots did they fire?"

"Four. Two each from two sentries. Three hit Rumford."

"Will he live?"

"Yes. He'll stand trial as soon as he's recovered."

"And I have to find a new Yeoman Gaoler as well as a Chief Warder. We'll need two new men on the strength, too."

"There are plenty of candidates, sir," said Webster, waving a list.

"Do you expect to arrest any more of my fellows, Fletcher?" the general asked with a touch of sarcasm.

"I doubt it, sir."

"Good. Well, you and Mrs. Fletcher have cleared that one up nicely. Unfortunately, as far as I can see, it doesn't help with Crabtree's murder, does it?"

"No," Alec admitted with a sigh. "It doesn't."

When Alec returned to the room set aside for the detectives at the Guard House, Piper jumped up, waving a piece of folded paper.

"A note from Mrs. Fletcher, Chief," he announced.

"The sergeant of the guard gave it to us when we arrived," said Tom.

"We've been dying to read it."

"But it's addressed to you."

"What do you bet she's solved Crabtree's murder?"

"The pair of you sound more and more like Brenda and Fay Carradine!" Alec unfolded the note and read it. "Great Scott!"

"What does it say, Chief?"

Alec sat down, flattening the sheet of paper on the table. "She wonders whether we're aware of the bridge between St. Thomas's Tower, the residence of the Keeper of the Regalia, and the Wakefield

Tower, where the Crown Jewels are kept. She's seen Sir Patrick Heald use it."

"What did I say?" crowed Piper. "She's done it again!"

"Now wait a minute, laddie," Tom cautioned. "No jumping to conclusions. But I must say, Chief, this looks like the breach in the walls we've been looking for. Heald was one of the names Rumford gave us, the only one we haven't talked to yet."

"It's been niggling at the back of my mind," said Alec: "Why hasn't Heald made more of a fuss about missing that important engagement of his? General Carradine didn't mention just now that Heald had been pestering him again. Yet he's a member of the Royal Household, an eminent and influential man."

"He could have raised a real stink." Tom stroked his moustache. "Or just walked out."

Piper's eyes gleamed with excitement. "He didn't want to draw attention to himself!"

"You could have it, laddie."

"There's a P.S.," said Alec. He picked up Daisy's note. " 'According to the Res. Gov., his money is his wife's.' "

"Then whatever shenanigans Rumford was blackmailing him for," Tom said, "he'd be desperate to keep it from Lady Heald. But at the same time, as long as she didn't know, he'd have plenty of money to keep paying Rumford."

"Until," Alec theorized, "Rumford's final demand was just too much to manage without going to her, cap in hand."

"And he couldn't do that, Chief, without telling her what it was for."

"All right, it all holds together. Let's just take a dekko at the plan of the Tower."

Piper produced a plan in an instant.

Alec put his fingertip on St. Thomas's Tower. "Here's the Keeper's residence. And here's the Wakefield Tower. These dotted lines represent the bridge."

"No wonder we didn't tumble to it," said Tom in disgust. "I thought it was just another archway."

"It's no excuse. We've all seen the damn thing, coming and going. Here's the door to the ground floor of the Wakefield Tower—labelled 'Entrance to Jewel House'—just opposite the end of the Guard House. All he'd have to do is come out here, cross the slope, and go up the shortcut steps, the fog hiding him from the Guard House sentry."

"What about the partizan?" Piper asked. "Where did he get that?"

"From Yeoman Warder Parkinson." Alec smiled at their puzzlement. "Parkinson asked my advice. He'd been on duty in the Wakefield Tower this week and left his partizan there overnight. He wanted it for patrolling. The tower was locked. He hoped I could help him retrieve it, but I said he'd have to approach the proper authorities. Tom, find Parkinson and ask if he managed to get into the Wakefield Tower and whether he found his partizan there."

"Doubt it, Chief."

"So do I. If he didn't, bring him to meet me there. I'm going to see what the Governor can tell me about Lady Heald's character. Ernie, you keep an eye on the Keeper's residence and make sure our bird doesn't get the wind up and flit before we're ready for him."

"Unobtrusively, Chief, or d'you want him to know about it?"

" 'Unobtrusively,' is it, laddie? I'd better watch out or you'll be using words I don't know myself."

"Be as obtrusive as you like. If we've got it right, he's already in a blue funk, and a bit more pressure before we strike can't hurt. Post a couple of yeomen at the Wakefield Tower entrance, just in case. Let's go."

24

"Not Lady Heald," said the Resident Governor. "Lady Julia. She's the daughter of an earl. Keep this under your hat, but it's my opinion that's the only reason he reached the rank of general officer. But my dear man, you're not proposing—"

"I have to ask him a few questions, sir," said Alec. "I ought to have done so sooner. I can do so more effectively if I know a bit about his wife."

"If you say so," Carradine said dubiously. "I must assume you know your own business best. What do we know about Lady Julia, Jeremy?"

"I've never met her ladyship, sir. I gather she rarely comes to town."

"That's it, exactly. Lady Julia doesn't care for London. I believe she is a great horsewoman—rides to hounds and so on—and a scratch golfer. Shoots, too, if I'm not mistaken. And I do believe she's a magistrate."

"A lady of some force of character, in fact."

"That about sums her up. Can't really blame Sir Patrick for wanting his own little foothold in town.

But look here, you're not suggesting he smuggled her into the Tower to do in Rumford for him?"

"Great Scott no!" All the same, the notion gave rise to other possibilities: Suppose Rumford had caught the Keeper smuggling in a chorus girl, or a merry widow, or, still more reprehensible, another man's wife. Offhand, Alec couldn't think of any secret Heald would be more anxious to keep from a domineering wife who held the purse strings. "Thank you for your frankness, General." He stood up.

"You'll tread gently when dealing with Sir Patrick, won't you? After all, he is a man of some consequence in the world. I'm rather surprised he hasn't been round here again demanding to be allowed to leave."

"So are we, sir. When did you last see him?"

"Quite early this morning. He hasn't even made any enquiries about this latest dreadful business. For all I know, he's not even aware of it."

"Surely his servant—"

"He's not likely to have heard," Webster interrupted. "His man is a surly, silent type, who doesn't so much as pass the time of day with the Yeoman Warders. He considers himself above the common herd. Like his master," he added resentfully.

"Sir Patrick *is* above the common herd, Jeremy."

"Not when it comes to the history of the Crown Jewels, sir. He may be Keeper, but he has no idea of academic rigour."

"Academic rigour, whatever that may be, is hardly a requirement for his position. I'm sure the Chief Inspector is not interested in your dispute over the Black Prince's ruby. Is there anything else we can do for you, Fletcher?"

"Have any of the yeomen asked to get into the Wakefield Tower for any reason since last night?"

The Governor looked at Webster, who said, "No, no one."

"I'd like to borrow the key."

Carradine chortled. "Want to check the ruby for yourself, eh? You'd better go with him, Jeremy, even if he is a Scotland Yard man. We're not supposed to let that key out of our sight." He extracted a bunch of keys from his pocket, unlocked a drawer of his desk, and took out a large iron key.

In the meantime, Webster had taken down a painting of a gaily caparisoned procession setting out from the Tower, banners waving. Set into the wall was an ancient iron safe that would have made any competent burglar snicker. Carradine opened it, took out another large key, and handed it to his aide.

As Alec and Webster left the study, Brenda and Fay inevitably popped out of their sitting room opposite.

"Are you arresting Mr. Webster?"

"Aunt Myrtle will be devastated!"

Webster turned a fiery red.

"No, I am not arresting Mr. Webster." Alec was glad to note that Fay, though a bit pink around the eyes, didn't seem too devastated by Dr. Macleod's grisly demise. "He's coming with me, on your father's orders, to make sure I don't steal the Crown Jewels."

"Not really!"

"Do you think they've already been pinched?"

"May we come too?"

"Certainly not. Go and reassure Miss Tebbit that Mr. Webster is not in imminent danger of arrest."

Alec waited until he and the secretary were beyond the hearing of the sentry outside before he asked, "Is there the slightest possibility that Sir Patrick had dishonest designs on the Crown Jewels?"

"Which Rumford might have discovered? Such is our mutual antipathy that I'd happily say yes, but I'm afraid it's most unlikely. He may have—as General Carradine puts it—little in the way of brains, and even less guts, but even he could hardly fail to realize he couldn't get away with it. Do you still want to get into the Wakefield Tower?"

"Oh yes. We'll meet my sergeant there."

They reached the bottom of the shortcut steps and turned down the slope towards the Bloody Tower. Beside the tower, between it and the Guard House, a flight of steps (no wonder Daisy had complained about endless steps!) led down to the door of the ground floor of the contiguous Wakefield Tower. From the top, Alec saw Tom Tring waiting outside the door. He dwarfed his companion, a by no means undersized yeoman. Another pair of yeomen, armed with partizans, stood guard.

Parkinson gulped visibly when he saw Webster. He stepped forward manfully as they descended. Tom winked at Alec over his head.

"I know I didn't ought to 've, sir," the yeoman said to Webster. "But everyone does it."

"And did you ever accept that as an excuse when you were in the army, Mr. Parkinson?" Webster enquired acidly.

"No, sir."

"Well, then! As it happens I have no idea what you're talking about, but no doubt I'll find out shortly."

Webster led the way to the door of the Wakefield Tower, unlocked it, stood aside for Alec to enter, and followed him into the gloomy circular room. Tom ushered Parkinson in after them and took out his notebook.

Alec turned to ask, "Where exactly did you leave your partizan, Mr. Parkinson?"

"Strewth, it's gorn! Right here beside the door it was, leaning up against the wall, like, so's I could grab it as I come in next morning."

"The night before last, you left it here?"

"'Sright, sir, when I went off duty. Polished it down nice with a shammy I keep in me pocket, and leant it right here."

"You may have to testify to that in court."

"It's true, sir, s'welp me, if it's not. D'you mean—was it my partizan Mr. Crabtree was skewered with?"

"It may have been."

"Let that be a lesson to you," Webster said sententiously.

Alec took pity on the sweating Parkinson. "Mr. Crabtree was dead before he was . . . skewered. You're not to say a word about this to anyone."

"Mum's the word, sir, I swear it."

"All right, you can go. Mr. Webster, I don't know what the penalty is for his dereliction of duty, but it's not to be carried out until after any court case arising from this investigation is over. Mr. Tring, make sure the two yeomen outside understand they are absolutely not to talk about what they have seen and may have overheard. And after we leave, anyone coming out through this door is to be arrested."

"Right, sir."

Tom went out and Alec turned back to Webster. "Who else has a key to this door?"

Webster grinned, an unnerving sight. "The Keeper

of the Regalia. No one else. He also has the *only* key to the door on the first floor, communicating between the jewel chamber and the bridge across to St. Thomas's Tower."

"Thank you."

"My pleasure," said the secretary with relish as they moved outside.

"You may report to General Carradine, of course, but to no one else."

"Of course." He closed and locked the door behind them. "The net closes. Good luck, Chief Inspector."

Alec and Tom followed him up the steps. He went up the slope and they turned under the Bloody Tower.

"Do we have enough circumstantial evidence?" Tom asked.

"Enough to take him in. Whether the public prosecutor will consider it sufficient to try a peer's son-in-law for murder is another matter."

As they walked down through the murky tunnel, a shadow detached itself from the wall at the end.

"No sign of life across the way, Chief," Piper reported. "I strolled up and down the street a few times. Dunno if anyone saw me. If they were watching they kept well back. 'Course, a uniformed bobby'd've been more use to put the wind up him."

"Not at all, laddie," said Tom. "You're enough to frighten the living daylights out of a scarecrow."

"Cor, ta, Sarge."

"Both of you come with me." Alec stepped out from under the arch, looking across Water Street at the half-timbered dwelling above the long, low arch of Traitors' Gate, between the two stone projections of St. Thomas's Tower. "How does one get up to his place?"

"I asked, Chief. It's that door, the one to the right of Traitors' Gate." Piper pointed out a heavy iron-bound door set back in the thickness of the stone wall.

"If he refuses to open it, we'll need a battering ram!"

Ernie yanked on the bellpull. No sound was heard from inside. They waited.

Nothing happened.

"Maybe it's not working," said Piper, reaching for the handle.

"If it's not working," said Tom, "there's no use pulling again. And if it is working, likely it'll take 'em a while to get here."

They waited.

"I wonder whether the Resident Governor has a key to this door," Alec said at last. "It's within his domain. Give it another try, Ernie."

But just then the door swung open. Inside, the only light was a flickering gas lamp turned low. The black-clad manservant's white shirtfront stood out in the gloom.

"Yes?"

"Police," said Alec, his foot over the threshold. "I'd like a word with Sir Patrick."

Without a word, the man turned and led the way upstairs. Piper closed the heavy door behind them with a reverberating thud.

The Keeper's quarters could not be described as cosy. However, though the gas lights were turned down low, Alec saw at a glance that his sitting room was furnished in somewhat old-fashioned but luxurious comfort, like the smoking room of a very expensive club.

"The police, sir," said the servant, and faded away. From the depths of a leather armchair beside the crackling fire, a terrified voice squeaked, "It was an accident!"

Piper already had his notebook out. Unobtrusively, he moved a straight chair to a position to one side and slightly to the rear of Sir Patrick's. No sense letting an already-frightened suspect see that every word he uttered was being written down.

Tom stationed himself with his back against the door. No one would be intruding or escaping that way.

Alec, without waiting to be invited, sat down in the chair across the fireplace from Sir Patrick. "What was an accident, sir?" he asked gently.

"Rumford falling down the stairs. Crabtree. He slipped. I didn't push him. Touch him."

"I must warn you, sir, that you need not say anything, but anything you choose to say may be used in evidence. You're entitled to have your lawyer—"

"*My* lawyer! He's Julia's, her family's. Tied up all her money so I can't touch a penny without begging."

"Someone else?"

"They're all the same. Damn parasites!"

Alec interpreted this as declining the right to have a lawyer present. "You were there when Crabtree fell."

"You don't need to tell me," Sir Patrick said petulantly. His hands were in constant motion, fingers scrabbling on his thighs like a cat flexing its claws. "I can't imagine how you found out. No one could have seen me in the dark and the fog. I didn't mean to push him. I just wanted to talk to him, to explain I simply couldn't come up with five hundred pounds. Julia would never have given me so much at one time, not without a damn good reason and something to show for it."

"You went to talk to . . . ?"

"To Rumford, that damn leech!"

"You went to talk to Rumford. If you spoke to him, how was it that you didn't realize the man you met was in fact Crabtree?"

"They look alike. In the dark and the fog, I assumed it was Rumford. I wouldn't have pushed Crabtree down the steps. Nothing against the man. Didn't know him."

"You went out at midnight on a cold, foggy night to speak to Rumford. What made you think he'd be there?"

"I knew it was his week on duty. Watched him often enough from here, and I'd seen which way he went from the King's House once when I spent an evening there. The other chap shouldn't have been there. It was his own fault he got pushed down the steps."

" 'Got pushed,' " said Alec.

"I mean he slipped." Sir Patrick was whining now. "I wanted to talk to Rumford, that's all."

"In that case, sir, may I ask why you took a partizan with you?"

"Partizan? Partizan? What the devil is a partizan?"

"A pike, sir."

"Well, why didn't you say so? I took it to defend myself, of course, in case he fought back. He was a big man, much bigger than I am. The fall might not have killed him, and I couldn't have him attacking me, could I?"

Enough, thought Alec. He'd had enough of the Keeper's feeble lies, sickening self-justification, and unintended admissions. Surely the man had sufficiently damned himself out of his own mouth.

He glanced at Tom, who nodded.

Alec stood up. "Sir Patrick Heald, I arrest you for the murder of Chief Warder Crabtree," he said wearily.

"It wasn't my fault!" cried the Keeper of the Regalia. "It was supposed to be Rumford!"

"An invitation?" said Alec, spreading marmalade on his toast. "From whom?"

"General Carradine and Mrs. Tebbit. It looks as if I'm going to have to go back to the Tower barely a fortnight after swearing never to darken its gates again. An engagement party for Myrtle Tebbit and Jeremy Fisher."

"Webster. So they're actually going to get married!"

"Why not?" Daisy looked up from the note Mrs. Tebbit had included with the formal invitation. "You were there."

"I thought it was just the old lady's mischief making. I wasn't paying much attention. You may recall I had other matters on my mind at the time."

"Ugh, don't remind me."

"Dare I hope that they don't want to be reminded, either, and have therefore omitted my name from the invitation?"

"Of course not, darling. It's for both of us."

"I'm afraid I shall be out of town on a case that day."

"I haven't told you what day it is."

"Nevertheless, I shall be out of town on a case."

"That's all right, I'll go with the Germonds. Mrs. Tebbit says they're invited, to make sure the promised tennis party for the girls comes off. Actually, Melanie told me she's at last settled on a date. She says she's found some suitable young men for Brenda and Fay."

"They could hardly be less suitable than Dr. Macleod!"

"By the way, did Rumford tell you what Sir Patrick did that gave him a hold over him."

"A sordid story—he smuggled a girl in. He simply couldn't afford to have Lady Julia find out."

"And General Carradine? What happened in Mesopotamia?"

"That, I'm not going to tell you."

"Beast!"

Alec grinned. "To tell the truth, he managed to avoid revealing his awful secret."

"Oh well, I suppose it's better not to know, in his case, especially if I'm going to this party at the King's House."

"I'm glad Mrs. Germond will be with you, but are you sure you'll be all right going back to that place, love? You were so determined not to."

"I know, but I feel I can face anything at all after yesterday's victory."

"Daisy, what on earth . . . ?"

"You came home too late for me to tell you last night, but I've taken Sakari's advice. She couldn't understand how I could let a servant lay down the law, so I screwed my courage to the sticking place and tackled Nanny."

"You didn't!"

"I did. We're allowed to call her Mrs. Gilpin instead of Nanny, because of the dog. I must say she was rather put out that we didn't just change the dog's name, but we couldn't do that, could we, Nana?" The dog looked up from where she was lying by the window, being frightfully good about not begging at table. Her tail thumped the floor. "She'd never answer to a different name. And I told Mrs. Gilpin *I* shall take the twins for their afternoon walk in the perambulator whenever I want to."

"Daisy, this is mutiny," Alec said with a grin, "if not insurrection!"

"And what's more, *you're* allowed to go and kiss them good night, however late you come in."

"Great Scott, weren't you afraid she'd give notice?"

"Not really," said Daisy complacently. "According to Melanie, nannies consider it most frightfully prestigious to be in charge of twins!"